Part One

Ellen

If there's no hatred in a mind
Assault and battery of the wind
Can never tear the linnet from the leaf.

W.B. Yeats

CHAPTER 1

FOR A LONG moment you could have heard a pin drop in the manager's office. Even the ticking of the clock on the wall seemed to have been shocked into silence, although perhaps it was just the roaring in Ellen's ears which shut out every other sound.

'I've never heard such nonsense, Miss Richards!' The poor man had got his breath back now, although his face was still a horrid shade of magenta. She hoped he wasn't about to have a stroke. 'You come in here,' he roared, 'having the gall to ask me for an indefinite leave of absence. The impudence of it! Just who do you think you are?'

'Compassionate leave, Mr Evans, that's all I'm asking for. I've told you about my brother being killed at Ypres. I thought I'd die when I got that telegram. Bertie was the only relation I had in the world, you see. I need time to come to grips with his death. If I could just get away for a bit to think things over, I know I'd be all right.'

The manager seemed to be struggling to control his temper. His office window overlooked the street and the sound of distant voices and the clip clopping of horses' hooves could be heard in the distance.

'And I'm sorry for your loss, my girl,' he managed at last, 'but you're not the only one who's lost someone near and dear to them, you know. Young Bryn Jones in Packing went off to fight for king and country just last month, and now he's dead. What about his poor mother, eh? She's not asking for days off! And then there's Mrs Rogers in Ladies' Modes. She has two sons at the front, and every day the poor woman expects to get bad news. No, Miss Richards, I'm not prepared to give you time off. I'd be a fool if I did. Everybody would expect the same treatment. I wouldn't know if I was coming or going. This is a department store I'm running here, not a charity!'

Ellen clenched her hands inside the pockets of her cardigan. Of course there was something in what he said but she only knew she had to get right away before she went stark, staring mad.

'I'm sorry, Mr Evans,' she gulped, 'but in that case I'll have to hand in my notice.'

'On your head be it, then,' he grunted, making no attempt to try to talk her out of it. 'You needn't think we'll take you back when you've come to your senses! Now, if you've quite finished, you can get out. I can't stand here all morning bandying words with the likes of you.'

Ellen blundered out of the room, half blinded by tears.

'How did it go?' Her friend had been loitering outside the room.

'I could have saved my breath, Mari! For all the sympathy I got I might have been reporting a missing dog, not explaining how I've just lost my only brother.'

'Well, don't say I didn't warn you! The question is, what are you going to do now?'

'I'm not staying here, for a start. I've given old Evans my notice.'

'You didn't! Was that wise? What on earth are you going to do without a job?'

'I've got enough saved up to tide me over for a bit. After that, well, I can always go into munitions, or sign on as a bus conductorette.'

Mari pulled a face. 'You don't fancy being a VAD, then, going out to France to look after all those poor wounded soldiers? That's what I'd do if I ever got up the nerve to pack it in here.'

Ellen shuddered. 'Not likely. Seeing those poor boys would only make me think of what happened to Bertie. I mean, the letter I had from his commanding officer said he died instantly and didn't suffer, but he would say that, wouldn't he? He wouldn't dare to write the truth to all those wives and mothers. But it stands to reason they don't all go quickly and pain-lessly.'

'Sorry, Nell, I didn't think. Come on, let's skip down to the canteen for a cup of tea before Miss Morris notices we've been gone too long. When she asked me where I was going I made out I've got the collywobbles, but knowing her she'd sneak into the Ladies to see if I've gone there for a quick smoke!'

'I could do with a cup,' Ellen admitted. 'I haven't eaten much since I got the news about Bertie. It felt like there was a lump in my throat. I couldn't seem to swallow.'

'Then I'll stand you a currant bun if you're good,' Mari said, grinning, 'and you can tell me what you mean to do with this holiday of yours. I hope you don't plan to stay in your room at old Ma Rutherford's, moping.'

'No, I don't want to stay in Cardiff at all. I think I'll go down to Barry.'

Mari's eyebrows rose. 'Are you mad? There won't be a soul on the beach at this time of year. Why don't you wait until summer when it's nice and warm? P'raps we can get our holidays at the same time, and I'll come with you. Keep you company, eh?'

'Thanks for the offer, Mari, but I don't want to be there when the place is crawling with trippers. It'll be peaceful just now. I'll find a nice boarding house up in the town and I know I'll enjoy walking around and just relaxing.'

'Rather you than me! I bet it's a real dead and alive hole at this time of year. Still, I suppose you know best, and you can always come back to Cardiff if you get fed up.'

'Mm.' Ellen agreed with her friend for the sake of peace, but she knew in her heart she was doing the right thing. Even though so many people were losing loved ones in this terrible war, the accepted thing was to carry on as usual even after tragedy had struck. If you didn't, that meant you were giving in to the Kaiser. That, no doubt, was what had prompted Mr Evans to be so harsh with her, but she couldn't possibly go on selling gloves and scarves to harrassed shoppers when all the while her heart was breaking. She needed to think, to plan her future.

When Bertie and Ellen were quite young their parents had died of typhoid fever and after that the children were brought up by their Irish grandmother. Nan was a kindly woman who did her best to make up for their loss, but inevitably the brother and sister had become close to each other, best friends as well as siblings. After Nan died they'd depended on each other even more for comfort and support, and this state of affairs would most likely have gone on throughout their lives, had the war not intervened. And now Bertie was gone, having gasped out his life in the mud and turmoil of Ypres.

'I suppose the old devil's making you work out your notice,' Mari sniffed, as they hurried back to their counter. 'If it was me I'd walk out right this minute after the rollicking you just got.'

'For two pins I would, but then I'd forfeit my pay, and I don't want to do that. Better grit my teeth and get on with it.'

As was the case in many places, the employees of Lloyd's Emporium had their first week's wages withheld in trust until the day they left. The girls had often discussed the unfairness of this, but the fact remained that nothing could be done about it.

Walking back to Tredegar Road at the end of the day, in order to save the tram fare, Ellen mentally rehearsed what she was going to say to Mrs Rutherford. After Bertie had joined up, she couldn't stay on in the modest house in Plum Street where they had grown up. Even though he sent her an allowance out of his army pay, she couldn't afford the rent. Her only option was to move into a boarding house, where she had a pokey little room to herself and had to share the bathroom with several others. Still, 'Ma', as they called her, was a passable cook who supplied her guests with two meals a day, the sort of fare which one of the lodgers referred to as 'cheap and cheerful'.

Ma was vastly more sympathetic than Mr Evans had been. 'Ah, there's sad it is for you, Miss Richards, losing your brother at the war, poor chap. It will take you years to get over it, I'm sure. How long do you mean to stop away, then?'

Ellen sighed. 'I really can't say, Mrs Rutherford. Possibly until my money runs out.'

'So you don't want me to keep your room on for you, then?'

'I wish you could, but I can't afford that. I suppose there's no chance you could store my few bits and pieces, just until I know what I'll be doing? There isn't much; only my nan's old rocking chair and the rag rug we made together. Oh, and my winter clothes, of course.'

Ma pretended to consider this. 'They could go in my box room, I s'pose. I'd have to charge, of course. A shilling a week, maybe?'

Ellen frowned. That sounded like a lot of money just for storing a few items. On the other hand, where else could she keep them?

'I tell you what,' Ma went on, not wanting to lose her bargain, 'for that price I'll keep your room for you if I can, and I won't charge nothing for it while you're gone. How will that be? I won't put my "room to let" notice up in the front window like I usually does when somebody leaves. Course, if someone comes asking, I won't turn them away. I'm sure you understand that.'

Ellen was too tired and bewildered to work that one out. The satisfied smirk on Ma's lined face warned her that the older woman had got the better of her in some way, but she simply opened her small blue purse and selected a shilling piece, which disappeared into the landlady's apron pocket. There was no turning back now. It was time to take the first step into an unknown future.

Chapter 2

'A THIRD CLASS SINGLE to Barry, please.' Ellen held out the money to the young man behind the ticket window.

'Single, is it? Surely not, a pretty girl like you!' he smirked. She didn't appreciate his cheek but she gave him a weak smile. Unfortunately he wasn't finished yet. 'Sure you don't want a return? You must be coming back eventually. Not going down there to drown yourself, I hope?'

She'd had enough of this. 'None of your beeswax!' she retorted.

'Only being friendly, miss,' he shot back, not squelched in the slightest. 'Service with a smile, that's my motto. No call for you to get aerated, is there?'

'Shouldn't you be in uniform? Don't you know there's a war on?'

'I am in uniform, see?' He indicated his railway suit. 'I can't help it if Kitchener won't have me. I've got a gammy leg, see, so don't go giving me no white feather.'

Ellen boarded the train, inexplicably cheered by this exchange. She was grateful to find herself in an empty compartment. It wasn't a corridor train and she hoped that nobody else would get in when they stopped at the next station.

Now she was on her way she felt a sense of relief at leaving her everyday life behind. Ma Rutherford had managed to book a room for her in a Barry boarding house that just happened to be run by her cousin, a Mrs Fleming.

'She don't usually take people out of season, but she'll make an exception in your case,' Ma had said, waving the letter with an air of one bestowing a great favour. 'She says here she'll let you have a special rate, it being the beginning of September when you get there. You'll have to pay a week in advance, of course.'

'Of course,' Ellen murmured. What would it be like to go to the sort of hotel where they waited on you hand and foot and you didn't have to pay until the day of departure? People like her always had to pay in advance in case they flitted, leaving their bill unpaid. It wasn't a very nice feeling knowing that people didn't trust you, just because you were poor. Perhaps they had learned that the hard way, she conceded.

She loved Cardiff, where she had lived since babyhood. It was home to her as no other place could be. But the city had temporarily lost its ability to charm, and old associations drew her to Barry. Once, long ago, the family had gone there for a glorious outing. Oh, not a holiday as such; people like the Richards family could never have afforded to stay away overnight. Gwyn Richards worked as a stevedore on the Cardiff docks, helping to load and unload the merchant ships, and although the family never wanted for food or shelter, there was precious little money left over for luxuries.

Ellen had been six years old, and her brother Bertie eight, when they had gone on that memorable day trip to Barry Island. She had never been there since, but she had never forgotten the sheer pleasure of it all. Digging in the wet sand, with her frock tucked up in her knickers, and paddling in the sea, shrieking with delight when an approaching wave threatened to knock her over. Listening, wide-eyed, to the terrified screams of an older boy who had stepped on a jellyfish and received a painful sting.

'Just fill your lungs with that good sea air,' Mam had instructed. Taking a deep breath, Ellen had obeyed. The scents of the place were fascinating, a mixture of ozone and seaweed, and fried onions from the barrows which catered to the needs of the holiday makers.

Walking along the promenade – a halfpenny to get through the turnstile – was an added thrill. She loved the look of the kiosks selling sticks of rock, or brightly coloured tin buckets and spades. Tawdry souvenirs of all descriptions delighted her eye. To her, Barry Island looked like a fairy paradise.

As the train clackety-clacked its way out of Cardiff, Ellen could see it all as if it were yesterday. Dad sitting in a rented deck chair, his trousers rolled up to his knees and his shirt open at the neck. He had tied knots in the four corners of his spotted handkerchief and was wearing it on his head against the sun's rays. Mam, more formally dressed, was seated in an identical chair, knitting rhythmically. Once in a while she glanced up, squinting against the sun, then turning to look at her husband with a satisfied sigh.

'Mam! Dad! Come on in, the water's lovely!' Bertie shouted, but his parents shook their heads. 'You go on, love! Enjoy yourself!' Sitting idly by, watching their children at play, was a rare treat and they intended to make the most of it. A dog ran out of the water and stopped nearby to shake itself, causing Mam to utter ladylike shrieks as the droplets spattered her skirts. Ellen longed for the day to go on for ever.

Not long after that day both Mam and Dad had fallen ill with the typhoid fever, and in a frighteningly short space of time they were both dead. The children's grandmother had come from Ireland to look after the shocked and anxious children. Ellen's memory of the expedition to Barry Island was something to be treasured because when she finally emerged from that grief-stricken state, she thought of it as the last time they had really been together as a family. When they were at home in Cardiff their parents always seemed to be working, with little time for leisure. Ellen and Bertie were never neglected but children were meant to make their own amusements, while the grown-ups got on with the business of providing a home.

'Oh, do let me get on!' was Mam's favourite cry, when the youngsters complained of boredom. 'I can soon find something for you to do, if you can't! That stove needs black-leading for a start!'

For Ellen, therefore, this trip to Barry was something of a journey back in time. She had some vague idea that she'd find comfort there. Perhaps she would find her parents and Bertie there in spirit. She sometimes paid a visit to the crowded graveyard outside Cardiff to place flowers on their family graves, but she couldn't do the same for Bertie, who was buried so far away. Memories were all she was left with.

Mon Repos, the place where Ellen was to stay, was a modern house, its outside walls covered with what was known as pebble dash. The doors and window frames were freshly painted and late summer flowers were blooming in long borders on either side of the garden path. Mrs Fleming was a smaller, greyer version of Ma Rutherford, but pleasant enough. That is, until you crossed her, as Ellen was to find out in time.

'This is your accommodation,' she announced, showing Ellen into an aggressively clean and rather gloomy room. A large and straggling monkey puzzle tree just outside the window managed to cut off most of the light.

'It's a bit cold,' Ellen shivered, glancing at the fireplace which sported a pleated paper fan instead of the glowing coals she'd liked to have seen.

Mrs Fleming tossed her frizzy head. 'Yes, well, I can't help that. No fires after 1 May until the 1 October. That's my rule.'

Ellen wondered what would happen if they had St Martin's Little Summer in October. Would the inhabitants of the house swelter in the heat? Still, the summer visitors were gone by then and presumably the landlady's rules didn't apply to herself.

'If that's all, then, Miss Richards, I'll leave you to unpack. We'll expect to see you downstairs at six o'clock sharp for high tea. That's when my hubby gets in, and he doesn't like to be kept waiting.'

Ellen's heart sank. That was more than three hours away, and she'd had no dinner, having had to rush across the city to catch the train by the skin of her teeth. She said as much to her hostess, who greeted this disclosure with pursed lips.

'I don't do dinners, Miss Richards. You'll get your breakfast and the evening meal, and I don't mind making up sandwiches for you to take with you when you go out each day, if you like to pay extra. I don't allow food in the rooms, of course. We don't want mice, do we, now?'

'I'll think about that, and let you know later, Mrs Fleming. Having sandwiches, I mean, not the mice. In the meantime, I'm sure you can run to a cup of tea, can't you? Milk and two lumps, please.'

The woman's eyebrows rose and she flounced out of the room without replying. Ellen hoped she had gone to put the kettle on. It had taken a lot of courage to stand up to her. Mari would have been proud of her! Paying extra for a measly sandwich, indeed! There must be some sort of tea room nearby where she could have her dinners in comfort. Failing that, she could buy bread and cheese at the shops and take it to the beach. She wasn't about to line Mrs Fleming's capacious pockets even more.

She unpacked her few possessions and placed them carefully in the chest of drawers. Then she sank down on the bed, thoroughly disheartened. While she didn't think she'd made a mistake in coming to Barry, Mon Repos wasn't what she'd had in mind when she allowed Ma to book a room here on her behalf. Indoors it was far less inviting than the exterior led one to believe. This cramped and chilly room offered no comfort, and nothing had been said about where she was supposed to spend her evenings. She would have to ask. Would she be invited to join the Flemings in some snug sitting room? If not, she would have to think again.

She'd paid for the first week in advance, and as Mrs Fleming had been so careful to point out, the money was non-refundable, so she had no alternative but to stay where she was for the first few days. After that she'd ask around and look for more congenial lodgings. She was determined not to run back to Cardiff with her tail between her legs.

CHAPTER 3

HARRY MORGAN LOOKED at his friend with disbelief in his eyes. 'You mean to tell me there's nothing wrong with the woman? What are you saying, man, that my wife is as fit as you or I?'

'Physically, yes.' Dr Lawson nodded.

'But she's been lying about for months now, not even lifting a hand to take up that wretched embroidery she's so fond of. She's so weak it takes two of the maids to help her from her bed to that couch where she spends her days.'

'I'll warrant that if there was an outbreak of fire in the house, she'd move fast enough. I've done a thorough examination, Harry, and she's putting it on.'

'But in heaven's name, why? What's the point of it all?'

The doctor shrugged. 'To avoid facing up to life, I suppose. Cases of this sort were well known in the old queen's day. Ladies who wanted to avoid child bearing, or their wifely duties, took to their couches in darkened rooms. Oh, in some cases there was real illness behind it, of course, but there was plenty of the other sort of nonsense, too.'

'It's a wonder to me how they were able to get away with it!' Harry muttered.

'It's simple, man. They got away with it because they could! Women like your wife have servants to wait on them. They don't have to do a hand's turn. You live in comfort here, but it's not because of anything she does for you, hey? It's your staff who smooth the way, as well they should, when you're providing them with a roof over their heads.

'Your miners' wives, now, it's different for them. They can't afford to loll about. Most of them have a dozen or more children to bring up, those who've survived infancy, that is. Why, the amount of washing those women have to do in a week would break the back of a carthorse, yet they manage it, and much more besides. That's what some of your fine ladies need, Harry, a proper day's work to put them in order. Not much chance of that for your Antonia, though, is there?'

Despite his distress, Harry had to smile at the idea of his dainty, gently bred wife standing at the wash tub, threading heavy, soaking sheets through the mangle. Not that he would want her to have to tackle menial labour like that. He said as much.

'Of course you wouldn't, man, but there are other remedies. A family, that's what she needs. If she had half a dozen children it would be the making of her.'

'Fine for you to say, old man. She's already had three miscarriages, and since that last one she hasn't let me near her. Says she can't face going through all that, only to be disappointed again. The plain fact of the matter is that she never did like "all that dreadful business" as she refers to making love. Dammit, James; a man has needs, as you surely must know.'

The doctor raised his eyebrows. 'That's easily remedied. Take a mistress if you have to. Antonia would probably be grateful, if that's the way she views married life.'

An expression of distaste crossed Harry Morgan's handsome face. 'I didn't get married to keep some loose woman on the side, James! I want children. In particular I want a son; several sons if possible.'

The doctor grinned. 'You sound like that other Welshman, old Harry Tudor. He kept ridding himself of one wife after another, all because he wanted a son and had trouble getting one. Of course his case was a bit different. He needed a prince, to rule England after he was gone.'

'And it's hardly different in my case, is it? Here I am, with my own little empire, and there's nobody to hand it on to after I die. There's the colliery, and all my other holdings, to say nothing of this enormous house and the estate with all its farms.'

'You've plenty of time yet, man. Antonia is barely out of her twenties. That son you crave will come along one of these days.'

'The way things are going? I doubt it.'

'Look here, Harry; it's time you took action. Get her up off that couch! Take it carefully, mind. Softly, softly, catchee monkey! Go along with her pretence of being delicate; say I recommended sea air, and take her away for a few weeks. The change can't do her any harm and it just might do her some good. Now then, it's time I was off. I'd like to be able to spend an evening at home with my lady wife!'

Harry followed his friend out into the courtyard, where the doctor's horse and trap was waiting. Instead of going back inside immediately, he strolled to the front of the great mansion he called home. The fine Georgian house was imposing in the early autumn sunshine and the lawns looked sleek and green again after their treatment with the horse-drawn roller. He noticed that some of the shrubs looked somewhat unkempt and he made a mental note to get the gardeners to tidy them up.

He went in search of his wife. He found her engaged in an animated conversation with her companion, Miss Lavinia Phipps. It didn't escape his notice that as soon as he appeared she sank back on the love seat with a weary expression on her face. Miss Phipps glanced at him anxiously, no doubt wondering what the doctor's verdict on her mistress's health had been.

'You were talking to James for a long time, weren't you, Harry? I suppose he's told you I'm just lazy, idling away my days like this. He doesn't understand what it's like to lose one child after another. How can he, being a man?'

'On the contrary, he's quite concerned, my dear. He wants me to take you away for a while. He says you need sea air. I shall make arrangements at once. Hawkins is quite capable of looking after my interests while we're away.'

'What did you have in mind, then? We cannot go to the Riviera, of course. This dreadful war!' She pouted again, as if the war was merely an inconvenience.

'I can't leave the estate for that long. We'll have to stay in Wales, I think.'

Antonia pondered this. 'Why not Bath? I can take the waters there.'

'That would not give you the sea air that James prescribed. In fact, I've more or less decided that we'll go to Barry. It's not so far away, so we'll be able to motor down.'

'Barry!' she shrieked. 'Certainly not! Do you think I want to mingle with thousands of working-class day trippers, all of them eating fish and chips and watching Punch and Judy shows? Why not go the whole hog and hire an omnibus and take some of your miners' families along with us? Really, what on earth are you thinking of?'

'I'm not suggesting we go to Barry Island,' he replied, trying to hold down his temper. 'Although this late in the year there won't be any trippers, as you call them. I shall make reservations at a very pleasant residential hotel I know of at Cold Knap. It comes highly recommended and I'm sure you'll find the other guests quite congenial. Not that you have to mingle with them if you prefer not to. You and Miss Phipps can sit out of doors on warm days and breathe in that good sea air.'

Miss Phipps had been listening to this. 'It might be very nice, Mrs Morgan. Perhaps we could find someone to make up a four for bridge in the evenings.'

Poor old girl, Harry thought, in a rare moment of concern for one of his servants. She mustn't lead much of a life, spending half her days shut in a darkened room with Antonia! I don't believe she's been given a holiday since she came to us two years ago after we lost that last baby, and even her afternoons off are spent running errands in the town. She'll enjoy this change of scene. All the more reason for putting my foot down now.

'But what about you, Harry?' Antonia went on. 'Won't you be bored, in a hotel full of invalids and old fogeys?'

'I shall take long walks,' he announced. 'The sea air will be good for me, as well. Spending the whole year in a coal-mining district can't be good for the lungs.' This was an exaggeration, of course. Carmarthenshire, where both his colliery and his estates were situated, boasted some beautiful countryside, encompassing sheep farming lands and glorious mountains, as well as the coal tips and slag heaps which admittedly defaced part of the landscape.

He gave a small cough to underline his point. There was nothing wrong with Harry Morgan's lungs but he was determined to talk his wife round to his way of thinking. Not that she would openly defy him, of course, but anything for a quiet life.

Antonia and Miss Phipps should go to Barry and remain there for at least a month. He would travel down with them, staying for a week or so before returning home, pleading the pressure of business. If his wife made a fuss he'd come down to see her on weekends. After all, it wasn't part of his plan to alienate her. He still wanted those sons!

Actually, he looked forward to seeing Barry again. He'd been taken there for holidays as a boy and it would be pleasant to go exploring the area again. Barry had several fine beaches, of which Porthkerry was his favourite, with its high cliffs and pebble beach. He was heartily sick of the round of social engagements he was forced to endure at home. Dinners and card parties, and those dreadful social evenings where caterwauling women with little talent tried to entertain the rest of their social circle.

'We'd better think about what we need to pack, Mrs Morgan,' Miss Phipps was saying as she fluttered about. 'Shall I get Jones to bring the big trunk down from the attic? Or will we need two trunks? I suppose people will dress for dinner at the hotel, so you'll need several gowns. And September can be so chilly, can't it, with the sea breezes – that is, unless it turns warm for a change. Oh dear, it's so difficult to know what to take!'

Harry hid a smile. With any luck the exercise would keep his wife fully occupied so that she had little time to make a fuss about being forced to spend a few weeks' convalescence in Barry instead of going to the continent as she would have preferred.

He was becoming bored with their company. 'I shall make arrangements and let you know when we are to leave,' he announced, and left the room.

CHAPTER 4

'THIS SIMPLY WILL not work out!' Antonia Morgan insisted. Her husband ignored her peevish complaint and continued to examine the sheaf of papers his secretary had sent him. 'Did you hear what I said, Harry?'

'Mm? What was that, my dear?'

'This business of going to Barry by car! How are we supposed to pack everything in that motor of yours, besides the four of us? My two trunks, the servants' bags, not to mention your things.'

'No problem. The baggage can go by rail.'

But his wife continued to find fault with the arrangements and he let her fuss on until she had herself thoroughly worked up. Miss Phipps fluttered about, practically wringing her hands as she tried to decide whether she dared interrupt. When Antonia was on the point of tears, Harry remarked, as if the thought had just occurred to him, that the three women could go by train and he would follow on by car.

'There's no point in having a private railway coach if it's never used, is there?'

Lavinia Phipps brightened at once. She knew that her employer had investments in one or two railway companies (something to do with stocks and shares, she believed) and that was why he owned this coach, which could be connected to any passenger train. They would travel in style – quite like royalty – and she looked forward to writing to her sister in Bournemouth, mentioning that they had gone to Barry in this special conveyance. Ruth was inclined to look down on her for being an old maid and it was good to be able to put this younger, married sister in her place occasionally. Lavinia might be 'only a companion', as Ruth put it, but what was wrong with that? She was earning her own living, and there was the reflected glory of serving Antonia Morgan, who was third cousin to an earl.

'Won't you be coming with us on the train?' Antonia pouted. 'I can't see the point of taking the car as well.'

Harry had his answer ready. 'Days out, my dear! If you're well enough we can take little jaunts into the countryside and it will save you walking to Sunday services if the church is any distance from the hotel. Besides, I mean to take Rex with me.'

'I don't see why you can't leave that dog at home,' Antonia mumbled, but he had managed to distract her and now congratulated himself on the success of his plan.

Miss Phipps went to find Daisy, who needed chivvying up. 'Haven't you got those velvet gowns steamed yet? You don't have much time left to finish everything. I hope you realize what a lucky girl you are, coming to the seaside with us.'

'Pooh!' The lady's maid was less than impressed. 'Staying in a hotel with a lot of old codgers won't be much fun! Better to stay here and get a rest, that's what I say.'

'A girl of your age shouldn't need a rest,' Miss Phipps reproved her. 'As it is, you've had very little to do recently, with Madam seeing nobody.'

'I've still had to do her mending and ironing, though, haven't I?'

'That's what you're paid for, my girl. If you don't like your job you can always give in your notice, can't you? There's plenty of young women seeking to better themselves who'd be glad to step into your shoes.'

'Not any more, there isn't. They're all nursing soldiers, or making bullets, not waiting on a rich woman who can't even manage to dress herself!'

'Shush!' Miss Phipps looked around in alarm. 'If anybody hears that kind of talk you'll be dismissed! I don't know where you get your ideas from, I really don't.'

'It's my brother, Sid. He says this war is going to change things, see? When this is all over there'll be no more rich and poor. No more tugging your forelock at them as thinks they're better than we are! And if they don't like it we'll have a revolution, like them Frenchies did, where they chopped people's heads off!'

'Nonsense! You know nothing about the French Revolution, Daisy Powell.'

'A lot more than you, Miss Phipps. I read them books about the Scarlet Pimpernel. Got them from the library, see? He's wonderful, that Sir Percy. So daring and brave.'

Lavinia didn't see how Daisy could adore Sir Percy Blakeney and sympathize with those wicked revolutionaries at the same time, but she let it go. Actually she was quite familiar with Baroness Orczy's hero, having read several of the books aloud to Mrs Morgan, but Daisy's words had started her thinking. Madam wasn't ill, so why should she need someone to read to her? She'd had a good education, so what was to stop her delving into the stories herself? Brought up in a Norfolk vicarage, Lavinia had read everything she could lay her hands on, and for her there was no greater pleasure than curling up with a good book.

Stop that at once, Lavinia Phipps! she told herself. It's not for you to judge what Madam does or does not do. She pays your wages – or at least, Mr Morgan does – so she's entitled to good service. And if she asks you to stand on your head, you'll do it!

Antonia Morgan graciously admitted that the small, private hotel seemed quite pleasant. There were several elderly occupants, retirees for the most part, including a colonel and his wife, two widowed sisters and a clergyman. There were a number of well-trained servants in the house, and within half an hour of their arrival Daisy Powell had her eye on a handsome footman who had obviously noticed her!

'I'm exhausted,' Antonia said faintly. 'I simply cannot face the thought of dressing for dinner. I shall have a tray sent up. You'll see to it, won't you, Phipps?'

'Certainly, Madam. I'll go down at once and speak to the proprietress.'

Harry looked at his wife in some distaste. 'Exhausted, my foot!' he muttered.

'What was that, Harry?'

'Just talking to myself, dear.' How could anyone be exhausted after a comfortable ride in a private coach? Especially when he'd met the train himself and his wife had only to walk a few steps to the car, with the companion in attendance.

Antonia sank down on the bed, wilting. 'See if you can find Powell, will you, darling? I need her to help me out of my things.' A piece of whalebone was protruding from her corset and jabbing her painfully in the ribs, but naturally a man could not be expected to understand that! None of them had the misfortune to wear corsets, apart from a few overweight old buffers, and that didn't bear thinking about!

Lavinia Phipps was in her element. In a larger establishment she might have been expected to eat with the servants, but here she was cautiously welcomed into the circle of residents. She joined the others in the lounge where in her most genteel manner she established her credentials in response to their gentle probing.

She managed to convey to the reverend gentleman that she was the daughter of a clergyman, now deceased, and was gratified when he nodded and said he believed he had met her father at a conference long ago: 'When I was a young man, of course.'

'Of course,' Miss Phipps agreed.

The two sisters, Mrs Davies and Mrs Grant, wanted to know where the Morgans were from and why they were here at this unfashionable time of year. Carefully Miss Phipps let fall a few nuggets of information about her employers.

'Madam is delicate and her doctor has prescribed sea air. Mr Morgan chose to come here because it isn't far from home and he'll be able to return to attend to business matters, if necessary.'

'What business is he in?' Mrs Davies asked, glancing down at her knitting.

Miss Phipps replied vaguely, explaining that he owned a colliery and a big estate with farms, among other things. She forebore to mention that she had travelled in a private railway coach with Madam and the lady's maid; that would have been construed as boasting.

Below stairs, Daisy Powell was having a much easier time fitting in. As a lady's maid she ranked higher up the social scale than the house parlour-maids, kitchen maids and the scullery maid, whose hands were raw and red.

'How many servants you got at your place, then?' the handsome footman asked.

'Only sixteen,' Daisy informed him. 'That's not much, really, for a place that size. Of course, there's no children yet, or there'd be a few more upstairs.'

'Newly married, are they, them Morgans?' the cook enquired.

'Oh, no. Been married nine years, they have, and I should know, because I started at the house the same year Madam came there to live.'

'You must be older than you look, then!' The footman grinned.

'Don't be cheeky, you! I started at the age of twelve, didn't I, like everybody else. Course, I wasn't a lady's maid then, was I?'

'Nine years and no children!' The cook went on. 'Funny, that.'

'They've lost three,' Daisy told her. 'Delicate, she is. That's why we've come here, see. The doctor reckons the sea air might do her some good.' Daisy turned her attention to the footman. 'What's a nice-looking young chap like you doing in a place like this, then?'

'Come here for the sea air, I s'pose!' He grinned.

'What's your name, then?'

'Tom Parry, if you must know!'

'Daisy Powell. Pleased to meet yer!' And she'd be even more pleased before too much longer, if she had anything to do with it, she vowed silently.

CHAPTER 5

IT WAS THE dog that Ellen noticed first. A large, noble-looking beast, trotting along with its head held high. From a distance it appeared to be blue in colour but as it came closer she realized that it was actually black and white. The ears were completely black and the tail was white, but the body was blotched with blue-black as if someone had dabbed ink on the fur. Long silky strands of hair hung down from the tail and body.

Ellen had never seen anything like it. The dogs who ran the streets of Cardiff had no known ancestry, and although lady customers sometimes brought their pets into the store these were pampered lap dogs, Pekingese or small poodles.

She wasn't used to dogs and she looked around wildly to see if there was any other human in sight to protect her. To her relief she saw a gentleman striding towards her; probably the owner of the beast.

The dog came to a halt in front of her, looking at her curiously. His mouth was open and she could have sworn he was laughing at her. Well, if he was planning to do her harm, it would have happened by now! 'Good dog!' she murmured, and the great plumey tail wagged slowly.

'Heel, Rex!' The dog trotted to his master, who raised his hat as he approached Ellen's bench. 'Good morning!' He nodded, striding on. Ellen did not reply. Only fast women spoke to strangers, gentlemen or otherwise. Nan had always stressed that; young women who were too familiar with the opposite sex deserved all they got.

Who could he be? Obviously not a working man, by his dress. Nor was he attired in typical vacation wear, such as they sold at Lloyd's – a striped blazer and light trousers. His suit was made of some brown tweedy material, as was his hat. His shiny brown boots looked as if they were made from the best quality leather, a far cry from the white sand shoes which were advertised as 'de rigueur for the promenade'.

He was tall, much like Bertie, who had been five feet ten. There the resemblance ended. This man had black hair, whereas Bertie's had been a fiery red that had given him the nickname of Carrot-top at school. Ellen's hair was a darker auburn, just as Nan's had been in her youth, although Nan's topknot had been steely grey for as long as Ellen could remember.

Bother convention! If the man crossed her path again, she would reply to his greeting. He looked to be twice her age and she had no doubt that she could outrun him if the worst came to the worst. And she'd love to see that beautiful dog again.

Harry Morgan had indulged in no such fantasies over the girl. It had been a surprise to see her sitting out there when a bitter wind was blowing in from the Bristol Channel, causing the waves to wash high over the beach, but who she was, or what she was doing there, was hardly his business. He had greeted her as a matter of course but had not been surprised when there was no response, as they had not been introduced.

Speaking of introductions, their stay at Cold Knap was beginning to pay dividends. The other guests had paid flattering attention to Antonia, and she had blossomed to the point where she was spending more time in the lounge than on her couch. This was due to the fact that Miss Phipps had indicated that Antonia was third cousin to an earl, and although Harry had winced on hearing this it did seem to have done the trick. The snobs in the group were thrilled by the Morgans' tenuous connection to high society.

Harry enjoyed the occasional chat with the colonel. Unlike some of his ilk, who bored listeners with endless tales of life in long-ago Poona, Bradshaw had an interest in country estates and showed a knowledge of sheep farming.

'Pity you've no sons to inherit all that in due course,' he mumbled. 'Not like me, old man. Three boys and not a penny piece to leave them when I'm gone. Only my pension, you see, and that dies with me. Never mind, never mind. Your lady wife is young yet. Plenty of time, what?' Harry didn't answer. The colonel was moving on, talking about horses. 'I suppose you're not interested in horseflesh now. Not when you have that fine motor out there to beetle around in.'

'Oh, I flatter myself I'm still a good judge of horseflesh. I have a decent Welsh cob for hacking around the estate and naturally I keep a couple of hunters. Then my tenants use horses for ploughing and so on. Yes, I can safely say that horses are very much a part of life at the hall.'

'Good, good. Though I daresay the car is the coming thing amongst those who can afford them, which doesn't include me, I'm sorry to say. Wouldn't mind having a run out in that machine of yours, though, if you'd be so kind. I'd like to see how fast she can go. I don't suppose she could beat those hunters of yours?'

'On a straight stretch of road, yes. The car doesn't do too well leaping hedges or five-bar gates, though!'

'That's a good one, old boy, what? Haw! Haw!'

Antonia sniffed when she heard that Harry was taking the colonel out. 'Really, Harry, why on earth? Surely you can't have anything in common with that old bore?'

'Actually, I do, but that's not the point. If it gives him pleasure to go for a spin, where's the harm in that? Why should you care what I do, anyway?'

'Because I'd like you to drive me into Cardiff. It's about time I had a new hat. And if you're feeling charitable we can take Mrs Davies and Mrs Grant with us. They've been kind to me and this would be a way to repay them. Surely there's somewhere in the city where they do cream teas? They'd like that, I'm sure.'

Lavinia Phipps had such an expression of longing on her face that Harry almost laughed. 'We could probably squeeze Miss Phipps in as well, if we leave Rex behind! When would you care to go, Antonia? Tomorrow afternoon, perhaps?'

This was something new. He could hardly believe it. His reclusive wife had not only made some friends but was prepared to go on a shopping expedition to the city! When at home she did not need to venture out to the shops, such as they were in Cwmbran. Hats and gowns were sent out to her on approval, so that she could make her selection without stepping out of doors. Garments which she didn't care for were sent back at once, while bills would be submitted in due course for anything she kept. This was a step in the right direction. The sea air and the change of scene must be doing her good.

Ellen had not been able to keep thoughts of the little encounter out of her head. Would they come this way again? When she had taken up her usual place on the bench overlooking the sea she jumped on hearing a loud bark. 'Hello, Rex! Good dog!' she murmured, when he came up to sniff at her outstretched hand. He sat down suddenly, laughing up at her. She pretended not to notice his owner, striding towards her.

'Good morning!' Once again the man tipped his hat. 'I see that Rex has made a friend. Do you like dogs?'

'He seems very friendly. What breed is he?'

'A setter, aren't you, boy?' Rex thumped his tail.

'Oh, but I thought that setters are red, aren't they?'

'You're thinking of an Irish setter. This is an English setter. They come in different colours. Rex is what is known as a blue belton.'

'He's lovely, with all that long hair hanging down, sort of like a curtain.'

'Those are known as feathers, which is appropriate in a way as these dogs are bred for field work. Unfortunately Rex is gun shy so he's no good for that. His breeder was thinking of having him put down, so I took him on as a companion animal.'

Ellen was shocked to hear that anyone could think of having such a magnificent creature destroyed, and said so. Harry Morgan laughed. 'Well, as you can see, it didn't happen. I've had him for six years now, and I hope we'll go on together for at least another six.'

Fondling the dog's ears, Ellen was disappointed to hear the man say they had to be off. 'I've promised to drive my wife and her friends to Cardiff this afternoon. They want to buy new hats or some such nonsense.'

'They have a good selection at Lloyd's,' she replied, to cover her confusion. 'A new shipment arrived just before I left.'

'You know Cardiff, then, obviously.'

'I work at Lloyd's. At least, I did. I don't know if I'll have a job when I go back.'

'I see,' he said, not understanding at all. 'Then I'll say good day to you.' He lifted his hat again, and strode off, with Rex at his heels.

Sadly, Ellen watched them go. She might have known he'd be married. A man like that, well bred, and obviously well to do; he'd be a catch for any woman. Lady, she corrected herself. She imagined him married to some society beauty, the sort who hunted all winter, and ran the local branch of the Red Cross.

Of course, they would have several children, little girls who wore pretty dresses under starched pinafores, and little boys who were away at boarding school. Unless, of course, the sons were old enough to be fighting in this terrible war. Come to that, why wasn't this man at the front, leading his men 'over the top'? They took them at all ages now, and he seemed fit enough. Perhaps he had already served, and been wounded, and was at the seaside to convalesce before returning to the fray. If he spoke to her again, she would ask him about that. Indulging in these fantasies, she was unaware that she was beginning to fall in love with Rex's owner.

CHAPTER 6

Harry Morgan hadn't been able to get Ellen out of his mind. It was quite silly, of course. They'd hardly spoken more than a few words; in fact, he'd done most of the talking! She seemed so unspoiled compared with the ladies he knew, and it was evident she'd been genuinely interested in what he'd had to say on the subject of field dogs.

He'd gathered that she was a shop assistant, so what was she doing on the sea front at this time of year, and on her own? He liked to get to the bottom of things, and his curiosity was piqued. He'd find out more about her the next time they met.

'Don't be such a fool, Harry Morgan!' he snapped, only realizing he'd spoken aloud when Rex scraped him painfully on the leg with an uplifted paw. 'It's all right, old boy, just thinking! And you need your claws clipped. I'll do that for you when we get back.'

Harry was not the sort of man to play fast and loose with the affections of women. He also knew that he had to beware of giving the wrong impression to emotional young females, ladies or otherwise. A friend of his was even now being sued for breach of promise by an unstable woman, old enough to know better, who insisted that he had proposed marriage to her and then reneged. The man in question insisted there had been nothing at all beyond the bounds of friendship, but that didn't matter. His name would be dragged through the courts and his reputation sullied.

The best thing to do was to drive home to Cwmbran to see how things were going on the estate. He'd made up his mind to do that soon in any case; he would just set off a little earlier than planned. Antonia received the news with disinterest.

'I suppose you'll be coming back at the weekend? We'll want a drive to church.'

'Yes, yes; I shan't be away for long. Are you and Miss Phipps enjoying the books you bought in Cardiff?'

'Oh, yes. The new Baroness Orczy is quite exciting.'

'Another Scarlet Pimpernel adventure, I suppose?'

'Yes, but the authoress herself is a most interesting woman. The colonel was telling us at tea that she is very much involved in the Order of the White Feather, you know.'

'What? Oh, you mean that silly business that Admiral Fitzgerald started up last year? Women with nothing better to do handing out white feathers for cowardice to any poor chap they suspect of slacking. Naturally Colonel Bradshaw would approve of that. Having spent his youth wiping out rebel tribesmen in India he'd like to send everyone else off to fight the beastly Hun. In that case it's a wonder I haven't been presented with a white feather.'

'Don't be silly, dear. He knows that coal mining is a reserved occupation, and you're needed at home to keep everything running smoothly. You're already fighting the war in your own way.'

Harry laughed. 'Whatever you say, dear.'

Below stairs, Daisy was regaling the other servants with what she'd overheard while she was putting away Mrs Morgan's newly washed lingerie.

'Ever so clever he is, that Sir Percy Blakeney. He gets disguised as a washerwoman and rescues aristos from under the noses of them Frenchies before they get sent to the guillotine. That's a machine that chops their heads off.'

'What's an aristo when it's at home?' Cook demanded.

'Them lords and ladies in France, so Madam told me.'

'You're pulling my leg, girl. If anyone's killing people in France it's that there Kaiser, and when there's a war on, people get themselves shot. Chopping their heads off, indeed! I never heard such nonsense.'

Daisy realized she was on thin ice here, although she wasn't sure why. She changed the subject. 'That baroness must know what she's talking about, or she wouldn't put it in a book. And Mrs Morgan says that the baroness is a great believer in handing out white feathers to men who won't go and fight. Then they go and join up. The more men that go to the war, the quicker that Kaiser will cave in. Stands to reason, see?'

'I'm surprised nobody give you one of them feathers yet, Tom Parry,' the parlour maid said slyly. She regarded him as her own property but ever since this upstart lady's maid had arrived he'd been flirting with her instead. He needed taking down a peg or two.

Parry's face reddened, but he made no reply.

'Now you leave the boy alone, my girl!' the cook snapped. 'He's needed here. It takes all sorts to win a war, and what would happen to all the ladies and gentlemen if they found themselves with nobody to wait on them?'

'Do them a power of good, lazy so-and-sos,' Muriel muttered under her breath.

'What was that I heard you say?'

'Nothing, Cook. I just wondered who'd cook the food.'

'Me, of course, you fool. I'd not be going off to war, would I, white feather or no white feather.'

Muriel giggled at the thought of Cook wearing a tin hat and armed with a sword, or would it be a rifle? There had been a drawing in the newspaper depicting Britannia, whose build, according to the artist, was much like that of their cook.

But Daisy was staring at Tom, whose complexion had gone from red to white. Something was up with him, and she vowed to find out what it was.

That afternoon, when many people in the house were enjoying a nap, she went in search of him. Having run him to earth in the stables, where he was glumly talking to the coachman, she favoured him with a flirtatious smile.

'There you are, Tom! Fancy coming for a walk, then? I'd love a bit of sea air.'

'Oh aye?' The coachman grinned. 'You got it made, haven't you, boyo! Off you go then, and show the lady the sights, and make sure she don't see one sight too many!'

Red around the ears once more, Tom followed her outside, none too pleased at the interruption. 'What you playing at then? I was just about to get a tip on a horse from old Raymond there. I need a bit of luck, see. A fellow can't live on the mingy wages they offer at this place. I have to make a bit on the side.'

'More likely lose a bit. Backing horses is a mug's game.'

'It's none of your business what I do. And like I asked you, why'd you follow me out here? I never asked you to come.'

'I came because I think you're in trouble and I reckon I can help. I saw the way you looked when we said about white feathers. Somebody pinned one on you, have they?'

'No, they haven't, then,' he blustered.

'That's a surprise, then. Footman isn't a reserved occupation as far as I know.'

'It's my eyes, isn't it. I tried to join up and they turned me down. Told me I'd never be able to see the Hun in the distance, let alone shoot one. "You go back where you come from, lad, and leave the fighting to those who can manage it," they said.'

But Daisy had seen him reading the newspaper and he didn't seem half blind to her. She said as much. She was shocked by the fury on his face.

'It ain't none of your business, Miss Nosy Parker! And don't you go spreading lies about me all over the place, or you'll get what's coming to yer!'

But Daisy had grown up in a mining village and had learned to stand up to the boys she went to school with. 'You don't scare me, Tom Parry! You're in trouble, aren't you? Why, I bet you're a deserter. That's why you're frightened of your own shadow!'

She hadn't believed this for a moment, and was shocked when he sank down on a nearby bench with his face in his hands, and began to sob.

'You don't know what it's like at the front, Daisy. Nobody does, unless they've been there. It's not just the blood, and the mud and the wounded horses screaming. It's the noise. It's those guns, it never stops. It gets so you wish your number was up, so you'd never have to go over the top again. I had good mates over there, and every one of them's dead now. One of them was only sixteen. He got shot out in no-man's land and he lay out there all night, calling for his Mam. I couldn't stand it no more, Daisy.'

Perhaps this was what they called being shell shocked, Daisy thought. She put her arm around his shaking shoulders in a clumsy attempt to comfort him.

'So what did you do? How did you get away from there?'

'It was the retreat from Mons. It was like a scene from hell, Daisy, confusion everywhere. I just kept walking. Then I came face to face with a Hun.'

'No! What happened next?'

'I shot him and he shot me. We must've both fired at the same time. I blew his head off and he got me in the shoulder. I lay there dazed for a bit until a stretcher party come along and scooped me up. "You've got a blighty one, mate," they said, and took me to a casualty clearing station, and eventually I finished up back in England.'

'So you're not a coward,' Daisy told him firmly. 'You didn't desert in the face of the enemy. In fact, you polished one of them off.'

'But I walked away from the hospital when they were getting ready to send me back. And I'm hiding here because I know what they do to deserters. I'll be shot.'

'Well, we'll have to see that doesn't happen,' Daisy said, all sympathy now.

'You mean you won't tell on me?' He had a look of hope on his face.

'No, but you can't stay here. I'm surprised you've lasted this long. I know what you can do. I'll send you down to Cwmbran and our Sid will look after you.'

CHAPTER 7

ELLEN HAD TAKEN to walking to another part of the coast, and for his part, Harry Morgan had avoided going in the direction of the bench where the girl usually sat. Therefore, when they finally came across each other, Ellen thought of it as fate, while he considered it a damn nuisance. They were unable to avoid each other, particularly when Rex bounded joyfully to Ellen's side, displaying his appealing doggy grin as he came.

'May I join you?' A pebble had somehow worked its way inside Harry's well-polished boot and was rubbing against his ankle bone. He needed to sit down to remove it.

'Yes, please do,' Ellen murmured. 'Isn't it a lovely day?'

'Yes, indeed, Miss er ...'

'Richards. My name is Ellen Richards.'

'And mine is Harry Morgan,' he responded. He was annoyed with himself, for this put them on a different footing, one he had been determined to avoid. She was looking at him with wide grey eyes and he realized that something more was needed.

'My wife and I are staying at a private hotel over at Cold Knap, Miss Richards. Mrs Morgan is delicate and her doctor prescribed sea air for a few weeks.'

'I'm sorry. I hope she'll feel better soon.' Ellen felt a pang of disappointment. The Morgans would be returning home soon, and she'd never see him again. On the other hand, that very knowledge seemed to allow them a certain amount of freedom. Ships that pass in the night; wasn't that how the saying went?

'Are you here on holiday, Miss Richards?'

'I suppose I am, Mr Morgan. I gave in my notice at work so I could get away. I wasn't due any holidays and they wouldn't give me compassionate leave, you see.'

'Ah, this wretched war!' he nodded. 'Forgive me for asking, but was it your sweetheart who was killed? Or your father, perhaps?' She looked too young for it to have been a husband.

'It was my brother Bertie. He fell at the third battle of Ypres.'

'Ah.'

They sat in silence for a while, and then she said simply, 'Bertie was all I had, you see. I had to come away to try to make sense of it all. Does that sound mad?'

'Not at all. Although how anyone could make sense out of slaughter and destruction is beyond me. But you're all alone, you say; have you no parents?'

'They died of typhoid fever when we were small. My grandmother brought us up, but she died two years ago, which left just Bertie and me. And now he's gone as well, and I don't know what to do next. He was the one who always made the decisions, you see. I'm lost without him.'

'I know it's hard, but you'll learn to make your way eventually,' he soothed. Unfortunately this girl wasn't the only young thing to be left on her own. The orphanages were full of bereaved and abandoned youngsters and the situation was likely to become much worse before this war was over.

'Pardon me for asking, but how old are you, Miss Richards?'

'Nineteen. I had my birthday in February.'

He sighed. The worst possible age. Too old to be looked after by the state, yet too young to have learned much in the way of self-sufficiency.

'I know what you're thinking, Mr Morgan. I should go and be a VAD and nurse wounded soldiers. Lots of girls my age are doing that, but I don't think I could face it. Every time I saw a dying man or one with terrible injuries I'd imagine it was Bertie. I know I'm a coward, but it's no good trying to make myself do it.'

'I wasn't thinking that at all. Not everyone is cut out to work with the sick and injured. I probably shouldn't be much good at it myself. Perhaps you should consider going into service? Good parlour maids are much in demand, with so many women going off to make munitions.'

He was alarmed to see the look of hope in her eyes. Good grief! Did she imagine he was offering her a job? He could imagine what Antonia would say if he presented her with an untrained girl he'd picked up on the beach!

'You'd better give it some thought,' he said hastily. 'It doesn't do to make sudden decisions in times of crisis. You must have friends back in Cardiff who could advise you. One of the young women you work with, for instance?'

'There's Mari, I suppose, but she doesn't really understand. She's still got both her parents, as well as a horde of brothers. If one got killed she'd be sad, of course, but she'd still have all the others.' Tears welled up in her eyes and she began to sob.

Now what was he supposed to do? Feeling awkward, he placed an arm around her thin shoulders. She flung her arms around him and looked up at him. Afterwards he was unable to decide whether he had kissed her first or if she had made the first move.

Tom Parry had recovered from his momentary panic. When he next saw Daisy he took her aside and spoke urgently to her.

'Nothing can go wrong if you keep your mouth shut!' he warned.

'I won't say a word, cross my heart and hope to die.' She admitted to herself that she fancied him rotten, so why would she want to get him shot?

'That's all right, then.'

'But you can't trust that Muriel, and that means you're not safe here.'

'Oh, her! She don't know nothing.'

'She fancies you, and she doesn't like you speaking to me. If she could see us now, I bet she'd fetch a white feather to pin on you, quicker than you can say knife!'

He shrugged. 'So what? I'll just say what I told you. I tried to join up but they turned me down on account of my eyesight.'

'You'll have to do better than that. She's not stupid. She's seen you reading them newspapers, same as me. Can't you think of something more convincing than that?'

'I'll say I've got flat feet or knock knees or something, all right?'

'I don't know as I could fancy a chap with knock knees,' Daisy said, pasting a coy expression on her face.

'Is that so? What makes you think I'd show you my knees anyway, huh?'

'If you was to go swimming I'd see your legs,' she countered.

'Not in this weather, you won't.'

Daisy sidled closer. 'But you do like me a bit, don't you, Tom?'

He pretended to consider this remark. 'Maybe I do, maybe I don't.'

'I've promised to keep your secret, haven't I? A person should always seal a bargain with a kiss, you know.'

'I never heard that.' He grinned, but he obediently put his arms around her and gave her a smacking kiss.

'Here, can't you do better than that?' She raised her mouth to his once more and this time he demonstrated what he was capable of with a lingering embrace.

*

'What you looking at, Muriel?' The kitchen maid had noticed the older girl standing at the window with a face like a wet week. 'Something going on outside, is there? Move aside and let me get a look-in, do.'

'It's Tom Parry and that Miss Powell, as she calls herself. Kissing, they are, and in broad daylight, too! Lady's maid, indeed! If Mrs Morgan could see the way she's been carrying on she'd be out on her ear and no mistake.'

'You could go and tell on her,' Betsy suggested.

'I could, but that wouldn't do me much good with Tom Parry if he's sweet on the trollop and Mrs Morgan gives her the sack.'

'For all he knows Mrs Morgan could have seen them at it, just like you done.'

'And since when do the ladies come down here to the kitchen? The guest rooms look out over the sea. No, I'll have to think of something else.'

Muriel had come up with a plan that could have far-reaching consequences for Tom Parry. It would put paid to her chances, but he deserved to get into trouble after the way he'd treated her. She'd been good enough for a kiss and a cuddle in dark corners until that stuck-up Powell floozy arrived on the scene.

She had a white feather in her pocket, and when the guests were assembled at dinner that evening, served by herself and Tom Parry, she would step forward and pin it on him.

Usually, any lack of decorum would pitchfork her into trouble with the management, but on this occasion she didn't see how she could go wrong. All the ladies loved those Scarlet Pimpernel books and had been loud in their praise of the authoress, who, when she wasn't penning her books, was busy handing out white feathers to every man between fifteen and fifty who was not in uniform.

Surely the colonel and the reverend would be all for it. The colonel! That was a thought. In for a penny, in for a pound! When the deed was done she'd turn to him and ask him outright if he didn't think that the footman should be fighting for king and country. He could hardly disagree. With any luck he'd speak to the management and encourage them to let Tom go. That would teach the fool to mind his manners. Instead of kissing bold hussies like that, he should be off killing Huns, like any proper man.

CHAPTER 8

'SOMETHING MOST EXTRAORDINARY happened at dinner last night,' Harry remarked. He and Ellen were strolling along the prom, oblivious to the rain spitting on their faces. Rex bounded ahead of them, stopping occasionally to lift a leg when he located an interesting smell. 'The footman was serving the Brussels sprouts when all of a sudden the maid walked over to him, calm as you please, and pinned a white feather on his jacket, telling him he should be ashamed of himself, skulking around at Barry when he should be in France!'

'Oh, dear,' Ellen murmured. She wasn't sure how Harry felt about this so she didn't want to commit herself. After all, he wasn't in uniform himself.

'The funny thing was, all the ladies clapped enthusiastically,' he went on. 'One would have expected them to be affronted by such a display, but they seemed to feel that the sentiments expressed by the girl excused her. Or so my wife led me to believe when we discussed the matter afterwards.'

'I see.'

'Of course, as Antonia said, the girl quite overstepped the bounds of propriety when she then addressed Colonel Bradshaw and instructed him to investigate the poor lad's background, in case he was hiding something!'

Antonia. So his wife was called Antonia. We shouldn't be meeting like this, Ellen reminded herself. Harry was smiling, recalling the scene. The footman had rushed from the room, still clutching the vegetable tureen. The maid had stood back, panting, to let him pass. Harry would have given a lot to witness the scene in the kitchen.

'Where would you like to go today?' he asked. 'I feel we've seen enough of Barry Island, and we've gone over to Porthkerry twice. Would you like a spin in my car?'

'Oh, I don't know! I've never been in a motor car.'

'Well, as my old nanny used to say, you'll never be younger to learn!'

'But what about Rex?'

'Oh, he loves to go for a drive, don't you, old fellow?' He scratched the dog's ears, and Rex looked up at him adoringly. 'Come on, Ellen. You're not frightened, are you?'

'No, but …' she left the words unsaid. He understood at once.

'You're afraid that someone might see us, is that it?' Ellen nodded silently. If someone reported back to Antonia it would be hard to explain what he'd been doing, driving about with a strange young woman in his car. Now he thought quickly.

'You stay here and wait for me, while I nip back to the hotel to fetch the car. It won't take me long. All right?'

Ellen agreed. She badly wanted to spend more time with him, and the idea of driving somewhere else appealed to her. Only last night she'd had a nightmare in which the two of them had been standing on the prom, staring out to sea, when a large woman had come up behind them and started to scream that she was Harry's lawful wife and that if Ellen knew what was good for her she'd walk into the water and let herself drown. When she woke up, relieved to find that none of this was true, she admitted to herself that the dream was probably the result of a guilty conscience.

But had she really done anything so wicked? Apart from that one kiss – which was a chaste sort of affair when all was said and done – they'd only walked along the sea front together, talking. Even though he was a married man there wasn't anything wrong with that, was there? Not really wrong!

She could imagine what Nan would have said, though. She was full of little moral sayings, any one of which could be trotted out as the occasion demanded. 'Avoid the appearance of evil' was one of them.

What Ellen failed to admit to herself was that she had fallen in love with Harry Morgan. She'd even indulged in a little fantasy where the two of them were married, but what could be more ridiculous? For that to happen, Antonia Morgan would somehow have to disappear from the scene, and she was very much alive. Nor did Ellen wish her any harm.

Divorce was impossible. Some people did manage it, if they were wealthy enough, but it finished them in society, especially the women. Antonia Morgan would never agree to such a thing, even if she no longer wanted her husband. People did die unexpectedly, of course. Harry would be free then. Would he marry Ellen? Of course not. It was highly unlikely that a wealthy man would marry a shop girl, because that would give society another reason for turning its collective back on him. The gulf between the classes could never be bridged.

The gulls rose screaming into the sky as the car made its noisy approach. She climbed in, resolving to live for the moment.

'In the back, Rex! Get in the back!' Harry instructed. The dog panted in her ear as Ellen settled herself in the passenger seat.

The hotel had been in an uproar, ever since that astonishing scene where the maid, Muriel, had disgraced herself. Grimly watching the events unfold, the proprietress had vowed to sack the girl as soon as the meal was over. However, she changed her mind when she understood how everyone present supported what the chit had done. 'Just wait until I get hold of her later, though,' she sniffed. 'I'll give her a piece of my mind she won't forget in a hurry!'

But before that could happen, Muriel had to run the gauntlet of her fellow servants.

'What's up with you, lad, coming back down here with those sprouts? Nothing wrong with them, is there? And don't tell me you've finished handing everything else round; you haven't been up there long enough.' Cook glared at Tom, her face red.

'I'm not going back up there to be insulted, so you can put that in your pipe and smoke it!'

'Don't you speak to me like that! Now, are you going to tell me what's going on, or do I have to lambaste it out of you?' She threatened him with her wooden spoon.

'I've done nothing wrong!' Muriel came into the room, carrying an empty platter. 'I gave this layabout a white feather, and about time, too!'

'That's not all you done!' Tom barked, turning back to face the cook. 'She told the colonel he should look into my background in case I've got something to hide!'

'Oh, well, that's just hot air, and so he'll find out, so no harm done, then.'

But Daisy Powell knew better. She jerked her head in the direction of the garden door, indicating that Tom should follow her out.

'Now you've got to go!' she urged him. 'That colonel may not be in the army any more, but he'll find out about you leaving that hospital. I bet you're not the only one who's disappeared and they've probably got a long list of such men up in London. They'll have you clapped in irons before you can say Jack Robinson!'

'I'll go up and speak to him after dinner,' he muttered. 'I'll tell him I was hurt at Mons. Show him my scars. I'll say the doctors told me I'm not fit to serve no more.'

'Don't be an idiot! He'll want to see your discharge papers.'

'Then I'll say I lost them.'

This was so obviously silly that Daisy didn't dignify it with an answer. 'You wait till tonight and then get down to the station. There's a train to Cardiff at 8.10. I already looked up the timetable in case. In the morning you can hop on another one and go down to Cwmbran. I'll write you a note to give to my brother. He'll hide you.'

'How do I know I can trust him, then?'

'Course you can trust him! He's against this stupid war, isn't he? He was engaged to this girl, see; Sian, her name was. She went off to be one of them VADs and got herself killed in France. It isn't only you men who die, you know. After that he went around saying he was a Conchie.'

'All right for him, though, isn't it? He's a miner. They can't do nothing to him.'

'That's all you know, Tom Parry. Mr Morgan don't like miners what speak out of turn. Working down the pit is like any other job. If you don't keep your place you're thrown out on your ear with nowhere to go.'

Tom stared at her in horror. 'You mean your Sid works for them Morgans upstairs? You didn't tell me that, Daisy.'

'What's the matter with that, then? You know I work for the mistress; Sid works for Mr Morgan too, only not in the house, of course.'

'But I didn't know you come from the same place as the Morgans, did I? I thought you only went there when you went into service. And surely Morgan has something to do with the railways? I thought he owned them, maybe, what with you lot coming here on a private coach.'

'He owns a lot of things. He has a finger in every pie, Miss Phipps says.'

'Then don't be so daft, girl! What am I going to do, move into his house and work as a footman, after he sat there listening to what Muriel had to say tonight? Going to this Cwmbran of yours is the worst thing I could do.'

'No, of course not, but there's other places you can work. Sid'll think of something. The first thing we've got to do is get you away from here. You get back upstairs and pretend everything's all right. I'll meet you out here at half seven and give you the letter for Sid. All right?'

'I suppose it'll have to be. What are you going to do in the meantime?'

'I'll have to go and attend to Madam. I'll keep my ears open for any sign of trouble.' After a hasty embrace they returned to the house by different routes so as not to be observed. Daisy was well pleased with the way things had turned out. It had been wicked of Muriel to do what she did, but it had worked in Daisy's favour. Now she and Tom would be living in close proximity in Cwmbran, and that could only be good!

CHAPTER 9

'WELL, I DON'T rightly know what to say.' Sid Powell scratched his head with dirt-encrusted nails. 'Our Daisy wants us to hide you, but what are we going to do with you? I suppose you've no other place to go?'

'Oh, I can move on if you can't help me,' Tom said stiffly, getting up to leave, but he subsided when the other man raised a hand to stop him.

'I didn't say that, man. It says here our Daisy is sweet on you, and she's depending on me to help. Give us the truth, now; do you feel the same about her?'

'Um, yes, I do.' In fact, Tom wasn't at all sure how he felt. He was grateful to her, but women had a way of twisting things to pin a man down. Still, he needed a bolthole.

'What's your story, then? Wounded at Mons, it says here. That right?'

'Aye, and I've got the scars to prove it.' He unbuttoned his shirt to reveal his injured shoulder. 'I was in hospital for weeks with this. One of the doctors told me I'd never have the full use of my arm again, and I thought I'd be back home for good. Then I made such an improvement they started talking about sending me back to fight, and I couldn't face it. Call me a coward if you want, but only those who've been in the thick of it can know what it's like. I just walked out of that hospital one day and never looked back. I tramped all the way into Wales, thinking I'd be safe here, and I would have been but for that blasted Muriel. Jealousy, that's all it was. I'll swear she didn't know my story, but I knew that once that old colonel got on the scent it'd be all up.'

'I can see that. I'll help you, Parry, for our Daisy's sake. We can't have her sweetheart sent to face a firing squad at dawn, can we? But where are we to put you? In a pinch, we could hide you in a disused mine shaft, but I don't suppose you'd fancy staying down there for the duration of the war, would you?' He was only half joking.

Tom shuddered. If he had to spend weeks far below the earth, he'd go stark staring mad. They might as well send him straight to an asylum and have done with it.

Sid saw the expression on the other man's face and regretted his words. 'That's no good, then. If you're sure you want to stay here we'll have to find you a job. Then you won't stand out as much. I don't suppose you've got any experience at mining?'

'I'd try anything but that. It's my right shoulder, see? I'm not fit to swing a pick. It'd give out in no time.'

'Perhaps a clerical job, then, in the colliery office.'

'And what do I do when the boss turns up? Don't forget he knows all about me!'

'I'm only thinking aloud, boyo! Can't you see this has caught me on the hop? The only other work round here is farming, but unless you stayed in a shepherd's *bwth* up the mountain, that's no good, either. All the farmers are tenants of old Morgan, and the man calls on them regularly. You'd spend half your time dodging him.'

'I told Daisy this wouldn't work,' Tom grunted, his disappointment plain.

It was then that a grin spread over Sid's face. 'I've had an idea! Now don't interrupt until I've spelled it out.'

Tom listened carefully, slapping his knee when Sid had finished. 'It's a crazy notion, but it just might work!'

Three days later, Tom Parry presented himself at an army recruiting post.

'You're here to join up, are you? Good man!'

'Yes, sir!' Tom forced himself to grin at the sergeant.

'What do you do in civilian life, son?'

'Coal miner, sir,' Tom lied.

'Splendid, splendid! We could do with more like you, but miners are hard to recruit, being in a reserved occupation.'

'Sir?'

'Sappers and miners, boy, sappers and miners!'

Seeing Tom's puzzlement, the man went on to explain. 'We need experienced men to tunnel underneath enemy lines, son.'

'Whatever for?'

'To set explosives where they're needed, and possibly for other reasons I'm not allowed to divulge. You'd like that, wouldn't you, son?'

Tom bit back an oath, cursing Sid Powell to hell and back. The big idea had been to pretend he wanted to join up, in the certain knowledge that the army doctors would see his injuries and turn him down. Then, armed with a letter saying he was unfit for service, he could walk out a free man. Thomas Parry was a common enough name; he could then get a job anywhere as someone who'd tried to join up without success.

Now, though, he was in real trouble. Suppose the army was so desperate for recruits that the doctors turned a blind eye to his well-healed wound? He'd find himself engaged in that tunnelling business! He'd almost rather go back to facing the guns than go underground like a mole. And surely the Huns had the same idea? What if you were going along on your hands and knees and you came face to face with one of the other side? It didn't bear thinking about!

Ellen's holiday at Barry was coming to an end. She couldn't stay there until her money ran out because she'd need something to live on after she returned to Cardiff. She might find work at Barry – presumably some of the guest houses would need maids when the next holiday season started – but what was the point of that? Harry would be leaving for home. There would be nothing to keep her here.

'We always knew this had to come to an end sometime, didn't we, *cariad*,' Harry murmured when she confided her distress to him.

'I know, Harry, but it's so hard!' Ellen blinked back the tears, determined not to break down in front of him.

'Besides,' he added, in an attempt to make her smile, 'what would you want with an old man like me? I'm forty years old and you're only nineteen. I'll be an old man when you're still in the prime of life.'

'It wouldn't make any difference to me. I'd love you no matter how old you were!'

'Even if I was hairless with no teeth?' he teased. 'Let's not spoil the day by thinking sad thoughts. Come on, Rex is desperate for a walk. Shall we join him?'

They had driven over to Wenvoe. The warmer weather had brought people down to the shore and they ran the risk of being seen together. On top of that, Ellen relished the idea of having another outing in Harry's beautiful car.

They strolled down a leafy lane, with Rex racing ahead. Absorbed in each other's company, the pair failed to notice the clouds racing across the sky, and within minutes the rain was lashing down.

'We'll get soaked if we try to get back to the car,' Harry groaned. 'Thank goodness I put the hood up or the upholstery would be ruined. Look, there's some sort of farm building over there. What say we take shelter until the worst is over?'

Ellen was timid at the thought of trespassing and perhaps being accosted by some irate farmer, but the rain was already running inside the neck of her blouse so she allowed Harry to help her over the fence. Hand in hand they raced across the sodden grass and fell inside the building, which proved to be half full of hay.

For a while they made small talk, glancing anxiously across the fields to see if the rain showed any sign of abating, but then Ellen began to shiver. 'It was silly of me to leave my jacket in the car,' she murmured, 'but the weather was so nice when we started out on our walk.'

'If I'd known this was going to happen I'd have brought a rug and some food.' Harry grimaced. 'Next time I'll provide a picnic.'

'Next time!'

'Oh, poor Ellen! I don't know what made me say that. I suppose I can't bear the thought of never seeing you again either.'

She waited, hoping he was going to tell her it wasn't over, that they would manage to see each other somehow. He could tell Antonia he had to go to Cardiff on business....

'You really are cold, aren't you, *cariad*,' he said eventually. 'Come here and let me warm you up.'

He held out his arms and she sank into them gratefully. She raised her face to his and he kissed her, softly at first, and then more intensely. It was inevitable that one thing should lead to another. Afterwards he asked himself why he had let it happen. He hadn't meant to take advantage of such a vulnerable young girl. He was a cad, a rotter.

The very fact that Ellen was gazing up at him with such adoration in her eyes only made him feel worse.

'I love you, Harry,' she whispered. 'I'll love you till I die.'

'I love you too, *cariad*,' he answered, for what else was there to say? She was a decent young woman and he could not bring himself to leave her with the impression that their coming together had been a mistake.

'Look, there's a rainbow,' she told him. 'Isn't it beautiful?'

'It is indeed, *cariad*. Now, since the rain seems to have stopped, we'd better make our way back to the car. And I'm afraid it's time we started back to Barry.'

Ellen was very quiet all the way back, and when he let her out of the car around the corner from her boarding house he didn't dare to kiss her goodbye, in case hostile eyes were watching. 'Take good care of yourself, *cariad*,' he said instead, and then was gone.

CHAPTER 10

THE DISAPPEARANCE OF the footman was the talk of the hotel.

'This is all your fault, young Muriel!' Cook snapped. 'Until the mistress can find a replacement you'll just have to do his work as well as your own, and serve you right!'

'I don't care! Able-bodied men should join up. Lord Kitchener says so.'

'Phooey! What do you know about Lord Kitchener then, eh? Kitchener would be the first to tell Tom to stay on and work out his notice, like a Christian should. But where is the boy now? That's what I want to know.'

'I expect he went to join up,' Daisy said. She was waiting to take a break-fast tray up to Antonia, who had decided to have a day in bed. Nice for some people!

'Muriel must have put the wind up him good and proper, then, if he had to run off in the night like that. There's something here that don't meet the eye.'

Daisy said nothing. She knew that Tom had slipped away to catch the evening train but she hoped it would be a while before anyone found that out. They might learn that he had taken the Cardiff train but after that, with any luck, the trail would go cold.

As it happened nobody bothered to track him down. The ladies shared the view that he had gone 'to do the right thing' having been shamed into it by the patriotic Muriel.

'More likely the young rogue has run off to avoid nagging women,' the colonel grunted, in a tone which suggested that he wished he might do the same.

'But aren't you going to try to bring him back, Colonel?' Mrs Davies flut-tered.

'What for? The chap's done nothing wrong, as far as I know. If he chooses to avoid serving his country that's his business, reprehensible though it might be.'

43

Two days later a letter arrived, brought up with the Morgans' post on a silver salver by the proprietress herself. Daisy was arranging Antonia's hair and she waited with growing impatience while her mistress sorted through the bundle of letters.

'Why, Powell, this one seems to be addressed to you. How strange!' Antonia turned it over in her hand while Daisy prayed that the woman wouldn't slit it open. 'Who could be writing to you, I wonder? I hope it's not from a young man. You know I don't allow followers.'

'Thank you, Madam.' Daisy took the envelope and pushed it down inside her apron pocket. 'It's from my brother, Madam.'

'And why would your brother be writing to you, Powell?'

Biting back a rude answer, Daisy forced herself to answer meekly, 'I expect he's writing to thank me for the birthday card I sent him last week, Madam. Shall I open it and see?'

'No, but I see it's postmarked Cwmbran. Isn't your brother in the army, then?'

'He works down the pit, Madam. He's employed by Mr Morgan.'

Antonia lost interest. 'I don't think I like what you've done with my hair, Powell. I'd like to try something different. Take it down and begin again, will you?'

'Yes, Madam.'

Daisy's stomach was tied up in knots by the time she could get away to read Sid's letter. Apparently he'd suspected that the letter might be read by other eyes, for the message was cryptic. 'Parcel received safely. Your loving brother, Sid.'

It was highly unsatisfactory, but for the moment it would have to do. Of course she would have preferred a chatty letter but her brother knew as well as she did that servants had no privacy. Antonia Morgan would have died rather than read someone else's mail when it came to her own class, but servants didn't count. If pressed she would no doubt have said that employers had the right to pry because they were responsible for the moral welfare of the people in their charge.

'Wait there, son, until you're fetched.'

Tom Parry sat on the hard wooden bench, his mind whirling. What if things didn't work out as planned? He'd have to go on the run again. Perhaps it would be best to do a bunk now, except he'd have to get past that eagle-eyed sergeant first.

'Next!' A thin chap, wearing a corporal's stripe on his arm, glared at Tom. 'Come on, then, let's be having yer! Quick, sharp!' Tom followed him through the double doors into a room full of half-naked men, where he was told to strip off.

'What's this, then?' the doctor prodded the scars on Tom's shoulder, making him wince. 'Looks like you've been in the wars, lad!'

'No, sir. I mean, yes, sir.'

'Come on, man, I don't have time to waste. Which is it, then?'

'I mean, I've been hurt, but I haven't been in the army.'

The doctor peered at the wound suspiciously.

'This looks like gunshot wounds to me.'

'Yes, sir. I got shot when I was working as a beater. In the wrong place at the wrong time, if you get my meaning.'

'Indeed, yes. This must have been very nasty at the time, although it seems to be well healed now.'

Tom held his breath. The doctor seemed to be pondering his decision.

'I suppose you're quite eager to go over and take pot shots at the Hun, hey? Shoot up a few people for yourself.'

'Yes, sir.' Tom nodded, mentally crossing his fingers.

'Sorry, lad, it can't be done. The army needs willing volunteers, but you're in no fit state to serve with that shoulder of yours.'

'That's too bad, sir. Are you sure they won't take me?' Steady on, Parry, he told himself. Carry on like this and you'll have him changing his mind!

Minutes later he was out in the street, clutching a paper marked 'unfit for service'. His heart was hammering but he'd done it! Now to get back to Cwmbran!

'This is what we'll do,' Sid had explained. 'We'll get you into the office here; a mate of mine has been working there but he's gone to join the army, stupid fool, so there's a vacancy. His Mam will take you in. She'll be glad of the money. When people hear you're our Daisy's sweetheart, they'll make you welcome, especially if you start attending the chapel with the rest of us.'

'But old Morgan; he'll recognize me and then the fat will be in the fire.'

'Na, na. Say you were ashamed because of that white feather nonsense and you tried to join up but they wouldn't have you on account of your shoulder, and here's the paper to prove it.'

'But the first thing he'll want to know is what I'm doing in Cwmbran. He'll say it's too much of a coincidence.'

'Our Daisy!' Sid said. 'You've taken a shine to her, see? Nothing wrong with that!'

Should he, or shouldn't he? If Morgan swallowed his tale it would be like hiding a tree in a forest. The military police wouldn't bother with a little place like Cwmbran, where practically every man was in a reserved occupation. He'd better risk it.

The Morgans were preparing to leave Barry. Leaving Daisy and Miss Phipps to do the packing, Antonia went to say goodbye to the elderly sisters.

'I do hope we see each other again,' Mrs Davies said, smiling. 'Perhaps you'll come back next year?'

'I'm not sure,' Antonia murmured. 'This has been most pleasant, but I'm determined to spend next winter on the Riviera if the war is over by then. Barry is much too close to home for my liking. My husband will keep popping back to Cwmbran to see to things, as he puts it. Why we employ men to manage our affairs if Mr Morgan cannot bring himself to leave the work to them I cannot think. Even when he's here he spends very little time with me. He's always out walking with Rex. He stays away for hours sometimes.'

'The dear doggy,' Mrs Davies murmured. 'I have sometimes wondered why you don't accompany Mr Morgan on these expeditions.'

'Oh, no, I couldn't do that!' Antonia sniffed. 'My health simply won't allow it. That's why we came to Barry in the first place, you know. I've always been delicate and my doctor prescribed sea air for me. He didn't suggest that I should march about out of doors in all winds and weathers.'

If Mrs Davies had been less of a lady she might have remarked that the sea air could not have done Mrs Morgan much good, when she had hardly set foot outside during her stay. There had of course been the outing to Cardiff, and most enjoyable that had been, but that was hardly the same thing.

The sisters had pumped Lavinia Phipps for information and had learned that her employer took hardly any exercise at all when she was at home, despite the fact that there was a stable filled with very good horses, as well as lovely gardens to walk in. It sounded marvellous, and the impoverished ladies had angled for an invitation to Cwmbran House but Mrs Morgan had been vague and they were forced to realize that they had been given a polite brush-off.

Harry Morgan took a last walk with Rex before driving his wife and her attendants to the train. Then he would get into his car and prepare to drive home. He considered taking a detour to Cardiff, but there was no point in that, since he had no idea where to find Ellen. No, face up to it, Morgan, he told himself. That episode in your life is closed.

Chapter 11

'OH, YOU'RE BACK, then!' Ma remarked. 'I did wonder if I'd see you again, but then you would come back, wouldn't you? I'm still keeping an eye on your things.'

'I'm wondering if my room is still available.'

'As a matter of fact it is. I did let it to a gentleman, but he didn't stay long. To tell you the truth we didn't take to each other and I had to give him notice to go.'

'Oh, goodness. What was the matter with him, then?'

'Funny habits, dear!' Ma lowered her voice. 'It was all a question of hygiene in the end. He must have had kidney trouble, I think, because he was up and down to the lavvy all night long. Of course, he had to pull the chain after himself every time and that sent the pipes clanking and groaning all through the house. People complained. Why can't you use the chamber pot, I asked him, that being what it's there for, but no, he wouldn't hear of such a thing. The upshot is, he's gone, and you can have your room back. It's funny how things work out for the best, isn't it?'

Ellen nodded. She hadn't looked forward to trudging around the city trying to find accommodation and although her room at Ma Rutherford's was cramped, and that lady herself inclined to be awkward at times, it was a question of better the devil you knew.

'There, then! I'll just take your money and you can go up and leave your case. I'll put the kettle on and you can tell me all about Barry. It's years since I've seen my cousin though we're only a few miles apart. Landladies can never get away.'

Ellen was eager to go and see Mari, but she had to sit in Ma's kitchen, drinking tea.

'Well, you don't seem to have done much while you've been away, I must say! Walking around Barry all day, sniffing the sea air. No wonder you've lost weight!'

'Have I? I hadn't noticed.'

Bored, Ma took herself off to fetch her knitting, and Ellen seized the opportunity to escape. Mari greeted her with shrieks of delight.

'You're back, then! Meet any nice fellows down at Barry, did you?'

'There weren't any around.'

'Well, don't say I didn't warn you! What will you do now you're back?'

'The first thing is to find myself a job. I've just paid Ma my rent in advance and I haven't enough to see me through the second week. I don't suppose you know of anything that might be going?'

Mari shook her head. 'There's nothing at Lloyd's. Anyway, you wouldn't want to come back after that bust-up you had with old Evans. You said you might go for a bus conductorette. I wouldn't mind that myself. At least you'd see a bit of life there.'

'Perhaps.'

'Or munitions. That would pay better. Tell you what, you go and see what you can find out, and I'll chuck it in at Lloyd's and come with you. We could share a room somewhere if it means leaving Cardiff.'

Cheered at the thought of joining forces with Mari, Ellen walked back to Tredegar Road in a much happier frame of mind. How she longed to tell her friend about Harry Morgan! But although Mari usually had half a dozen young chaps on her string at any given time, she was a very moral person and she certainly wouldn't approve of what Ellen had done. She had been involved with a married man and, a hundred times worse, she had given herself to him. She didn't even have the excuse that other girls had, when their sweethearts were about to go off to war without ever having experienced any form of loving. The one good thing about it was that she had got off lightly; their coming together had only happened once and as everyone knew, you couldn't get pregnant the first time.

Night after night, lying in her narrow bed, Ellen acknowledged that going to Barry had been a mistake. It had done nothing to ease her grief for Bertie, and now she was lumbered with a different grief as she longed for Harry Morgan. She loved him, and now she'd lost him as well.

Sometimes she thought they'd done the honourable thing in agreeing not to see each other again. At other times she felt a burning resentment towards him. He had used her and left her. In her more rational moments she understood that this wasn't really the case. He hadn't made any attempt to seduce her, or to force himself on her. What had happened in the old barn had happened on the spur of the moment.

Within a week Ellen had located a munitions factory on the edge of the city and been interviewed by the harassed man in charge.

'I suppose you're like all the rest,' he sighed. 'Your sweetheart has joined up and now you want to help him win the war. This is hard labour, *bach*. By the look of your hands you've never done anything like it before. Are you sure you're up to it? It's no good you coming here for a few weeks and then walking away, just when we've got you trained. Do you understand what I'm saying?'

'My brother was killed at Ypres,' she informed him.

'Sorry, *bach*. I didn't know.'

'Yes, well, my friend wants to come with me. Can you find her a job as well? And does the factory do anything about helping us find accommodation?'

She left the place walking on air. On the way home she couldn't resist calling in at Lloyd's, where she found Mari putting gloves away.

'Oh, it's you, Nell! Just look at this, will you! I've had every glove in the place out to show some beastly woman who didn't buy anything. Then she had the cheek to ask me if I knew of a better-class shop where she might find more of a selection. Honestly!'

'Never mind that. We've got jobs at the munitions place, Mari. Not immediately, but according to the boss there'll be vacancies coming up in a fortnight. I'm to go back next week to confirm. What do you think?'

'Wonderful! I'll hand in my notice here at the end of the week.'

'So shall I look around for a bedsit for us?'

'You do that! It'll be bliss to get out of that crowded house, though I'm sure Ma will be sorry to see me go. Every time I turn round I either bump into one of the kids or step on something they've left lying around.'

'If that's the way you feel, I don't know why you haven't moved out sooner.'

'You don't know my Dad. What, let me leave home to go living on my own? That's not what decent girls do. But if I'm doing war work and moving in with you, well, that's different. Everything's changed since this rotten war started. Dad knows that, or he will do, by the time I've finished with him!'

So Ellen had something to look forward to at last. The factory work would be hard but she was determined to succeed at it. Nothing could help Bertie now, but the lives of other men might be saved, and all those mothers, wives and sweethearts would be spared the anguish of loss that she had endured. Furthermore, falling exhausted into bed at night would be good for her. She'd have less time to think about Harry Morgan.

Harry Morgan was furious. He'd walked into the office that morning, asking to see the account books, only to have Llew Roberts, the manager, say he'd send the new chap to fetch them.

'New chap? I didn't give orders for someone else to be taken on, did I?'

'No, sir, but young White went off at a moment's notice, saying he was going to join up. While you were away his sister had a telegram saying her husband had been killed at the front and White promised he'd go to fight the Hun in his place. What makes you think you can beat the Kaiser single-handed, I asked him, but there was no reasoning with him. Young and hotheaded, of course. This other man – Parry, his name is – came looking for work at just the right moment. We had to have somebody, sir. Can't manage otherwise.'

'All right! Stop rambling, man. It's done now, so he can stay here on trial.'

'Yes, sir. Thank you, sir.'

'What the devil!' Tom had just entered the room, his arms loaded down with ledgers, when Harry caught sight of him.

'I know you! Wait a bit – don't tell me! You're that footman, aren't you? The one who was given the white feather. You've got some explaining to do, I think!'

'What's all this? You didn't tell me you've met Mr Morgan before!'

'No, Mr Roberts. I didn't think it was necessary.'

'I'll decide what's necessary and what isn't,' Harry roared. 'Out with it, then! You ran off without giving notice so I'll hear your explanation now, if indeed there is one!'

'Yes, sir.' Tom took a deep breath before launching on the story he'd cooked up. 'I was so ashamed when Muriel gave me that feather, I couldn't face anyone after. I went straight out to a recruiting centre and tried to join up. Unfortunately they turned me down. Wouldn't have me because of an old injury I got.' Just in time he stopped himself from repeating his tale of working at a shoot as a beater. A landowner like Morgan would know all the other bigwigs and might demand the name of the estate.

'And I'm supposed to believe that, am I?'

'He's got the papers, sir, I've seen them. Unfit for service, it says.'

'All right, Roberts, that will do. Bring them in tomorrow, Parry, and let me have a look. There's one thing that bothers me, though! What brings you here to Cwmbran?'

Tom mumbled something about wanting to be near Daisy.

'Daisy? Do you mean my wife's maid, Miss Powell?'

'Yes, sir, that's it.'

'And does this young woman return your affections?'

'I don't know, sir.'

Harry stared at him through narrowed eyes. 'You must have got it badly, then, to follow the girl all this way if she hardly knows you exist!'

Tom shrugged. 'I couldn't very well go back to the hotel after what happened. Yes, I fancy Daisy, and that made me try my luck here. If she turned me down, or there was no work hereabouts, why, I'd move on and no harm done.'

'That's not what my wife will say if you turn up at the house, asking to see the girl. Mrs Morgan is very strict about the servants' welfare. Do you understand me?'

'Yes, sir.'

'I'll look at these books another day, Roberts. I've just remembered something I have to do.'

Harry strode out to his car, thinking furiously. Parry had spoken politely enough, but he had a mutinous look in his eyes. There was something not right here, although he couldn't put his finger on it. He was a great believer in nipping trouble in the bud, and instinct told him that it might be necessary here.

The lady's maid would have to go. Antonia wouldn't like it but servants were ten a penny and could easily be replaced. She had Lavinia Phipps; perhaps one of the parlour maids could be trained to mend gowns and dress hair. Daisy was a pert little miss. If Parry wanted to marry her, let him get on with it. Better than having the household disrupted by a chit who might very well find herself unwed and in the family way in the very near future.

CHAPTER 12

'YOU ARE NOT going to dismiss Powell! I won't have it!' Antonia turned her back on her husband, her face contorted with fury.

'I believe I'm still master in my own house, my dear. I have the last word as to who comes and who stays.'

'In most cases, yes, but Powell and Phipps are *my* servants, not yours. Besides, it simply isn't fair to dismiss Powell just because a besotted young man follows her to Cwmbran. There is no evidence of her having a tendresse for him. She hasn't had time off since we returned home, so when are they supposed to have met?'

'I'm not suggesting that they have, but they may have other plans. We know very little about him. For all we know he may have a criminal background. Powell will let him into the house some night and he'll make off with the silver, or worse!'

'Parry must have good references, or Roberts would never have taken him on.'

'References can be forged, Antonia. And Powell has been reliable enough up to now, but it wouldn't be the first time a girl's head has been turned by a handsome rogue. We can't afford to take that chance. You may give her a small gift of money for services rendered, and I'll write her a decent reference, and she can leave at the end of the week. She does have family in the district so she'll hardly be destitute.'

'I've said no, Harry, and I mean no! I'm going to need Powell more than ever now. I should think you'd want to grant my every whim at a time like this.'

'What? What on earth are you talking about?'

'What do you think I'm talking about? I'm pregnant, Harry. Isn't that what you were hoping for?'

'Oh, my dear girl!' Overjoyed, Harry raised her hand to his lips. 'I'm absolutely delighted, of course. I trust that you are happy too?'

'I don't know about that! You don't have to endure nine months of

misery and discomfort, with possibly nothing to show for it at the end. I'd
hoped never to be in this state again, but no! You had it all planned, didn't
you, Harry? Taking me to Barry and pretending it was all for my good. Sea
air will strengthen you, you said. Meeting new people will jog you out of
your depression, you told me.'

'All true, my dear! And of course you must keep Powell, if that is what
you want, and I'll speak to James and make sure you get the very best of
care. Everything will turn out well this time, you can count on that.'

If Antonia had come from a different social class she might have replied
that pigs might fly, but not being given to vulgar expressions she simply
pressed her lips together and picked up her hairbrush.

Too filled with emotion to settle down, Harry whistled for Rex and was
soon striding across the meadow. He disappeared into the wood with the
dog racing ahead of him. He was ecstatic about Antonia's news. The longed-
for son was on his way at last! Nothing should go wrong this time; his wife
should be pampered and petted to the utmost extent. There should be no
miscarriage and no stillbirth. And then, if she managed to carry the pregnancy to a successful conclusion, other children might follow.

He began to plan what he would give her as a reward, once the child was
safely in the old nursery upstairs. A diamond necklace, perhaps, or a stay in
Biarritz. A nanny must be engaged, and a nursery maid as well. The nursery
must be completely refurbished, and the old toys replaced. Next time he
was in London he might order a splendid train set. The boy must grow up
to appreciate everything to do with the railways, since his father owned
stock in one of the foremost companies.

'You've been listening at doors, I suppose,' Cook sniffed, although she loved
to hear the latest gossip. Seldom upstairs, she did not have the same oppor-
tunities as Daisy.

'I had to. He wanted me sent packing!'

'I assume you mean the master. Why, what have you done?'

'Nothing.'

'Come off it, girl; you must have done something.'

Daisy hesitated, wondering how much to say. 'There was this footman
down there at Barry. I think he fancied me.'

'Oh, no! Don't tell me you've gone and got yourself in the family way!
You might have known you'd be given your marching orders on account of
that!'

'Na, na! Listen to me, will you? We got talking and he wanted to know
where I was from. Now he's turned up here and got himself taken on as a

clerk in the colliery office. It's not my fault. I never told him to do it.' She crossed her fingers behind her back.

'Followed you here, did he? And the master found out. I don't see why you had to get the boot, though. A bit harsh, isn't it? What will you do now, then, *bach*?'

'Oh, the mistress talked him out of it.'

'That's a surprise. He always gets his own way, does Mr Morgan.'

'Maybe so, but this time she had a surprise for him. She's expecting, you see!'

'Never!' Cook dropped her rolling pin and it landed on the flag floor with a clatter. 'And them married nine years with nothing to show for it. Well, he'll give her anything she asks for now, you may be sure.'

'So there we are, James! A miracle has happened at last!' Harry had sought out his doctor friend, beaming all over his face.

'Not quite a miracle yet, old boy. Antonia is delicate, you know that. She'll have to take special care from now on. No excitements, no worries, and a long rest every afternoon. And don't talk about the coming child too much, or she'll start to fret, having been disappointed in the past. Time enough to celebrate when she's holding the child in her arms.'

'A son, at last!'

'Or a daughter,' James reminded him.

'Yes, well, we'll see!'

Antonia began as she meant to go on. When her husband mentioned that he was about to get the decorators in, to refurbish the nurseries, she utterly refused to allow it.

'The odour of paint will make me feel sick.'

'Come now, the nurseries are on the top floor. You won't smell a thing.'

'Yes, I shall. I'm nauseated enough as it is. If I can't keep food down it will harm the baby. Do be reasonable, Harry!'

And she got her way. Daisy and Miss Phipps were at her beck and call at all hours of the day and Cook was always being asked to prepare delicacies to tempt her appetite.

'Such nonsense!' Cook muttered, when Miss Phipps came down with yet another request for arrowroot mush or lemon barley water. 'Having a baby is a perfectly natural thing. My mother gave birth to twelve and managed to bring up seven of them, and she didn't take to her bed wanting sips of this or that. The mistress hasn't enough to do with her time, that's her problem.'

'I don't think you have the right to criticize, not having had children, Cook, and she pays our wages so she has the right to good service.'

'No need to get on your high horse, Miss Phipps. I was only saying. If you ask me she'd be better off not lying around all day. Weakens the muscles, that does, and she'll need hers in working order when the time comes to bring the child into the world.'

This was getting into the realm of matters that Lavinia Phipps preferred not to think about, so she merely grunted what might be taken for an agreement and left the room. Cook was wrong, though, if she believed that her mother wouldn't have loved to exchange places with the gentry. Imagine having to wash and scrub and cook meals and nurse children while constantly being pregnant or recovering from childbirth.

'You've been a long time, Phipps!' Antonia was bored and peevish. 'You know I don't like you gossiping with the servants below stairs.'

'No, Mrs Morgan. The butcher's boy came to the door and I had to wait until Cook had finished with him. Can I help you now I'm here? Shall I read to you, perhaps?'

'That last book you got at the library is not at all interesting. You can go back this afternoon to see if you can find something more amusing.'

'Certainly, Mrs Morgan. I'll go directly after lunch, shall I?'

'Yes, do. And call at the draper's and get me a different shade of pink embroidery wool. I don't care for the look of this tapestry. The old rose makes it appear too dull. You can unpick all the stitching in that colour, and do be careful not to cut the canvas.'

'Yes, Mrs Morgan.'

Lavinia Phipps looked down at her skirt so that Antonia couldn't see the flare of resentment in her eyes. Unpick the old rose, indeed! Surely she could have seen it was not what she wanted before getting started! At least the walk into town would come as a relief. She'd go into the Copper Kettle and treat herself to a cream tea, and if Madam complained that she'd taken too long she'd say she had to wait in the draper's.

'You're turning into a dreadful liar, Lavinia Phipps!' she told herself. 'It's not as if you haven't been brought up to know better, and you a clergyman's daughter!' Perhaps she should forego the cream tea, as a penance. But then Antonia began to rail at poor Daisy, saying her newly laundered nightgown had wrinkles in it.

'I'll go and heat up the iron and touch it up, Madam.'

'That's not good enough. You must rinse it through again.'

Daisy was rash enough to suggest that this might not be necessary, and was told she must forfeit her next afternoon off, for insolence.

Miss Phipps decided that no penance was necessary. She deserved a treat when Antonia was in a mood. She'd have to spend the evening dealing with the aftermath.

CHAPTER 13

M A'S COOKING WAS quite good, even if she was fond of serving boiled cabbage every second day. Unfortunately she also had a thrifty habit of trying to find bargains, such as day-old bread, or scrag end of mutton which, bought just before closing time, she could talk the butcher into selling her at a discount. Last evening's fish was definitely off, Ellen thought, as she tried to hold down the nausea which threatened to overwhelm her.

She couldn't wait to move. The girls would get their midday meal in the works canteen, which meant they could make do with a sandwich and a cuppa when they reached home in the evening. Breakfast would be tea and a bacon roll bought from a workman's stall on the way to the factory. It sounded blissful.

Meanwhile, there wasn't much to do. There was no longer any need to go job seeking, and she wanted to spend as little money as possible in case the munitions post fell through. So, on this bright morning, she decided to walk out along the river.

All went well until she arrived there after a brisk walk along the city streets, with bruised feet inside her worn shoes. Whether it was the smell of the water, or the dizzying appearance of the fast-flowing Taff, she couldn't say, but in moments she was bent over double, retching her heart out.

'All right, are you, love?' A young woman had come up behind her, unheard because of the chuckling of the water. She pulled a shabby perambulator to a halt, staring at Ellen in concern. 'Is there anything I can do?'

'Thanks, I'll be all right in a minute,' Ellen gasped, wiping her mouth on her sleeve. 'I ate some bad fish last night and it's kicking back on me.'

'Oh, aye? You sure that's all it is? Not expecting, are you?'

'Oh no. It can't be that; I'm not married.'

The other girl roared with laughter. 'You don't have to be married for that to happen, and I should know! I've got this little devil here to prove it!' She pointed to the pram where a toddler stared back at them with a toothy grin.

The young mother's gaze was full of pity as she noticed Ellen's white face. 'Given you something to think about, have I? You take my advice, then, and get after the father as soon as you can, and pin him down before he does a bunk. Went back to sea, my chap did, and never been seen since. Yes, you do that, and don't let him give you no nonsense about maybe it isn't his!'

'I told you, it's the fish. My landlady cooked something that was going off.'

'Oh, yes? And are there any men living there, then? See if any of them aren't feeling too well this morning. I bet the answer's no!'

She sauntered off, leaving Ellen in a panic-stricken state. She'd have liked to ask the girl whether you could indeed get caught as a result of your first experience, but that would have meant admitting she had been with a man, and she was deeply ashamed. And as for Harry, how could she possibly 'pin him down' as the girl had recommended? He was a married man.

Now she had to face facts. Her monthly visitor was overdue, something she'd put down to the fact that she'd been under stress since word had come of Bertie's death. There were other signs, too, but she had refused to think about them.

'Oh, Nan!' she whispered. 'Why did you have to die? I need you so badly now!'

But if Nan could hear her – and some people believed that the dead see us and watch over us – she was unable to answer her beloved granddaughter. And if she had been alive, and if Ellen had gone to her in disgrace, what would she have said? How would she have acted? But if Nan had been alive, none of this would have happened. They'd have been able to comfort each other after Bertie was killed, and Ellen would never have gone to Barry, and certainly never have come across Harry Morgan.

Trembling with distress, she made an appointment with a doctor on the other side of the city, not old Dr Lester who had seen Ellen and Bertie through attacks of mumps and chickenpox, and attended Nan in her last illness. This other physician, a harassed older man, briskly confirmed that Ellen was pregnant.

'This will be your first, of course. Will your husband be pleased about it?' He appeared not to have noticed that she wasn't wearing a wedding ring.

'He's away, Doctor,' she lied. 'Fighting in France.'

'Then you'll have to write and tell him all about it, won't you? I'm sure he'll be delighted to have good news from home!'

And let's hope and pray the man comes safely home to see his child, he thought, ringing the bell to summon the next patient from the crowded waiting room.

Ellen stumbled out of the surgery, sick at heart. She desperately wanted to talk to somebody about this, but who was there? Mari was her best friend, but she couldn't bear to confess to her what she'd done. At times like this she wished she was a Catholic, then she could go and unburden herself to a priest. On the other hand, perhaps not. He'd only rant on at her about mortal sin, which was what they were trained to say. Hearing that she was doomed to perpetual hellfire wouldn't help her at all. As a youngster she'd refused to go back to Sunday School after the Methodist minister had preached about the flames of hell that awaited evil doers, and that was only in connection with children who told lies, or stole sweets. Well, she was certainly going to have to tell some fibs now.

'I've had a letter from a girl I met while I was staying in Barry.'

'Oh, yes? I don't think you mentioned her.'

'No, well, it was just one of those holiday things. We exchanged addresses but I didn't really expect to hear from her again. Perhaps a card at Christmas, that sort of thing. Dorothy, her name is.'

'It's just as well she's written now, then. You won't be at Ma's after next week.'

Ellen bit her lip. 'The thing is, she's in trouble.'

'Trouble as in shoplifting, or really in trouble? Either way, what does she expect you to do about it? It's not as if you really know her, is it?'

'That's it, see. She's in a fix and she daren't tell them at home. Her dad is really strict and he'd show her the door. She's asking me for advice. I can't think what to tell her.'

'So you came to Auntie Mari for advice. The first thing is, tell her to forget trying to get rid of it. By what I've heard, drinking gin and jumping off park benches doesn't work, or the kid could be born deformed. She shouldn't go and see someone, either.'

'What sort of someone?'

'You know, some old woman in a back street hovel that takes the baby away with a knitting needle. A girl down our way did that and she ended up bleeding to death.'

Ellen felt faint. 'I can't imagine anybody trying that.'

'Well, there's plenty who do. But forget about that. You can tell this Dorothy, or whatever her name is, that if her parents won't see reason she has two choices. Either her chap has to face up to his responsibilities, or she has to go into the workhouse and give birth to the brat there. Of course, if she does she'll be stuck in there for years, working off her debt to the authorities for their tender loving care, and the child will be brought up in an orphanage.'

'That's awful! What if the man can't marry her?'

'You mean he's married already?'

'I don't know. She didn't say. Surely there's something else she can do?'

Mari shrugged. 'Not that I know of. She could always leave the baby on the church steps, but then it would still end up in an orphanage, so what's the difference?'

Ellen was shocked to the core. She'd never known Mari to be so hard. Cruel, really, but that was how most of society would view the situation. Naturally she had no idea it was Ellen who was in this mess, or she might have chosen her words with more care.

'Then I'll write back and encourage her to tell the baby's father about the situation.'

'That would certainly be best.' Mari nodded. 'Have you done anything about finding out where we'll stay once we start work at the factory?'

'I went to see the billeting officer yesterday. She can squeeze us into a hostel they have for female workers. She says we can share a room together.'

'Aw!' Mari was disappointed. 'I was looking forward to us getting a bedsit. It won't be much fun in a hostel. They'll have a warden who'll make us sign in and out.'

'I tried to find a bedsit,' Ellen fibbed, 'but there isn't anything going. P'raps we'll be able to find something later.'

'I suppose so.' Mari frowned. She had no idea that Ellen had plumped for the hostel because she had no idea what was going to happen. If she suddenly had to disappear from Cardiff, Mari would be stuck with paying the whole rent for the bedsitter which Ellen had promised to share. Leaving her friend in the hostel was the lesser evil.

Feeling no hope at all, Ellen sat down that evening to write to Harry Morgan. The lover of the mythical Dorothy might be persuaded to pay for his fun and marry the girl; there was no possibility of that with Harry. On the other hand, there was just a chance that he might provide for the coming child. He had confided to her that he desperately wanted children but his wife had been unable to provide them.

Perhaps some arrangement could be made; Harry would find a childless couple who would be glad to give a good home to an unwanted baby. In due course he would reveal himself as the child's true father. Ellen cried out in frustration. Oh, what was the point of thinking up silly scenarios? It would be up to him to find a solution.

'Dear Harry,' she began. 'I really need to see you. Can you possibly come to Cardiff? We could meet somewhere where nobody knows us. Yours faithfully, Ellen Richards.' She sealed the envelope and ran out to the pillar box. There! It was done!

CHAPTER 14

'THIS ONE'S MARKED personal, sir, so of course we didn't open it.'
'Thank you, Roberts.' Harry accepted the small, cheap envelope that the colliery manager held out to him. He noticed with a sinking feeling that the letter was postmarked Cardiff. He wasn't able to examine it more closely until much later, when he was sitting in his car with Rex breathing eagerly down his neck.

Damn! It was from Ellen, of course, and she wanted to see him. Well, that wasn't going to happen. After the regrettable incident at the barn they had to make a break for good. He hoped she wasn't going to be a nuisance, but at least she'd had the sense to send it to the office rather than to the house. Not that Antonia would ever knowingly open his post, but she might want to know who it was from.

Should he ignore the letter, or would it be better to write a firm note in response? Either way was fraught with hazards. If he didn't reply she'd try again. A rejection letter might prompt an unfortunate reaction. In his student days at Oxford they had read something that fitted the case now; by Congreve, wasn't that it?

> 'Heav'n has no rage, like love to hatred turn'd,
> Nor hell a fury, like a woman scorn'd.'

Nothing must be allowed to upset Antonia. If anything went wrong this time, he might not get another chance. He would have to deal with this situation in person.

'I have to go to Cardiff,' he told his wife. 'I'll probably be gone a day or two.'

'Yes, Harry. What do you think of this?' she held up a small gown for his inspection, obviously something she was stitching in preparation for the baby.

'Very nice. Is there anything you'd like me to bring back for you? Books, perhaps?'

'That would be lovely. Help me make a list, would you, Phipps?'

Antonia had never been interested in business, which worked in his favour now. Another woman would have asked why he was going and when he would be back, but she simply accepted that going away occasionally was what men did. She had no wish to enter their world or to interfere in any way. She also accepted his statement that he meant to drive to Cardiff instead of taking the train. 'Shall you be taking Rex?'

'I think not. He'd be on his own while I'm in meetings. He's better off here.'

Again she showed little interest, turning to Miss Phipps to have her needle threaded. Harry swallowed a feeling of impatience and went to his study to smoke. He found women's pursuits cloying.

Ellen opened the envelope with a trembling hand. The message inside was terse. He would meet her outside City Hall on Thursday at ten in the morning. This was followed by a scrawled signature.

City Hall was a fine, modern building, less than ten years old. Its construction had begun shortly after Cardiff was declared a city in 1905. As ill luck would have it, the rain was teeming down when she left the house, and although she had an umbrella her feet were soon soaked. Water had seeped through the cardboard with which she'd lined her worn shoes, and by the feel of it she would soon have to contend with blisters.

She'd set out much too early, too jittery to stay in the house, and as a result she found herself at the meeting place by a quarter to the hour. There was no sign of Harry and she looked around for somewhere to shelter. There was nothing else for it; she had to step inside the great building and hope that nobody asked her to state her business. There was a man seated behind a wicket, but although he looked up briefly, nothing was said, so he must have concluded that she was no threat. She stayed close to the door, pretending to be invisible. Long moments passed, and then Harry was there.

He looked just as she remembered him, which was a silly thought, for how much could he have changed in a few short weeks? The one thing that was missing was his boyish grin; his jaw was set and she knew he was far from pleased. He'll be even crosser when he hears what I have to tell him, she told herself.

He wasted no time on polite greetings. 'Come on, we can't talk here. My car's outside. It's pouring out there; we'll have to make a run for it.'

'I've got my umbrella.'

'Never mind about that. Just come on!'

With water dripping from her hair and clothing, Ellen settled herself in the passenger seat. Shaking with cold and nerves, she hoped he'd suggest going somewhere for a hot drink, but instead he piloted the car expertly through the city streets without looking at her or speaking a word.

'Where are we going, Harry?'

'What? Oh, out to the country, somewhere we can park the car and talk without being overheard.'

'Couldn't we do that here? Surely nobody can hear what we're saying with the door shut?'

'We might be seen, and recognized.'

She shivered again. This didn't sound promising. She waited until they were some miles outside the built-up area, with green fields on each side of the road. Then she took a deep breath and began. 'Are you angry with me, Harry?'

'Angry! Let's just say I'm none too pleased. I thought you understood when we left Barry that our relationship – such as it was – had come to an end. What happened between us was wrong. A mistake. You should not have written me, Ellen. What if my wife had seen your letter? How could I possibly have explained that?'

'That's why I sent it to your office, marked personal.'

'Even so, there was no point in your contacting me. What's this about? Are you hoping to beg me to continue seeing you, or is this an attempt at blackmail, perhaps?'

'How dare you suggest that! I thought you ought to know you're going to be a father, that's all! Now I wish I hadn't come!' She was furious. The car was going too fast for her to make her escape but as soon as it stopped she was going to jump out, no matter how far she had to walk to get back to Tredegar Road. Hobble, she reminded herself, bending over to massage her sore ankles.

'You thought I ought to know?' Harry was amazed. 'Well, of course I know! I was the first to be told, naturally!'

Now Ellen was puzzled. 'I don't understand. Nobody knows apart from the doctor, and I haven't told anyone else, not even my friend Mari.'

Light dawned in both of them simultaneously.

'You mean to tell me you're expecting a baby? That I'm the father of your child?'

'Your wife is expecting a baby? You told me your marriage has been over for years, but that you stayed together for the sake of appearances.'

Carefully, Harry drove the car to the side of the road and brought it to a halt.

'Oh, *Duw!*' he muttered, sinking his face in his hands. 'What have we done, child?'

Ellen refused to look at him. She'd fallen for what, according to Mari, was the oldest line in the world. His wife didn't understand him! Now the day of reckoning had come. Twisting her sodden handkerchief in fingers stiff with cold she forced herself to keep quiet. She wanted to scream at him, to call him every name she could think of, but she didn't dare. If she was to have any hope of being rescued from her predicament she mustn't drive him away.

Harry thought rapidly. He would not sink to asking her if the baby might conceivably belong to some other man. He knew that their coming together had been the first time for Ellen, and that was just a few short weeks ago. What a ghastly, awful muddle! For years he'd longed for a child, prayed for it, even, and now there were two on the way, with different mothers. Antonia, his lawful wife, and this girl who now sat trembling beside him. Under different circumstances she might have been his daughter.

'I must have time to think,' he muttered. 'I'm going to take you back to Cardiff now, Ellen, and I'll let you know when I decide what must be done.'

'I won't get rid of it!' she cried, her eyes wide.

'I'd never suggest you do that!' he snapped. 'It's dangerous and it's illegal. You can put that right out of your head!'

'But you will come back?' she faltered.

'I'll book into a hotel overnight, and come for you in the morning.'

'Don't come to the house! If Ma Rutherford catches sight of you there's no telling what she'll think. Shall I wait for you at City Hall?'

'No, we'll go somewhere different this time.' They settled on a pretty little park where they could meet at the bandstand.

Harry Morgan was at heart a moral man, and although he would have given much to turn back the clock he was loath to desert the girl now, when she had no family. He was well aware that many a woman in her position wound up selling herself on the streets, ending up diseased, or dead, at an early age. Could he condemn Ellen to that?

At the hotel he stretched out on the bed, fully dressed. He hardly noticed the passing of the hours, and neither did he make any attempt to order food, although he had eaten nothing since breakfasting at seven. He examined many ideas in turn, rejecting each one. At some point a maid knocked at the door, wanting to turn down the bed, but he sent her away brusquely. By the time dawn's first rays appeared in the sky, he thought he had found a solution.

CHAPTER 15

Daisy Powell was extremely annoyed. Antonia Morgan had made it clear that it was only her intervention that had prevented the master from giving her the sack.

'And I must say you're a very lucky girl, Powell. If it wasn't that I need you with me because of my present condition, I'd have dismissed you myself.'

'I've done nothing wrong, Madam.'

'That's not what I've been told. My husband was extremely surprised to come across that young footman from Barry, actually working in the colliery office! By the man's own admission, he came to Cwmbran because of you.'

'That's news to me, Madam. I certainly didn't ask him to come here.' Trembling in her button boots, Daisy managed to brazen her way out of her dilemma.

'You must, of course, be given the benefit of the doubt, Powell, but I urge you to bear in mind that we do not allow followers in this house.'

'Of course, Madam. We all know that.'

'It's not right nor fair, though,' she grumbled to Miss Phipps, when Antonia had gone to bed. 'What's wrong with getting to know a nice chap and settling down to married life, same as anybody else? What right do people like the Morgans have to keep us in bondage like heathen slaves?'

'You'd do well to watch your tongue, Miss Powell. And of course they are responsible for the moral welfare of their servants. That is how it should be.'

'Pooh! That's all very well for you to say, at your age. No man is going to look at you. I'm still young and I deserve a chance.'

Miss Phipps was so taken aback that her mouth dropped open in horror. 'How dare you speak to me in that manner! Mr Morgan certainly knew what he was about when he spoke of dismissing you! A lady's maid should be lady *like*, Powell.'

Daisy was aware she'd made an enemy, but the words could not be taken back And she hadn't said anything that wasn't true. Lavinia Phipps was long past it. She tossed her head and flounced out of the room.

Tom Parry had hardly been near her since he'd come to Cwmbran; they'd just had a few country walks. He could have written to her, or sent a message asking her to meet him somewhere. Well, if Tom Parry wouldn't come to the mountain ...

Daisy's mother was still living in Cwmbran, and even the mistress couldn't find anything wrong with a daughter visiting an elderly parent. Not that Mam was doddering. She could run rings round Madam, any day of the week. Mrs Powell always provided a good tea when Daisy went there on her afternoons off. And if Tom Parry happened to be present at the same time, what was wrong with that? She'd get Mam to invite him. So on the following Wednesday Tom came to tea, and did justice to the *bara brith*. Daisy made up her mind to push him into a commitment when he walked her home, but she was disappointed. When they rounded the corner of the lane, which brought them within sight of the house, he stopped abruptly and said he wouldn't come any further.

'You can come as far as the door, surely!' she protested.

'Not a good idea, see? Don't want you losing your job, do we?'

'There's nobody to see us. And if they did, where's the harm?'

'References. You'll never get another job unless they're willing to swear you're sober and honest and all the rest.'

'Perhaps I don't want another job, then. I won't be going out to work when I'm married, will I? My husband will want me at home. And with the hours a lady's maid has to keep, no one will employ a married woman.'

This was Tom's cue to speak up. If he didn't make an outright proposal, at least he might hint about the future. Even a little show of jealousy wouldn't have come amiss. 'Have you been seeing someone else?' But no. He merely looked uncomfortable and said he must be going. Then, without so much as a kiss, or a see you later, he was off, running as if the seven devils were hot on his heels. Daisy spat out a word which Miss Phipps would most definitely not have approved of, even though the companion would probably have no idea what it meant.

Some days later Sid Powell learned something which gave him pause for thought. He and his work mates were sitting in a dimly lit cavern, far below the ground, eating their midday meal. Slabs of bread and dripping, washed down by a bottle of cold tea, gave them the strength they needed to carry on with the rest of the long, weary shift.

'What's your Bron up to these days, boyo?' he asked his friend Gwilym, more for the sake of conversation than anything. Bronwen Pugh was a pert, lively girl, known by some to be 'fast'. That's what the old tabbies in the chapel said, although there was no harm in her really.

'I just want a bit of fun before I settle down,' she was often heard to say. 'Look at our Mam, eight children like a flight of stairs, and old before her time. And how does a girl know who to pick for a husband unless she sees a few boys, just to compare?'

There were some who said she was a sinner who ought to be brought into chapel and sat down on a stool, to be ranted at by the minister, like in the old days, but nothing could be proved against her. Sid himself had taken Bronwen out once or twice and knew she was a decent girl at heart. A bit flighty, yes, but nothing worse than that. Not the sort of girl you'd pick for a wife, but then he was particular.

'Oh, you know our Bron,' Gwil laughed. 'Happy as a lark. Going up in the world, seeing that new man they've taken on in the office. She's too good for a common miner now, wants a chap who wears a collar to work.'

Sid frowned. 'Tom Parry, is that who you mean?'

'That's the one. Why, do you know him?'

'We've met. I'd tell your Bron to watch her step there, if I were you.'

'Jealous, are we, boyo?'

Sid did not reply. Should he say something to Daisy? No, perhaps there were other ways of going about this. He might seek out Tom Parry, ask him what his intentions were. If it wasn't for Daisy, Parry might be in a pickle now, and it still wasn't too late for the authorities to get wind of what the man had done.

Still seething over her rebuff, Daisy plotted her revenge. When a timid maid knocked on the door of Antonia's bedroom, it didn't register for a moment that the girl had a message for her, not for their mistress.

'There's a man at the kitchen door asking for you, Miss Powell.'

'Then he can just go away again,' Antonia snapped. 'What on earth were you thinking of, Powell, to permit this interruption?'

'I don't know, Madam. I mean, who is it, Ada?'

'He says he's your brother, Miss.' Ada was not a local girl, and if the man in the moon had knocked at the back door she wouldn't have recognized him either.

'Can't you see I'm dressing for dinner, you silly girl? Tell him to return on Powell's afternoon off,' Antonia directed, but Daisy was already on her way to the door.

'I'm sorry, Madam, I'll be as quick as I can, but I must go and see what he wants. This isn't like him, you see, so something must be wrong at home. It's my mother, I expect. She hasn't been well lately and perhaps I've been sent for.' She was through the door before Antonia could call her back.

Miss Phipps hid a grimace of disgust. As her pregnancy advanced, Antonia was becoming more and more demanding. Daisy could certainly be annoying, yet the time spent in chastising the girl would have been better spent letting her go on her way.

'Sid! What's the matter? Is it Mam?'

'Nothing wrong with Mam. It's that Tom Parry I want to talk to you about.'

'Oh, him!'

'Where do you stand with him, *cariad*?'

'I wish I knew! Mam invited him to tea the other day, lovely it was, mind, and I expected him to say something when he walked me home, but not a word out of him.'

Sid nodded. When a girl was walking out with a man, taking him home to meet her parents meant something. If they expressed approval it was a milestone on the road to an engagement, an acknowledgement that they were pledged to each other.

Sid had spoken to his mother, who had agreed that she had nothing against Tom Parry. Marriage to an office clerk would be quite suitable for a young woman who had risen to the dizzy heights of being a lady's maid, and to the wife of the owner of the colliery, no less. She didn't want her daughter married to a man who worked down the pit. She had lost her husband in a cave-in and been left to bring up a family on her own.

'With Da gone, I've decided it's up to me to speak to Parry, and ask him what his intentions are towards you, Daisy.'

'I don't mind, but why come here, landing me in trouble with the mistress?'

He sauntered off then, leaving Daisy puzzled. On getting back upstairs she had to invent a story about Mam having slipped on a wet floor she'd been scrubbing, and the doctor had to be sent for. Doctors cost money and Sid had come to see if Daisy could make a contribution towards his fee. Mrs Morgan received this news coldly. It was fortunate that she was not the sort of woman who visited the poor when they were ill, bearing jars of beef tea, or poor Daisy would have been caught in a lie.

CHAPTER 16

'DO BE CAREFUL with that! If you chip that paint I'll see that you pay for repairs!' Ma Rutherford watched sourly as the carter manoeuvred Ellen's rocking chair on to the path. By the look of his wagon he wasn't the sort of man who'd be concerned with a few chips. Only a few smears showed that it had once been painted red. The patient horse looked as ancient as the wagon itself.

Ma offered to keep Ellen's bits and pieces in storage again, but Ellen had refused. She was determined to hoard as much money as she could, and handing over hard-earned shillings to Ma was not part of her plan. Somehow they'd manage to squeeze Nan's chair into their room at the hostel. The room was sparsely furnished, with only one cane chair standing between the two narrow beds. The rocker would be useful.

Ellen pictured herself sitting in it, lulling her baby to sleep. But where would that be? Not in the workhouse, if that was where she finished up. They would take it from her to sell, saying it was to pay for her keep.

Ma kept saying she would miss Ellen. 'One of my best guests, you've been, dearie. If ever you find it's too much for you, manufacturing them bombs or whatever it is, you come right back here. If I can squeeze you in somewhere, I will!'

'Thank you. You're very kind.'

'They're hard work, them factories. I'm sure you don't know what you're letting yourself in for.'

If only you knew, Ellen thought. You'd change your tune in a hurry. You wouldn't touch me with a ten-foot pole. But her problems faded into the background temporarily when she and Mari were ushered into the room they were to share at the hostel. It was cramped and cheerless, yet the fact that they were about to do something to help the war effort filled them with excitement.

'And if what I hear is true, we'll be too exhausted after a day's work to notice what the place looks like,' Mari said cheerfully. 'I'll fall into bed and go out like a light!'

'Are you glad you made the switch, then? Won't you miss working at Lloyd's?'

'Not on your life! And think of the money we'll be making. I still can't believe they're paying us thirty bob a week.'

'Minus deductions for food and that.'

'Then we'll just have to stuff our faces and get our money's worth.'

As far as Ellen was concerned, all this was easier than they'd anticipated. When they reported to the foreman in the morning, she learned that she wouldn't be working on the assembly line at all, although Mari would.

'You're for the canteen, Richards. One of the married girls has gone off sick. In the club, she is, and she won't be coming back. Doesn't she know there's a war on?'

'Here, I didn't sign on to wash dishes! My brother was killed at Ypres and I want to do my bit to help win this war!' Ellen was furious, but the man merely shrugged.

'You won't be washing dishes, love, take it from me.' He was an elderly man, possibly called out of retirement. By his accent she judged him to be from northern England; Yorkshire, perhaps, or Lancashire. Not having met many Englishmen, she didn't know the difference. 'You'll be standing behind the counter, dishing out sausage and mash and toad in the hole, followed by jam roly-poly. And you'll be helping to win the war, all right. You know what they say about an army marching on its stomach.'

Ellen's mouth watered at the thought of such delicious food. She hadn't had any breakfast, and her stomach was rumbling. There was no point in arguing so she went where the man directed her to go and soon found herself wearing a gingham apron while somebody called Ruby Entwistle showed her the ropes.

'You dish out a good helping every time, mind, Nellie. A lot try coming back for seconds, but there isn't always enough left. Then we get complaints, so my motto is, ram as much down them as possible first time around. Then fill them up with gallons of tea. Understand? And when it's your turn to brew up, don't make the tea so it's like dishwater. Most of them like it so a spoon will stand up in it without falling over.'

She soon got on to the routine, discovering that it was a happy place to work. The workers arrived in shifts, and those who doled out the food were able to take a five-minute break in between, for a welcome cup of tea. They would have their own meal when everyone was finished.

'I hope there's enough left over for us,' Ellen moaned to Ruby, who laughed.

'Don't you worry, the cook makes sure of that, else she'd have a riot on her hands. There's nothing worse than smelling good food and dishing it up for others to give you a roaring great appetite! And if Cook likes you, she'll make you up a little packet to take with you when you go off. A lump of spotted dick or a bit of bread and dripping.'

Ellen's mouth watered. 'I could do with some of that now! I came away without breakfast and I could eat a horse!'

Ruby laughed. 'See that tin over there? It's full of bikkies. Go and help yourself.'

'But won't I get into trouble?'

'Course not. They're ours, see? For us that works on this side of the counter, not for them at the tables!'

Ellen had just enough time to swallow an arrowroot biscuit, washed down with strong, sugarless tea, when the rush started. Then it was slapping the food on to thick chinaware plates while the laughter and banter wafted over her head. By the time her shift was over her feet were killing her and she had a wicked headache. She managed to stumble over to the hostel, longing to lie down and close her eyes.

'You're new here; are you Richards, by any chance?' The warden, or housemother, or whatever she was called, stopped Ellen as she trudged across the main hall. 'There's a letter come for you; it's in your pigeonhole over there. Look under R.'

Ellen's heart skipped a beat. There was only one person likely to be writing letters to her. When she had the thick, cream-coloured envelope in her hand it was some time before she could bring herself to open it. When she did her reaction was a mixture of relief and disappointment. The contents offered her a temporary way out of her dilemma, yet it was clear that Harry had no intention of publicly acknowledging her or her coming child. Well, what else had she expected?

What would Nan think of all this if she were alive? Ellen had a clear memory of her grandmother speaking disparagingly to a neighbour about a woman known to be some man's mistress. 'A kept woman', she'd sniffed, unaware that her young granddaughter was crouching under the table, hidden by the red chenille cloth.

This had conjured up a picture of a sinful person, dripping with diamonds, living in palatial surroundings, feasting on cream cakes and hot house peaches. How wonderful it must be to be 'kept', the child had marvelled. Hardly what she was being offered now!

Ellen should have received his letter by now. Harry Morgan wondered if he was doing the right thing. He owned several terraces of two-up, two-down, back to back houses of dwellings for the miners and their families. The house at the end of one of these streets had been converted into a small shop selling sweets and tobacco. The front room in what was normally the parlour was where these items were sold; it had a wide window which could be slid open in order to serve customers. A canopy protected people from the worst of the weather as well as keeping the sun off the merchandise inside. A counter, holding a till and various small items, stood beneath this window, while shelves holding cigars, cigarettes and large glass jars of sweets were clearly visible from outside.

An old woman, the widow of a miner who had died years before in an accident in the pit, eked out a meagre living from this shop. Now she was mumbling about it being time for her to retire and move to Llanelly to live with a married daughter. The premises would be vacant in December.

Bringing Ellen here would be the ideal solution. He'd been careful not to say too much in his letter, in case it fell into the wrong hands, but when he spoke to her next he'd have to make it clear that he had no intention of continuing a relationship with her. Cwmbran, with its chapel gossips, was no place to harbour a mistress, even if he'd wanted one. He would, of course, keep an eye on her and the child, and that would not be a problem because he often went to the shop to buy his cigars; nobody who saw him going there would suspect a thing.

She would have to promise to give no hint to anyone of their connection. He had a cover story ready; he was doing a favour for a friend he'd known at Oxford. Ellen could 'become' the daughter of a tenant farmer, an unfortunate girl who'd had to leave home when she got into trouble, or perhaps it would be kinder to explain her as a young war widow who wanted to make a new start far away from the place where she'd been happy with her husband before the war ruined their chance of happiness.

Harry was well aware that bringing the girl to Cwmbran was a risk, but it was better than leaving her in Cardiff. Antonia was self-absorbed but even she would become suspicious if he made too many trips to the city. She might even decide that he was keeping a mistress there which, given the circumstances, would be ironic!

The sweet shop was ideal because Ellen could keep the child with her in the room while serving customers. That would not be possible if she had to support herself with some other kind of work. He was rather pleased with himself for having thought of it.

Chapter 17

ANTONIA MORGAN HAD reached the stage of pregnancy where she could not get comfortable, no matter how she arranged herself on her couch. She longed for someone to rub her aching back and to sponge her face and hands in the heat of the day, but Lavinia Phipps had responded to such requests with a look of distaste, plainly indicating that this was not part of a paid companion's role.

'Can't you find me a nurse, James? Harry can well afford to hire one and I do need more help these days.'

Her doctor grimaced. 'Stuff and nonsense, Antonia. It's quite unnecessary at present. Time enough for the nurse to move in a week or two before your confinement. Childbirth is a perfectly natural function. Every day I see women who are on their feet, attending to their families, up and about until almost the last moment, and then they are scrubbing floors within a week of giving birth.'

'Miners' wives!'

'Yes, and you might learn from their example, Antonia. It won't do you any good to lie about, waited on hand and foot by those two attendants of yours. Muscles must be exercised to keep in trim. Take walks in those lovely gardens of yours.'

'I'm afraid to do too much in case it harms the baby. You know how many we've lost already, James, and Harry is determined that this one shall survive.'

'Of course it will survive if you do everything you're told. I've said before that tight lacing was most likely the cause of the problem last time. Why you women feel the need to truss yourselves up in whalebone corsets is beyond me. It's nothing but a sacrifice on the altar of fashion. Absolute madness!'

'It's because you men demand that we look presentable when we appear in public!' she retorted, but he only laughed and patted her hand, a mannerism she deplored.

He went on his way, saying he had other patients to see, people who were really ill! James always left her feeling foolish and diminished. He seemed to regard her as a little woman, frivolous and unintelligent. How could he understand the dread that came over her every time she contemplated the business of giving birth? It was all very well to say it was a natural function and a woman's lot; that didn't lessen the pain.

It was no good discussing matters with her attendants, either. Phipps was very much an old maid, who shied away from any mention of things she found unfit for a lady's ears; she belonged to that breed of women who cooed over sleeping babies but would have no idea how to change an infant's napkins. She enjoyed reading the sort of romance novels which ended with the heroine tiptoeing into the sunset on the arm of the masterful hero. She didn't want to know about what went on between the couple after the strains of the Wedding March had died away.

Daisy Powell was inclined to be coarse. Wanting to shock Miss Phipps, she'd been overheard saying that a neighbour had just given birth to her tenth child, the process being 'as easy as shelling peas'. Antonia didn't believe a word of it.

Harry had been more attentive since she'd given him the news of the coming child, but even he tended to be bracing and hearty rather than sympathetic. It would serve him right if she died in the process, then he'd be sorry! She wiped away a tear with the scrap of lawn and lace which served as a handkerchief.

'Did you ever think of getting married, Phipps?' she asked suddenly.

'Oh, when I was a girl I expected that some young man would come along and sweep me off my feet, Mrs Morgan. It just didn't happen. My father was a rector in a small country parish and there were very few suitable young men in the district. I do remember one curate who paid me a little attention, but Papa said he'd never amount to anything, so that was that! He's an army chaplain now, serving in France.'

'And are you happy as a spinster, do you think?'

'Oh, yes, Mrs Morgan. I'm able to earn my own living, in pleasant surroundings; what more could I ask?' Lavinia was amazed that her employer should ask such a question. It wasn't like her to concern herself with the feelings of others.

'I sometimes think that I'd have been happier if I had remained single, Phipps.'

'Oh, surely not, Madam!'

'I loved my home and my family, you see. I should have been glad to spend my life there, I know.'

'But you fell in love with Mr Morgan,' Lavinia prompted, shying away from what revelation might be coming next.

'I suppose I did, in a way. He was *suitable*, you see, Phipps. Wealthy, well thought of in society, well educated, well bred. It wasn't as if I had any choice. Women are nothing without a man.'

'I certainly do not believe that, Madam!' There was nothing of the suffragette about Lavinia Phipps, and she strongly believed in the Bible admonition about women being subservient to their husbands, but that didn't mean they were less than the dust in their own right.

'Oh, yes, Phipps.' Antonia nodded. 'Gentlemen can go out and rule the world, in one way or another. They make the Grand Tour when they are young; they are favoured with university educations and they can train for the professions if they choose. They manage their estates; they go into parliament and make laws. They even go to war, and all the while we women sit at home with our embroidery, because they think we are too unintelligent or too frail to do anything else.'

Lavinia gave her a long look. 'That doctor has upset you, Mrs Morgan. Why, your nerves are quite frayed! Shall I send for some chamomile tea to help calm you?'

Ashamed of her outburst and puzzled by her sudden passion, Antonia agreed. Public displays of pique signified ill breeding, and she was thankful that Phipps had been the only witness to her lack of control.

She sent up a silent prayer, to the God she no longer believed in, that her child should be a boy. If it was, then Harry would be jubilant, and she'd be able to say, 'You've got what you always wanted. Now let there be an end to this business. I've had enough. No more insisting on your "rights", as you call it. Take a mistress if you must, only leave me alone.'

Yes, that is what she would say and do. First, however, that business of the birth had to be undergone, and it was with mounting dread that she faced the thought of that.

December was well advanced when Ellen felt a curious sensation in her lower body. She was frightened at first until she realized what it meant. Her child was stirring inside her, letting her know it was alive and well. She was overcome with awe. Until this point it hadn't seemed real. She had thought of it as akin to some parasite that had invaded her body, but now a real person was making itself felt. A child. Her child. And not an 'it' but a little boy or a little girl.

Harry had written to her – another one of his terse notes – to let her know that the old lady was leaving the sweet shop in the middle of the month and she, Ellen, was to move in as soon as she was gone. She was to travel to Cwmbran by train and walk to Jubilee Street from the station, a distance of half a mile. Any luggage could be brought on by the carrier's cart. Mrs Jones next door had the keys and had been instructed to hand them over.

Disappointed, Ellen accepted the fact that Harry wouldn't be fetching her in his car. She would have liked to spend time with him, instead of being jolted on the train, squashed into a third-class compartment with strangers, but she understood how it had to be. If she'd rolled up to the door in his car it would have raised more than a few eyebrows. She would have been the talk of the chapel in no time.

The only problem now was what on earth she was to do about Mari. The job was one thing; she could easily come up with some excuse for leaving, or even flit in the night. But it seemed cruel to disappear without explaining herself to her friend, and that was something she just could not bring herself to do.

Mari knew she didn't have any living relatives so she couldn't invent some elderly aunt or cousin who needed looking after. Could she say that she had decided to become a VAD after all and was off to some hospital to train? But what if Mari insisted on downing tools and coming with her? At the very least she would demand an address so they could keep in touch. The same would apply if she pretended she was going into service, or wanted to go back to shop work.

She remembered a sermon she'd heard at a long-ago camp meeting. The young preacher had leaned over the makeshift pulpit and thundered, 'Oh, what a tangled web we weave, when first we practice to deceive!' Well, she was in a tangled web now, and she didn't like it one little bit.

CHAPTER 18

HARRY TURNED OVER the envelope in his hand. Made of good-quality paper, it had been addressed in black ink in unfamiliar handwriting. He slit it open with his table knife, cursing when it became smeared with ginger marmalade. It was as well that Antonia took breakfast in her room, for she deplored what she referred to as 'filthy habits'.

He recognized the signature as that of Bradshaw, the retired colonel he'd met in the hotel at Barry. Neither had expected to see the other again but as Harry was the most important man in Cwmbran, no other address was necessary.

'You'll remember that footman whom all the fuss was about,' the colonel wrote, coming straight to the point as always. 'Something about the fellow intrigued me; I wondered why he bolted if he had nothing to hide. I still have connections at the War Office so I made enquiries, and the upshot is, I learned that a soldier by the name of Thomas Parry disappeared from a hospital at Bagshot, shortly before this footman took up employment at the hotel. He was wounded in the shoulder at Mons.

'The girl who presented our chap with the white feather maintains that your lady wife's maid had formed an alliance with him, and if that is the case there is every possibility that he will turn up in Cwmbran. While I have no proof that these men are in fact one and the same, it bears investigation. As you are the local magistrate I felt it only proper to bring this to your attention. I am sure you will agree that if we are to win this war, deserters must be apprehended and made an example of.'

Could it be the same man? Harry could have sworn that the certificate Parry had produced was perfectly legitimate. But what if the young clerk in his office was a deserter? In a way, he felt a sneaking sympathy for a young man who, having experienced the horrors of war and been wounded, did not want to go back. At the same time he agreed with the colonel. If proper discipline wasn't maintained, you'd have men running off all over the place and before you knew it Britain would be overrun by the Kaiser. Executing men who deserted, or who showed cowardice in the face of the enemy, was a terrible punishment, yet it served as a deterrent to others.

Was there any way to find out if Thomas Parry was guilty? Having been alerted by Colonel Bradshaw, Harry could not now let things slide. It would do his own reputation no good whatsoever if it came out later that he'd been harbouring a fugitive.

'You're looking grim,' his wife remarked, when he looked in to wish her good morning. He had taken to doing this since her pregnancy had been confirmed; James had warned him to keep her calm and happy if she was to carry the child to term. 'Is there trouble at the pit?'

'Yes and no. I've had a letter from Colonel Bradshaw, at the hotel.'

'Oh, no! Don't tell me they're angling for an invitation to come to stay! I couldn't bear it, Harry. You'll have to write and say it's just not possible.'

'No, no,' he soothed, 'it's nothing like that. It's about that young footman who was given the white feather that evening at dinner.'

'I remember him! We all agreed he was a slacker, disloyal to his king and country, and should be made to face up to his responsibilities. But surely you told me that he's now working in the colliery office? You wanted to dismiss Powell because you thought he'd followed her here.'

'That is so. It appears that the white feather did the trick; he went straight out and attempted to enlist. He was turned down because of some old injury. He has an official document to that effect.'

'So what is the colonel writing to you about?'

'He's made enquiries at the War Office and has learned that a Thomas Parry deserted from the army some time ago and is still unaccounted for.'

'Oh.' Antonia was disappointed that there was nothing more to the story. She'd been hoping for something to relieve the boredom of her days. 'The army must be full of Parrys, don't you think?'

'This is too much of a coincidence. According to the colonel the missing man was injured in the shoulder, and our Parry has a shoulder injury which he claims to have received while working in civilian life. I shall have to inform the authorities.'

'Of course you must, dear, and the sooner the better.'

Not meaning to stay for more than a minute or two, Harry had left the door ajar after entering her room. Daisy, coming upstairs with an armful of freshly laundered undergarments, had paused outside on hearing her sweetheart's name. Horrified, she knew that Tom must be warned, and soon. She had no idea how long it would take for the military police to arrive, but the Morgans had one of the new-fangled telephones which could connect them with far-flung places in a matter of minutes.

She slipped into the dressing room and slid the garments into a drawer. When she heard Harry's firm tread passing the door, she sidled into Antonia's room, putting a dying duck expression on her face.

'What on earth is the matter, Powell? You look as if you've swallowed a lemon!'

'Please, Madam, I've got one of my bilious attacks.'

'If you were in my position, girl, you'd know what feeling bilious really means.'

'I know, Madam, but I do feel so ill. If I don't go and lie down I think I might be sick all over the ...'

'All right, all right, spare me the details! Go if you must, but if you're no better by lunchtime you must take a good dose of syrup of figs.'

'Yes, Madam, thank you, Madam.'

Had the girl been listening at doors? It occurred to Antonia then that she might have overheard what Harry had said about Parry. It was too late to call her back to find out, and she might genuinely be ill, having had such attacks before. Antonia sighed. Life was difficult enough without having lovesick servants to contend with.

Daisy, meanwhile, was running through the grounds as fast as her legs would carry her. That doctor's certificate might be enough to convince Mr Morgan, but the police would quickly put two and two together, thanks to that interfering old colonel. Tom had to be warned, even if she did lose her job as a result.

The office was almost two miles away and it wasn't long before she was forced to slow down, with a stitch in her side. Bending over, she brought her knee up to her chin, willing the pain to go away.

Finally she came in sight of the ugly brick building where Mr Morgan's business affairs were carried on. It was with some relief that she noticed the manager, Mr Roberts, striding away from the office. This meant that Tom was probably alone inside. He could be safely away before the manager returned, and nobody any the wiser.

However, someone else was watching. Bronwen Pugh sidled out from behind a shrub and slipped inside the building. Cursing under her breath, Daisy wondered what to do next. She'd have to get rid of her in a hurry. Opening the door cautiously, she was appalled to see Bronwen standing with her arms around Tom's neck.

'Have you missed me, darling? I thought old Roberts would never go!'

'Of course I missed you, *cariad*,' Tom murmured. 'Give us a kiss while we've got the place to ourselves.' Without waiting for an answer, he planted a lingering kiss on the girl's pouting lips. Daisy leapt back, as if stung by a bee. The double-dyed rat! So this was why he hadn't been in touch. Well, he'd get no more help from her. Silently she backed away from the door and tiptoed down the steps.

She couldn't bring herself to return to the house. She'd call on Mam instead and get a comforting cup of tea. 'Might as well be hung for a sheep as a lamb,' she mumbled.

'What you doin' here at this time of day, our Daisy? This isn't your afternoon off!'

'I want to see our Sid. I thought he'd be off shift by now, him being on nights?'

'Of course he is. Just had his bath and gone out to see his ferret. I was about to put his meal on the table, see? How's that young man of yours, then?'

'He's not my young man, Mam!' Daisy tried to keep the bitterness out of her voice but there was no deceiving her mother.

'Fallen out, have you?'

'Worse than that, Mam. He's been carrying on with that Bronwen Pugh.'

'Never! And after you brought him home for his tea, too!'

'I could have told you that,' Sid said, as he entered the kitchen. 'I had it from the horse's mouth, see? Gwil let slip she was seeing Tom. He didn't know about you two, I suppose, or he wouldn't have said.'

'Shut up, Sid, and let me tell you what's going on. I'm not supposed to be here and there'll be hell to pay if I'm found out.'

'Language, Daisy!'

'Sorry, Mam. They've found out about Tom. When I came to warn him I saw him with Bron. Now he can just stew in his own juice!'

'Aye, that's the best way, Daisy. I wasn't happy about this from the beginning. It may be best all round if the police take him out of here.'

'I don't like to think of him being shot,' she began.

'Don't you think about that. You just pray he doesn't spill the beans. If they find out we were in on this, we're in for trouble, especially me. I don't know what the penalty is for hiding a fugitive, but I could find myself doing a prison stretch!'

CHAPTER 19

MRS JONES PROVED to be a chatty little body, full of good humour. Rosy cheeked and dark eyed, she looked typically Welsh, with her black hair braided into the style known as ear phones.

'You've come, then,' she said, smiling. 'Not too tired after the journey, I hope. It's Cardiff you're from, isn't it? I'll give you the key, and you can let yourself in and put the kettle on. I was round earlier to keep the fire on. I'll follow you in five minutes to show you what's what; I just have to get our Ifor off to school. He comes home for his dinner, see?' She ruffled the hair of the grinning youngster at her side.

Save for the ticking of a clock on the mantel, the house was silent. It was pleasantly though sparsely furnished. Perhaps the old lady hadn't wanted to take all her things with her and had sold them to Harry.

Ellen moved the kettle to the edge of the hob, where it immediately began to bubble and sing. The big fireplace with its wall oven would make the room cosy when the cold weather set in. She could imagine herself sitting in Nan's chair, holding her baby and rocking him softly to sleep. The chair and her trunk had yet to come, so she had only the one small travelling bag to unpack. She removed the framed picture of Bertie in his uniform and placed it lovingly on the mantel. It was the first thing Mrs Jones noticed when she came into the house, not bothering to knock.

'There's lovely!' she declared. 'That's your hubby, is it? Fine-looking man, he is.'

In that moment Ellen's new identity was born. She was Mrs Bertie Richards, poor young war widow. By the simple act of changing her title from Miss to Mrs she would become no longer an object of scorn but a respectable young mother-to-be whose husband had paid the supreme sacrifice in the war to end all wars.

'Yes, that's Bertie,' she agreed. 'He was killed at Ypres.'

'There's awful! Left all on your own now, are you?'

'I am expecting a baby, though,' Ellen confided.

'There's lovely! You'll have something to remember him by, though it's sad to think of the baby growing up not knowing his father. Mind you, I should think there'll be a good few like that by the time this war's over.'

Seeing Ellen's sad expression, Megan Jones hastened to change the subject. 'Well, now, if you've finished your tea I'll take you through to the shop and show you the ropes. You won't have customers this afternoon, it being early closing, but you want to be ready for the morning. They come in fits and starts, see. Children come on their way home from school, but you can expect a lot of old retired chaps dropping in at any time for a pennorth of baccy. In between you won't have much to do, so apart from dusting round first thing you can get on with your knitting.'

Ellen's mouth watered as she regarded the tall glass jars of sweets. Bulls eyes, pear drops, humbugs and boiled sweets were there in abundance, as were barley sugar twists and straps of liquorice. There were a few boxes of chocolates but Megan said there was little call for them, except at Christmas, which was fast approaching.

'Too expensive for most people, see. But when they do come in, oh, lovely they are, with pictures on the lids, and satin ribbon bows.' She showed Ellen how to manage the scales, and the till. Then she reached up to a shelf and took down some flat pans and a small hammer. 'If you're any good at making toffee, that's always popular with the young ones. Wait till the slab hardens and then smash it to bits with the hammer. Sell it for a farthing a piece and let them choose their own. That's the way to do it.'

'Do I have to sit here all day?' Ellen wondered, but Megan shook her head.

'Na, na. You can go in the back and get on with your work. They can ring the bell if they want you. A word of warning, though; don't leave the packets of fags too close to the window where the little boys can reach them. They've been known to disappear!'

'The cigarettes, or the boys?'

'Both!' Megan laughed. 'What happens is, the youngsters want the faggies, and their fathers can't afford to buy enough to satisfy them, so a few children steal. Then they sell the cigarettes for a few pennies to older boys who've taken up smoking and everybody's happy except the poor shop-keeper! Of course, they get a good hiding if their parents find out, but that doesn't always happen. Cunning, some of them are.'

Faggies were brightly coloured cards in the cigarette packages. There was an endless variety of ships, soldiers in uniform, flowers, royalty, and birds. Children traded these cards with their friends in an effort to complete a set.

'And send them on their way if you see them hanging about outside,' Megan advised. 'A lot of them wait until a man comes to buy so they can beg for his cards.'

Ellen thought this was harmless enough, but she nodded agreement. She knew she had a lot to learn. She was aware of how close-knit small communities could be because each street in Cardiff had been like a miniature kingdom, with unwritten laws, firmly adhered to by the residents. She would have to work hard to be accepted here in Cwmbran and she would need friends when the time of her confinement arrived.

'Now then,' Megan continued, 'about your front door. You must keep it locked, see? Nobody locks up their houses here, they don't need to. It's different in your case, though. People expect to walk into a shop without knocking and strangers don't realize about you selling through the window. You don't want to look up from your cooking some day and find some man looking at you! And of course those wretched children could fill their pockets while your back was turned!'

Ellen shivered. She had no doubt that most of the local men were pillars of the chapel and highly trustworthy, and she would get to know them all in time. But human nature being what it was, there was always someone who would prey on a defenceless woman, and they might see her as fair game.

Working at Lloyd's was a different kettle of fish. There was safety in numbers, with a big staff, and there were floor walkers as well, who kept an eye open for shoplifters. The takings were placed in small containers attached to overhead wires. These whizzed across the store to a small office where the money was removed and replaced with the correct change. There was little chance of theft by any of the assistants, even if any of them had been foolish enough to try it.

'No need to look so frightened, *bach*!' Megan told her. 'It's quiet here in Cwmbran, and I'm only next door if you need me. Just give a good thump on the wall and I'll come round at once, or send my Merfin. All right?'

The days passed and Harry didn't come. Then one day, when she was bent over the hob stirring a pot of soup, she heard a sound behind her, and there he was.

'Oh, you made me jump!' she gasped, clutching her chest. 'I wasn't expecting to see anyone. I'm sure I locked the door.'

'You did,' he said, grinning, 'but I have a key. How are you settling in?'

'I'm getting the hang of it now, I think.'

'And the living quarters are satisfactory?'

'Yes, thank you.' She wondered if he expected her to grovel, and say how grateful she was for having been given a roof over her head, but she was too proud to do that. It was the least he could do, being responsible for her present plight. A little voice in her head reminded her that many a man would have looked the other way, and she had to tread warily in case he changed his mind and put her out.

'Megan Jones next door has been very helpful,' she murmured.

'That's good. Now, we must put our arrangement on a proper footing. My agent will collect the rent each week, and you must keep a proper accounting of income and expenditure in the shop. If you can't manage I shall give you a little help. It is vital that no one should suspect there is anything more between us than the usual landlord and tenant relationship. Is that understood?'

'Of course.'

'If the subject ever comes up, I shall say that I've given you the job as a favour to an old friend, who wanted to do something for you. How you choose to explain your condition is up to you, as long as my name is kept out of it.'

'You don't need to worry about that!' Ellen's face was stiff as she spoke. 'Mrs Jones noticed my brother's photograph, and jumped to the conclusion that he was my husband. I told her he was killed at Ypres and she's been calling me Mrs Richards ever since. As far as the people hereabouts are concerned, I'm a war widow.'

'Good, good. That should solve the problem nicely. Well, if everything here is under control, I must be on my way. I'll call in again in a week or two, if I may.'

'Won't you have a cup of tea before you go? The kettle's on the boil.'

'No, no, I don't need anything, thank you.'

With that he was gone, leaving Ellen feeling thoroughly deflated. Why did he have to be so businesslike, so cold? Surely he must know she would not betray him. Apart from any loyalty she might owe him, she was in a most vulnerable position. Didn't he know that?

She wished she could hate him, but the way her heart had leapt up when he appeared in her kitchen showed her that she still loved him. And where could that lead her? He was married, and he'd made it clear that there was to be nothing more between them than this business arrangement.

Perhaps things would change when the baby came. He might spend more time with them then, and she would at least have that much. She asked nothing more than to be able to see his face, but would she be given even that? Suddenly overcome with despair, she sat down at the table with her head in her hands, and the tears began to flow.

CHAPTER 20

A BOY ON A bicycle arrived panting at the front door, and was ordered to go to the back.

'No, mister, they sent me to fetch Mr Morgan. He's to come at once!'

'Oh, all right, if it's that important, I'll make sure the master hears about it at once, but next time use the right door. We can't have every ragtag and bobtail running up the front steps.'

The child was not impressed. 'It's urgent, Mr Roberts said! He'll have your guts for garters if you don't deliver the message to Mr Morgan!'

'Now then, what's all this about?' Harry had been crossing the hall when he heard the boy's shrill tones and he now came forward to investigate.

'Please, sir!' the boy piped up. 'Mr Roberts needs you, sir! There's policemen all over the place and he doesn't know what to do!'

'Very well, boy.' Harry fumbled in his pocket for a coin, which he tossed to the child, who caught it deftly. 'Jenkins! See that Williams brings the car round at once.'

'Right away, sir!'

Police all over the place. They must have come in response to his report concerning Thomas Parry. He hoped the arrest could be made without causing too much disruption at the office. On arrival he found that the offi-cers were two ordinary constables rather than the military police he'd been expecting to see.

'We've orders to hold him at the gaol until the proper authorities have time to pick him up,' one of them stated. Harry ignored the man and glared at Tom, who was wearing handcuffs.

'Well, Parry, what do you have to say for yourself?'

'It's all a mistake, Mr Morgan,' Thomas protested. 'I was getting on with my work when these two burst in. What am I supposed to have done, anyway?'

'You know quite well what you've done, man! You're a deserter from His Majesty's army, having walked away from a hospital where your wounds were being treated.'

'That must be somebody else. You've seen my papers; I tried to join up and got turned down. Unfit for service, they said.'

'And what about that wound in your shoulder?'

'I explained that to Mr Roberts, sir.'

'I know, you were injured in a shooting accident on some mythical estate. Did you think I was born yesterday, man?'

'I tell you, it's true!' Parry was almost hysterical. Harry regarded him without pity.

'The military authorities will conduct a thorough investigation, Parry. If you are innocent of the charges, you'll be set free. If not ... well, whatever punishment you have to suffer will be through your own fault. Take this man away, Constable.'

Still protesting, Parry was led out of the building and pushed into the Black Maria which awaited him. Harry turned to Roberts, who, having stood by with his mouth open while the uncomfortable scene was being played out, was wringing his hands.

'Next time you take on a new hand you check him out more thoroughly, Roberts!'

'But how was I to know, Mr Morgan? His papers looked genuine enough. Was I supposed to write to the War Office to ask if they'd been forged? I'd no reason to believe they were.'

'Neither have I, Roberts, and they may well be genuine. It's what happened earlier that is the problem.'

'Sir? I don't understand.'

'Don't worry your head about it, man. The true story will come out in time.'

'What do you want me to do now, Mr Morgan? I'm a man short with Parry gone.'

But Harry had marched out of the office, leaving the manager staring after him in puzzlement. The whole thing was a mystery.

When Marged Powell next saw her son, she couldn't wait to pass on the gossip.

'Whatever do you think, son? That chap of our Daisy's has been taken away by the police!'

'Oh, aye?'

'Came for him with handcuffs, they did, two of them.'

'Military police, were they?'

'Na, na, ordinary constables. What would make you ask that?'

'Never mind, Mam. It's best you don't know, then you can't be caught out if they come around asking questions.'

'Sidney Powell! What have you been up to?'

'None of your business, Mam, all right?'

'No, it's not all right, and don't you give me no back answers or you'll get a good smack from me, big as you are!'

Sid had to laugh as he looked down at his tiny mother. Chirpy as a little sparrow, she was, and still ruled the roost.

'Was it you turned him in to the police, then, son?'

'No, Mam, it was not, although I could have done. I kept quiet for our Daisy's sake. In love with him, she is.'

'Was would be a better word. She saw the light in a hurry when she caught him making up to that hussy of a Bronwen Pugh! Mad she was, swearing she'd never look at him again. Mind you, when a girl is in love there's no telling. He'd only need to come begging for forgiveness and she'd take him back in a heartbeat. Just as well he's out of the picture now, if you ask me. A proper bad lot he is, to be sure.'

That was just like Mam, Sid thought. She didn't need to ask what Tom Parry had done to get himself arrested; he was bad because he had let their Daisy down, and in this house that was a hanging offence.

'P'raps I should go up to the house and let our Daisy know what's happened,' he suggested, but his mother was against it.

'She'll hear soon enough. Mr Morgan will tell the mistress, and she'll say something to Daisy, sure to. And you don't want to get involved, son. There's two jobs at stake here, don't forget, and if you lose yours we lose the roof over our heads as well. I'm warning you, don't risk it.'

'They can't sack a man for calling on his sister, even if she is in service,' he muttered, but nevertheless he took her words to heart. If it ever came out that he'd harboured a deserter, Sid stood to lose more than his livelihood. He didn't fancy a few years' hard labour in one of His Majesty's prisons.

'Oh, do stop snivelling, Powell, you're setting my nerves on edge! Go and wash your face and tidy your hair, and pull yourself together.' Antonia spoke more sharply than she intended, but she'd been feeling queasy all day and she hoped and prayed that she wasn't about to miscarry. A thought struck her.

'You seem especially upset about that young man, Parry, or whatever his name is. There's nothing more to it than that, I trust, is there?'

'Madam?'

'You know what I mean! Are you in a delicate condition?'

'What? Oh, no, Madam, of course not! I'm a respectable girl, Madam.'

'Well, I certainly hope you're right, Powell, because if you were found to be in a certain condition you'd be dismissed instantly, and sent back to your poor mother in disgrace. Do I make myself clear?'

'Yes, Madam.'

'Then go and do as you're told, and when you come back into the room I expect you to have wiped that surly expression off your face.'

I'd like to wipe that look off your face and all, you miserable old hag, Daisy thought. She wished now that she'd warned Tom. She could have got rid of Bronwen somehow and he could have got away in plenty of time. But then she remembered the crimson wave of fury that had possessed her when she'd seen the pair in each other's arms and another part of her was glad he was going to be punished.

That night, tossing and turning in her narrow bed, she tried to be honest about her part in their relationship. Had she made all the running? Worse yet, had she made a fool of herself? There was nothing more pitiful than a girl who threw herself at a man when the attraction wasn't reciprocated.

At Barry, they'd been mutually drawn to each other. Then, when he was in trouble she'd gone out of her way to help him. Had she been wrong in assuming that he'd accepted because he wanted to have a future with her? She hadn't forced him to come to Cwmbran! He could have gone to Ireland. They were neutral there.

They'd gone out together in Cwmbran on her afternoons off. What was unforgivable was that he'd obviously been seeing that slut of a Bronwen at the same time as he'd been leading Daisy up the garden path, telling her she was wonderful and how grateful he was.

She turned her tear-stained pillow over so that the wet part was underneath. She wondered whether Tom was lying awake in a cell somewhere. Was he thinking of her, and regretting the way he'd treated her? Worse than that, did he believe that she had betrayed him? 'I hate you, Tom Parry!' she sobbed, knowing at the same time that she loved him, more than she was ever likely to love a man again.

CHAPTER 21

'THERE'S BEEN TROUBLE at the mine office,' Megan Jones announced, letting herself into the kitchen where Ellen was doing the washing up.

'There's been trouble here, too,' came the response.

Megan wrinkled her nose. 'I smell burning! Trying out a new recipe, were you? That wall oven does take a bit of getting used to.'

'No, I left a pot of potatoes on the hob while I went through to mind the shop, and it boiled dry. An old woman couldn't make up her mind between two ounces of toffees or a penny bar of chocolate, and I didn't like to hurry the poor soul.'

'What did she settle for in the end?'

'Toffees, but then she said she'd forgotten her purse and would have to come back later. Mr Morgan won't let me give tick, so there was nothing more I could do!'

Megan laughed. 'That's life!'

Ellen suddenly realized what her friend had said. 'Trouble? Nothing happened to Mr Morgan, did it?' She had visions of him lying on the floor, felled by a stroke. She bent over to hide her reddened cheeks. She had almost given herself away there!

'He wasn't even there when the police arrived. They had to send for him, or so Mrs Prosser up the street told me. She just happened to be passing at the time, she said. That woman! Trust her to be in the right place when there's anything going on.'

'The police!'

'Yes, they'd come to arrest that new clerk.'

'What's he done, then?'

'Well, according to Mrs Prosser, he'd robbed the safe and stolen all this week's wages, but Roberts found out in time. Serve them right for hiring a stranger, she said. Of course, that's sour grapes because she hoped her son would get the job.'

'I expect he'll get his chance now, then.'

'Yes, but I think she's wrong about that Parry. How would he get the safe open, unless he got in at night and fiddled with the combination? Mrs Powell told my aunt he'd run off from the army and they want to court martial him, which is no more than he deserves because he's been going out with her daughter and has let her down.'

Ellen frowned. 'Powell. Isn't that the name of Mrs Morgan's lady's maid?' Harry had mentioned the girl to her in passing when they were at Barry.

'How would you know that?' Megan wondered innocently, and Ellen knew she'd done it again. She must be more careful and not let her tongue run away with her!

'Mr Morgan came in the other day to buy sweets for his wife,' she improvised. 'She was annoyed because she'd sent Powell to run some errands but she'd forgotten to come here. Apparently Mrs Morgan has a hankering for aniseed balls these days.'

Megan laughed and said that was pregnancy for you. She herself had taken a fancy for apple tart when she was expecting her first, and she'd eaten so much of it that half the weight she'd gained must have come from that.

'What I really came for was to ask if you'd like to borrow my Moses basket when your baby arrives,' she went on. 'I'm not giving it to you for keeps, mind. That would be asking for trouble!'

'What do you mean?'

'Oh, just an old wives' tale, I suppose.' Megan laughed self-consciously. 'They say that as soon as you give away your baby things you fall pregnant again, and I'm hoping the stork stays away from our house now! Four children is quite enough!'

'There's kind, Megan. I'd be glad to borrow it. I was thinking of buying a treasure cot, but they're so expensive in the shops.' A treasure cot was a sort of tiny hammock, suspended from a wooden frame, equipped with muslin curtains to keep off draughts.

'The Morgans have one in their nursery, I expect, but a basket is better for the likes of us. You can take it from room to room with you. Some folks in this street make do with an old drawer, and I don't suppose the baby cares, one way or the other.'

Sid Powell was suffering a massive attack of guilt at the thought of what could have happened to his sister as a result of his willingness to shelter Tom Parry. Heart-broken she might be now, but she would get over that. Poor Bronwen Pugh wasn't so lucky.

'Talking about drowning herself, she is,' her brother Gwilym muttered to Sid, who devoutly hoped that his secret was safe. Gwilym was a keen amateur boxer, and Sid didn't fancy getting his nose broken if it came out about his role in Parry's arrival in Cwmbran. Of course it wasn't his fault if the girl had succumbed to the man's blandishments, but Gwil wouldn't see it that way.

'Our poor Mam is half demented, with the other women from the chapel sticking their noses in the air and passing by on the other side of the street. The minister wants to have a word with Mr Morgan, him being the magistrate and having a bit of clout, like, to see if he can get in touch with the army and force Parry to marry Bron.'

'Oh, *Duw*, I wouldn't wish that on the girl, Gwil! If they don't put him to death he'll get sent down for years. He'd be no sort of husband for her.'

'Ah, but she'd be respectable, you see.'

'Oh, aye? Married to a gaol bird? This is Cwmbran, man! The old tabbies at the chapel wouldn't see past the end of their noses and she'd still be shunned.'

'The child should be born in wedlock, Sid. Mam wants him to have a name, and come to that, so do I. Our Bronwen may be a bit foolish, but she's not a bad girl. She's not the first to get carried away some moonlight night up the mountain.'

Sid relayed this piece of news to his mother, who had already heard the gossip. 'All over Cwmbran, it is, boyo! I always said Bronwen would go to the bad and she's proved me right. It's her poor Mam I feel sorry for. Talking about sending the girl off to her Auntie Ceinwen in Tonypandy, but what's the point of that? Everybody knows what's going on by now, so she might as well stay here and face the music.'

'What? And have a brick thrown through their window some dark night?'

Mrs Powell shrugged. 'At least our Daisy saw through the man, and thank the Lord for that! She'll forget all about him now, you'll see.'

Sid thought otherwise. He decided that he'd better put her wise about Bronwen before she heard it from someone else and gave herself away. Up there at the house the news probably hadn't reached her yet. Daisy was furious. 'I knew she was up to no good, the minute I caught them together at the office! The rotten slut! How dare she steal my man! I'm glad she's got what's coming to her!'

'Come on, Daisy, that's a bit thick.'

'Oh, it is, is it!'

'Look, I agree he treated you badly, but it's not as if you were engaged or anything. I know you're angry, but you're better off without him, and in time you'll accept it.'

'It's so unfair!' Daisy burst out. 'You don't understand anything.'

'Try me and see.'

'You know how it is in Cwmbran. Well, everywhere, I suppose. We're taught to keep ourselves pure, to save ourselves for marriage. That's the girls. It's different for men. You're all out for what you can get, but at the same time not one of you will marry a girl who isn't a virgin. Well, I held out against Tom Parry and he dropped me like a hot potato and took up with her instead, that Bron!'

'And now she's paying the price!'

'Not according to Gwil. She'll end up married, see, which means she's won.'

'Married and widowed, perhaps,' Sid sighed, but nothing would console his sister.

'I've a good mind to go and scratch that cat's eyes out!' she snapped.

'Now, Daisy, don't you go and do anything silly. Do you want to lose your place with the Morgans? Have a bit of dignity, *cariad*. The mistress won't like it if her maid is found brawling. There's stupid to fight over a worthless fool like that Tom Parry.'

Daisy was forced to agree, but she had a hard time keeping quiet when she heard her employers talking about Tom and Bronwen. Like many of their class, they ignored their servants as if they simply didn't exist and took no pains to moderate their voices when discussing their personal affairs.

'It's a damn nuisance, but I'll have to go up to London,' Harry told his wife, who regarded him languidly.

'Whatever for?'

'To attend this tribunal, or whatever it's called, when Parry's case comes up.'

'I thought you'd finished with all that.'

'I thought so too, but apparently he's got some local girl into trouble and her mother is pressing to get them married, to give the baby a name. Old Matthews from the chapel came up to plead with me to see what I can do, and I could hardly say no to the man.'

CHAPTER 22

HARRY HAD DEBATED with himself about the train journey to London. He would never have considered anything below first-class for himself, and he would willingly have purchased a similar ticket for the clergyman, who could not afford this luxury. The problem was Bronwen Pugh; pregnant, unmarried, and most definitely vulgar. He knew many people who were likely to be in London at the same time; he couldn't risk being seen by someone who might put the wrong interpretation on the matter. He reluctantly decided to use his private coach.

Bronwen was thrilled to the core. She had expected to travel third-class and now this! Wide-eyed, she took in all the elements of the coach, from the comfortable seats on the thick carpeting, to the velvet curtains on the windows. When an attendant appeared and helped her to put her legs up on a footstool, she leaned back and prepared to enjoy herself. This was the life!

The Reverend Matthews was torn two ways. It was very good of Mr Morgan to arrange this for their comfort; he'd been to London before and had experienced first hand the rigours of third-class train travel. On the other hand, the beliefs of his Puritan ancestors were lurking at the back of his brain, and he felt it wasn't right for a few men to have such wealth, while others had to struggle for survival.

He tried to reconcile these opposing ideas in his mind. Our Lord Himself had mentioned that the poor are always with us, and Matthews accepted the fact that God was responsible for calling each man and woman to their place in society. So why was wealth an affront to a right-thinking man such as himself? Could it stem from envy or greed, both of which were sins? Perplexed, he opened his Bible to search for answers.

Harry breathed a heavy sigh. With Matthews present, like the death's head at the feast, there could be no card game or talk of horse racing, and he had already told his steward that no wine could be served at luncheon. He unfolded his newspaper and turned to news of the war. That left him feeling more gloomy than before.

Only Bronwen was happy. She watched the countryside slide by, leaning forward to get a closer look each time the train raced through a town, or stopped at a station. She had never been out of Cwmbran before and she relished the experience. All this would be something to tell Mam went she returned home. As for London, well! She had never expected to go there. Of course, there would be no chance to see the sights as they'd be driven straight to a place called Whitehall for the hearing.

When the meal was served – enough to feed them at home for days – Bronwen hardly knew what to ask for. She'd never heard of half the things on the menu.

'Would you choose for me, Mr Matthews?' she asked meekly. 'I'm not so good reading English, see.'

The little clergyman bit his lip. He, too, was out of his depth. Were they meant to ask for all these courses, or make a selection of one or two? Harry saw his difficulty and moved in smoothly to solve the problem.

'Shall I order for all of us? You're hungry, I'm sure.'

'That would be most acceptable, sir,' Matthews replied.

'Then I think the chicken bouillon, then the turbot, followed by roast pork. We can decide on a pudding later, and of course I'll want the cheese board.'

'Very good, sir.' The steward disappeared, leaving Bronwen mentally licking her lips. She'd never heard of bouillon before, and what on earth was turbot? When the first course arrived she was disappointed to see that it was a clear soup, without even any vegetables floating around in it. Not a bit like Mam's soups, made from a good beef bone with a lot of carrots and pearl barley thrown in. The nobs didn't seem to know much about cooking, did they? Still, it tasted all right.

The turbot turned out to be a bit of fish, and again, it wasn't a patch on cod, fried in batter. However, the roast pork was just right, succulent and complete with crackling. She toyed with the idea of asking for seconds but decided it might not be the thing. Besides, she had to save room for afters.

Later, when she was seated in the hackney cab, she wished she hadn't eaten so much. She felt queasy. Surely she wasn't going to be sick here and now? What a disgrace that would be! Quick, now, Bron, think about something else. Think about Tom. You'll be seeing him soon. The steady drumming of the horse's feet as it trotted over the wet streets almost lulled her to sleep and then, suddenly, they were there.

In the tall, echoing building, that was even bigger than All Saints church at Cwmbran, they were met by a stern man who must be somebody high up in the army, to judge by all the bits and pieces on his uniform. Was he the one who would decide Tom's fate? Bronwen looked up at him with a pleading expression on her face.

'Mr Morgan, I presume? I'm Major Barnaby.'

'How do you do?' Harry nodded curtly. 'And this is the Reverend Clive Matthews from Cwmbran, and this is Parry's fiancée, Miss Pugh.'

'I'm afraid you won't be allowed into the room while the accused is being tried, Miss Pugh. You'll have to wait outside, and the hearing is likely to take some time.'

'Oh, but I wanted …' Bronwen's words were lost as the officer marched away, with Mr Morgan at his side and the minister trotting in their wake. Disconsolately she wandered into the waiting room, which was far less comfortable than the railway coach she had just left. Would she get to see Tom at all? A tear ran down her cheek and was angrily wiped away by the sleeve of her shabby coat.

In the courtroom, Tom Parry presented a very different picture from the cocky young man Harry remembered from the colliery office. His hair had been cut so short that he resembled the convicts Harry had once seen working on a chain gang. He was dressed in some sort of overall, similar to those worn by patients in military hospitals. He held himself stiffly, as if determined not to shiver. He was made to stand throughout the lengthy proceedings, while the tribunal, made up of several high-ranking officers, sat at a table facing him. Harry and Matthews were given chairs at the side of the room.

Harry was one of the first to give evidence. 'Would you state your name, address and occupation, sir?'

'Henry Morgan, of the Hall at Cwmbran, Carmarthenshire. I own the colliery there, as well as the estates surrounding my home. I am also the local magistrate.'

'And would you explain to us how and when you first met the accused?'

'It was when my wife and I were staying at the Sea View Hotel at Barry. He was employed as a footman there.'

'And how did he come to terminate his employment at the hotel?'

'A housemaid caused a disturbance when Parry was serving at dinner. She presented him with a white feather because she felt that such a healthy-looking young man should be fighting in France. She was quite clear about that, and said so firmly.'

'A very proper sentiment, if I may say so. And what happened after that?'

'The next morning he was gone. I was given to understand that he'd taken her words to heart and had gone out to enlist.'

'How did you learn this, if he did not return?'

'When I returned to Cwmbran I found him working in the office at my colliery.'

'Just a moment, sir!' The interruption came from one of the officers who hadn't spoken before. 'I don't believe I understand. You say he went out to enlist, yet he found employment at your colliery. Had you offered him a post while you were staying at the hotel?'

'Not at all. Apparently he had formed an attachment with my wife's maid, and knowing we would be returning to Cwmbran shortly, he decided to go there in order to continue seeing Miss Powell. I was most surprised to find that my manager had taken him on during my absence. Parry showed me a document which seemed to be quite authentic; he had indeed attempted to enlist but had been turned down as physically unfit for service.'

Other witnesses came and went. It was explained that Parry had served bravely at the front before being wounded at Mons. He had then spent some time in an English hospital before deserting. The officer in charge then addressed his remarks to Parry.

'It is most unfortunate that you chose to abscond from the hospital as you did. I have received a report from the medical officer at Bagshot which states that you were to have been given an honourable discharge, being considered unfit for further duty. He may be partly to blame for not having explained this to you. It is also in your favour that, having regretted your action, you then attempted to re-enlist. However, we cannot discharge you without punishment. Justice must be seen to be done.'

Parry went white, swaying on his feet. It came as a great relief to be told that he was not to be executed but would be sent to prison, there to be detained at His Majesty's pleasure. Before he could be led away, the Reverend Matthews asked permission to speak to the accused on behalf of the young woman he had come to represent.

Much, much later, Bronwen Pugh returned to Cwmbran with a ring on her finger.

'You've done it, then!' her mother observed sourly. 'I hope you're properly grateful to Reverend Matthews! That young man would have left you in the lurch, as he probably will when he gets out of prison. That's if he ever does.'

'It's thanks to Mr Morgan, too, Mam! He was the one who got us the special licence. He even got us the ring, seeing as Tom didn't have any money.'

Mrs Pugh pressed her lips together. All that mattered now was that the girl was married. She'd never live down the disgrace, but at least the child would be born in wedlock.

CHAPTER 23

CHRISTMAS CAME AND went in a blur. Ellen had never been so busy in her life, not even when she'd worked at Lloyd's. She had decorated the little shop with paper chains, the sort they'd made when she was at school, from strips of coloured paper stuck together with flour and water paste. Megan had contributed some sprigs of holly which she'd gathered while on a walk with her children. The whole effect was homely and cheerful.

Everyone wanted sweets or tobacco products for Christmas gifts. Ellen had ordered two boxes of sugar mice with string tails and these proved extremely popular with parents who bought them for their children's stockings.

The youngsters who gazed through the window with shining eyes were just as taken by the pink and white confectionery. Ellen had to smile at the antics of a little girl and her even smaller brother, who couldn't take their eyes off the mice.

'I want one of those,' the boy announced, holding up a penny and a ha'penny.

'Well, you can't have one, our Matthew! We've got to buy a present for Mam.'

'Get it with your money, then.' The child pouted. 'You've got more than me. It's not my fault I don't get as much pocket money as you do.'

'No! It's supposed to be from both of us, see!'

Matthew's mouth went square and Ellen hastened to intervene.

'Let's see how much you have to spend, then.' The girl displayed some coins. It was obvious that it wouldn't buy much.

'What about some homemade fudge, then?' she suggested. 'Do you think your Mam would like that?'

The children nodded solemnly and she put several squares into a paper bag, taking their money as she handed it over.

'But what about my mouse?' The boy still wasn't satisfied with the transaction.

'I can't let you have a mouse, but would you like a piece of treacle toffee instead?' After a long hesitation, he nodded. She gave him a chunk of her homemade toffee, large enough to clamp his jaws together to forestall any more complaints.

'*Diolch yn fawr*, missus,' the little girl said, as she popped her own share into a rosy little mouth. Ellen grinned. At least one of them was happy. She would love to hand out free sweets to all her little customers, but it just wasn't possible. As it was, young Matthew still thought he'd been cheated in some way.

On Christmas Eve she accepted an invitation to attend the carol service at the chapel with Megan's family. Her friend's husband was singing a solo and she didn't want to miss that. The shop had to be kept open until the last minute so Ellen did not arrive until after the service had started. As she neared the chapel, a great wave of music overflowed on to the street as the people inside sung their hearts out. She slipped inside the door and was escorted to a seat by a solemn-faced usher.

The gas lamps hissed, the little organ wheezed, the people shuffled in their seats, and the odour of wet clothes filled the room. The music swelled to the rafters, taking Ellen's heart with it. All her pain and sorrow were swept from her body in that instant. Everyone here had their own troubles, but in this joyous season they could set them aside for a little while, while they rejoiced at the coming birth of their saviour.

Christmas Day brought pleasure to Ellen, who stayed with Megan's family. It was a delight to hear the children's exclamations of pleasure over their simple gifts, which were mostly homemade toys produced by their parents.

'This time next year you'll be helping your own baby open presents,' Megan said, beaming.

The year 1918 arrived. Ellen got up early and put a few coins in her apron pocket, and sweets in a dish, ready for the boys who would come singing at her door to welcome in the New Year.

> *I say one and you say two,*
> *You say Charlie, how d'you do,*
> *So early in the morning, so early in the morning*
> *So early in the morning*
> *Before the break of day.*

Between that and the pennies they collected from singing Christmas carols round the doors, some of them would be quite well off, she mused. What would the New Year bring for them all? Would the war come to an end at last? It seemed as if it had been going on for ever.

Ellen entered a phase where she felt a bit like a dormouse. When she wasn't working in the shop, she spent long hours in bed, as she felt too tired to sit for long in her rocking chair by the kitchen fire. The cold, dark days of January dragged by, and everyone who stopped at the shop complained of chilblains or rheumatism.

February brought some relief and in parts of Cwmbran, where people had small front gardens, snowdrops emerged from the earth and bloomed defiantly.

'My sister's daffodils are poking up,' Megan announced cheerfully. 'With any luck they'll bloom for St David's Day. That's not far off.'

Ellen knew how important this was to the children. Every girl hoped to find a daffodil to wear to school, and every boy sported a leek on his jacket. Both were the emblems of Wales. There was always some naughty boy who chewed on his leek during morning lessons, calling forth a rebuke from the teacher. The afternoon was always a half-day holiday, so St David's Day was an occasion to look forward to, breaking up the cold months between Christmas and Easter.

'Are you all right, Ellen? You look a bit wan.' Megan had come in carrying a bottle of milk. 'Jones the milk left us an extra pint this morning but nothing on your step. I don't know what's the matter with him. It must be love!'

They both laughed. The elderly man had been walking out with a widow for at least six years and as far as everyone could see he was in no hurry to propose.

'Perhaps he's taking a leaf out of Jacob's book, serving seven years for Rachel,' Ellen quipped.

'Never mind that; you haven't answered my question. Are you feeling all right?'

'Oh, yes. I just didn't sleep too well, that's all. You know how it is when you're as big as a whale; you just can't seem to get comfortable in bed. And then when I do get settled I have to get out again to use the potty.'

'No pains, then?'

'Just a bit of wind. I should be more careful what I eat before going to bed.'

Megan nodded thoughtfully. 'It could be labour pains, you know.'

'Oh, definitely not. I'm not due just yet, and I'm not having actual pains, you see.'

'You take it from one who knows, Ellen Richards! A person can't always be sure of the date of arrival, and besides, there's what they call false labour, pains that come too early but don't amount to anything. I'd better let Mrs Bryant know, just in case.'

'There's no need to tell her anything yet,' Ellen protested. She had met the midwife, who was bossy and self-opinionated. No doubt she'd be glad to have the woman at her side when the time came, but meanwhile she could stay away.

'I'll send our Ifor round with a note after school,' Megan countered. 'It's only wise to put her in the picture so she can be prepared. How would you feel if you started when she was away from home? Once that baby is on its way you'll be glad to have professional support. Take it from one who knows!'

Ellen knew her friend was right. She was dreading her confinement and wondered if she'd be able to get through it. As schoolgirls, she and her friends had held whispered conversations about childbirth and they'd heard that it was ten times worse than the worst toothache imaginable. No older woman was prepared to discuss such matters with young girls, and they'd have died sooner than ask their mothers about it. And in Ellen's case, of course, her mother was dead.

As things turned out, Megan had been right and Ellen wrong. The next morning brought steady contractions, none of them painful, but it was obvious that the baby was eager to come into the world. After thumping on the wall with the heel of her shoe, Ellen sank back in the rocking chair and waited for Megan to arrive.

'This is it, then!' Megan was beaming with delight. 'It won't be long now, *cariad*. In a few hours' time you'll have a little one in your arms, and think how happy you'll be, looking at its tiny face!'

She took charge in the most efficient matter. Ellen was given a cup of tea and told to relax. 'Nothing much will happen for a bit. First babies always take their time coming.' The shop door was locked, and a hastily penned notice nailed to the outside: 'Closed due to illness'. Having seen Ellen's shape gradually expanding over the winter, regular customers would know what that meant. 'And anyone who doesn't will just have to go away and come again another day,' Megan laughed.

By midnight Ellen found herself wishing she'd never been born. How on earth did women go through this agony over and over again? Some women produced a dozen or more children. How did they manage to get through it?

Just as dawn was breaking over Cwmbran, Ellen gave one last, exhausted push and her child was born, complaining vociferously about the journey it had just undertaken.

'A lovely little girl!' Mrs Bryant said approvingly.

'Is she all right? Let me see her!' Ellen gasped, holding out her arms for the child. She looked down at her daughter's face, which greatly resembled a squashed rose. This was Harry Morgan's child, and hers. They had made this tiny miracle together. She promptly fell in love with the baby.

CHAPTER 24

ELLEN LAY IN an exhausted sleep. Her baby was in her basket nearby, well wrapped up against the cold. There was no fireplace in the upstairs rooms and Ellen was afraid that the shock of being taken from the cosy kitchen into the unheated bedroom might harm the child. She would have taken the baby into her own bed for warmth but was afraid she might roll over on the little one in her sleep.

Sensing that she wasn't alone in the room, she struggled to regain consciousness. When she managed to get her eyes open she was amazed to see Harry Morgan, bending over the basket to look at his daughter.

'Oh, you frightened me, Harry! How did you get here? Did Megan let you in?'

'I have a key, remember. I own the street, or have you forgotten?'

Ellen thought that landlords didn't usually burst into their tenants' homes without an invitation, but she didn't say it. Instead, she watched the expression on Harry's face, as he doted over his newborn daughter.

'I came as soon as I heard, *cariad*. Was it very bad?'

Ellen pulled a face. Honestly, men had no idea, no idea at all! Still, he was trying to be sympathetic, she supposed. 'I'm glad it's over now, that's all.'

'She's beautiful, Ellen. Have you chosen a name?' Again, this caused a pang in her heart. When his lawful child appeared, he and his wife would select his or her names together. It was different for this little half-sister.

'I thought Mariah, after my mother,' she murmured.

'Mariah Richards. That sounds good.' He had stumbled over the words, and for a moment she'd thought he was about to say Mariah Morgan, which could never be.

'I've brought her a present,' he said, delving into his overcoat pocket. It jingled when he handed it over, and when the wrapping was off a beautiful rattle was revealed, with tiny silver bells set into the top.

'It's real ivory,' he remarked, 'and see how the handle is shaped at the other end. I'm told it can be used to gum on when the baby's teeth are coming in. You'll have to keep an eye on those bells, mind you. I was assured that they are firmly fixed and will never come apart, but one never knows. We don't want little Mariah to choke, do we?'

'I wouldn't have thought they'd sell something as fine as this in Cwmbran.'

'Oh, I didn't get it in the village, *cariad*. I was in London some time ago and I bought it there.'

'It was kind of you to think of us, Harry, but I'm not sure I should use it where it can be seen. Megan is a good soul; she's always in and out doing things for me and she'd be bound to notice it. How could I explain where I came by it?'

He laughed. 'When you've something to hide the best plan is to tell the truth as far as possible. Say I bought it for you, of course. She already knows – or thinks she does – that you are here because I'm doing a favour for my god daughter.'

Ellen laughed. 'And the next thing to explain is how a man who unloaded ships at the Cardiff docks came to choose a university chap as godfather to his daughter!'

'Oh, that's simple enough. If your friend is so rude as to ask, just say you have no idea! In any case, godparents come in all shapes and sizes. I shall stand godfather to Miss Mariah Richards, if you'll have me.'

Ellen was delighted. Harry could never claim the baby as his own, but at least he had no intention of disowning her completely.

He stood up. Longing to keep him near her for a little longer, she cast about for something to say.

'I suppose you had business to see to in London?'

'I had to give evidence at a court martial. Do you recall my telling you about that footman at the hotel in Barry?'

'Oh, you mean the one who was given a white feather?'

'That's the man. He turned up here in Cwmbran, actually working in my office! To cut a long story short I learned that he had been in the army and deserted. Of course, I had to turn him over to the authorities.'

'So what are they going to do with him now? They won't execute him, will they?'

'No. There are mitigating circumstances so he's been given a prison sentence instead. He'll find that breaking up rocks in a quarry will be less to his liking than working as a footman in a hotel.'

'I'm glad,' Ellen said softly. 'It's bad enough being killed by the enemy without being put to death by your own side.'

'Unfortunately that's not the end of the story as far as I'm concerned. While Parry was here in Cwmbran he met a local girl who is now going to have his child. The Reverend Matthews from the chapel here brought the girl to London to face Parry, who was more or less forced to marry her. He also managed to stand up to the officer in charge, who kept saying that Parry didn't deserve any special consideration. The wedding took place in the prison chapel the next day, and a very shabby affair it was, too. Still, it was the best that could be done under the circumstances, and at least the young person has returned to Cwmbran as a married woman.'

'I see.'

'I don't think you do see,' he grumbled. 'My wife's maid is sweet on the wretched man. In fact, that was how he came to be here in Cwmbran. I don't know the extent of her involvement in his deception, but you can imagine how she feels now! Powell is going around the house with a face like a wet week, which is upsetting my wife. I'd give the girl the sack but every time I suggest it Antonia has a bout of hysteria. I've had my fill of fussy women, I can tell you!'

'I expect it will be different when the baby comes,' Ellen soothed.

'I certainly hope so. Now I mustn't tire you out. You must get strong again, so you can look after this little scrap.' He bent over the basket and kissed the tiny Mariah on the forehead, and then he was gone.

Little did Harry know it, but in his usually well-ordered house it was poor Lavinia Phipps who bore the brunt of the upheaval.

'For goodness' sake, pull yourself together!' she snapped, when for the fourth time that day she found Daisy weeping in the linen cupboard. 'It's your job to brush Mrs Morgan's hair, but you're never about when she wants it done. She said it soothes her nerves, but she doesn't like the way I do it. I'm her companion, not a lady's maid.'

'I can't help it. How am I supposed to work when my heart is breaking?'

'Don't talk nonsense, girl!'

'It isn't nonsense. I love him, Miss Phipps. I can't help it, no matter what he's done.'

'Then you'll have to help it. He's a married man now.'

Daisy broke into loud sobs. Goaded beyond measure, Lavinia grabbed her by the shoulder and shook her like a terrier with a rat. 'He's no good, you little fool. You're better off without him, and some day you'll thank your lucky stars for the way things have turned out.'

When Daisy came to her later, snivelling over a scorch mark she'd made in Antonia's peignoir, Lavinia wished she hadn't said anything.

'I've warned you before not to let the flatiron get too hot when you are pressing delicate materials. Now see what you've done! What Mrs Morgan will say I don't know. She was particularly fond of this blue one.'

'P'raps if we put it away and don't say anything she won't notice,' Daisy said hopefully. 'It's not as if she doesn't have others. Can't you say that the peach satin suits her complexion better?'

'Don't you get me involved, Daisy Powell! You go straight in there and confess what you've done, and get it over with.'

This Daisy did, with the result that both Antonia and her maid were in a temper for the rest of the day, and Lavinia was caught in the middle. She tried to calm Antonia down. Offers to read to her or to rub her back were curtly refused. The meals that were sent up were too heavy, or too sweet, and Lavinia was obliged to go down to the kitchen to have it out with the cook.

'But Madam ordered roes on toast with junket to follow! And I made it all just the way she likes it. And we've enough to do down here without Ruth running up and down stairs all day with trays of food that gets sent back! I don't know, I don't really!'

'Well, don't blame me, Cook. It's her condition, I expect. It's enough to upset anyone's digestion and that's why she can't manage to swallow your delicious food.'

The cook wasn't mollified. 'Perhaps you'd tell me what Madam does fancy, then!'

'Perhaps we could try a lightly boiled egg and a little blancmange?'

'I ain't got no blancmange made, and that can't be made all in five minutes. I can give her a bowl of arrowroot if she'll take that, and if she won't, then I'll have to think about giving up the job here and going some-where I'm appreciated!'

As she trudged back up two flights of stairs, Lavinia thought how wonderful it would be if she could only give in her notice and go away to some quiet place where she could be alone. She fixed a false smile on her face as she prepared to deliver the cook's message in suitably modified terms. She could feel a migraine coming on.

CHAPTER 25

THERE WAS MORE upheaval in the house when the midwife moved in. And this was not just any midwife, as Daisy reported to her mother. This was a highly qualified personage who had come all the way from London, if you please!

'I don't see why Madam Morgan can't send for Mrs Bryant, same as anyone else,' Marged Powell grumbled. 'Good enough for the likes of us, she's always been. And giving birth is the same awkward business no matter what your station in life may be. There comes a time when you don't care who is standing beside you, just so long as you can get it over with. And why is this woman here now, too early to be of any use?'

'Well, they can hardly wait until Madam goes into labour before sending for her, can they, not when this Sister Blaine, as she calls herself, has to come from England! According to Phipps, Mr Morgan wants to make sure nothing goes wrong this time.'

Her mother peered in to the teapot, frowning. 'I wonder if I can stretch these leaves to another cup or two? Tea is so dear these days.'

'I'll see if Cook will give me a packet or two next time I come, Mam.'

'You'll do no such thing, my girl. That's stealing, that is. I'd rather go thirsty than see any child of mine going off the straight and narrow.'

'It's not stealing, Mam! It's Cook's perks. It happens in all the big houses.'

'Perks, is it! Well, we'll have no perks here, thank you very much!'

'Please yourself, then. Anyway, you probably wouldn't like their tea. I had a sip of that stuff Madam drinks. Like dishwater, it was, and all scenty.'

'Huh! I don't suppose that Sister woman will drink it, then. Nurses likes their cup of tea. Keeps them going on the job. What's she like, this one?'

'Very hoity toity. Wants to be waited on every moment. Fetch this, fetch that. I had to tell her, I said, "I'm Madam's lady's maid. If you want a house-maid, ring the bell."'

'You want to watch your step, my girl, or you'll be sent off with a flea in your ear.'

'See if I care!' Daisy tossed her head. 'I'm thinking of looking around for something else, anyway.'

'There's nothing round here for lady's maids. You'd have to work as a parlour maid. A bit of a come-down, that, after what you've been used to, being taken away on holiday with the family and such.'

'Yes, and see where that got me!' She began to cry.

'Oh, come on, *cariad.* You're well out of it with that Tom Parry!'

'That's what everybody keeps saying, so why do I feel so sad, Mam?'

'You'll get over it. First love doesn't last. We've all been there.'

Daisy forebore to remind her mother that Tom was hardly her first love. There had been a series of boys during her schooldays with whom she'd fancied herself in love, only to have nothing come of it. Most of them didn't even spare her a glance. She was well into her twenties and if she didn't meet somebody soon she'd be an old maid, an object of scorn like poor old Phipps.

'Have you seen anything of Bronwen Pugh?' she asked, although it pained her to think of the smug cat married to Tom and expecting his child.

'Oh, she's round about, looking like butter wouldn't melt in her mouth. Of course, try as she might, she's not going to convince anyone she's a respectable married woman, even if she does have a ring on her finger. And what kind of husband is it that she won't see for heaven knows how many years?' Mam had conveniently forgotten that many another woman was in the same boat, with their menfolk away at the war.

Suddenly, Daisy had had enough. 'Thanks for the tea, Mam. I'd best be getting back. Madam is sure to squawk if I'm five minutes late, even though I did finish up all my work before I came away.'

Her mother nodded. She wanted to get on with her baking. Their Sid was bringing a friend home after work. Too bad it wasn't a nice young lady, she thought. It was time he settled down. The thing was, his friend was Gwil Pugh, brother to the hated Bronwen, and she wasn't sure how Daisy would react if she knew. Sitting down with the enemy was how she might see it.

Lavinia Phipps had another of her heads. She really was going to have to lie down, and if Antonia complained, that midwife could jolly well dance attendance on her. The woman had nothing better to do than read novels and drink endless cups of tea.

Even the uniform she insisted on wearing annoyed the companion. Her apron was so stiff with starch that it crackled when she moved, and as for her cap, with those great bows tied under the chin! 'Wouldn't a hat pin keep it on?' she'd asked, the first time she saw it, but apparently that was the wrong thing to say. The nurse told her loftily that 'strings' were a mark of rank at her training hospital.

Lavina longed to know how much this Sister, or whatever she called herself, was getting paid for being on standby. Had she been a betting woman she would have guessed that it far outweighed her own modest remuneration.

She had to admit, though, that the woman's presence in the house calmed Antonia.

'I feel safe just knowing she's here, Miss Phipps.'

Knowing nothing about motherhood, Lavinia expected that when the baby's arrival was imminent there would be a moment of high drama, with Antonia doubled over in pain, gasping for help. Thus she was unprepared when her mistress refused her breakfast one morning, saying she had a touch of indigestion.

'It must be that mushroom omelette Cook gave me last night.'

'Yes, Madam. Shall I fetch the peppermint water?'

By the time the gong sounded for luncheon the waves of pain were coming regularly, and Sister announced with satisfaction that her patient was in labour. Lavinia was banished, much to her relief. For once she didn't mind being ordered about by the bossy nurse.

'I shall take my book outside and sit in the arbour,' she told Daisy. 'It's such a pleasant day. You'll find me there if I'm needed.'

'Wish I could come with you,' Daisy grumbled, 'but the old she-devil says I'll be needed to fetch and carry. Hot water, I suppose, and more cups of tea for her! I'll be glad when this is all over, I can tell you that!'

Later that afternoon, Harry Morgan looked in, to find that all was quiet.

'Everything is progressing as expected, Mr Morgan,' the midwife said, putting down her knitting and standing up on seeing him.

'Good, good.' He bent over his wife, kissing her on the forehead. 'How are you feeling, *cariad*? Not too dreadful, I hope.'

'Sister says I'm doing well.' Antonia's voice was weary, and a faint sheen of perspiration showed on her forehead. 'I do wish you'd go away, Harry. I don't want you here now.'

'Mrs Morgan is quite correct, sir. This is no place for a husband at present.'

'I'll look in again later, then.' Harry went to his study, where he opened a drawer to examine, for the tenth time, a diamond bracelet inside a velvet-lined leather case. This should be Antonia's when she presented him with his son. He had purchased it at Garrard's, the Crown jewellers, when he was in London.

He could imagine the scene when they were out at some ball or the opera. A friend would admire the bracelet, and Antonia would reply airily, 'Oh, this? My husband gave it to me when little Henry was born. Isn't it pretty?'

The clock in Harry's study had just struck ten when the knock came at his door. He was calmly smoking a cigar and waiting for the summons that would tell him that Antonia's ordeal was over.

'Come in!'

Daisy stood framed in the doorway, her cap awry and tears running down her face.

'Oh, sir! Can you come? Sister Blaine says we've got to send for the doctor at once. No time to lose, sir! Something's not right with the baby and she can't manage!'

Harry leapt to his feet at once. 'Tell her I'll go myself. It'll be quicker in the car.'

'Yes, sir. Thank you, sir.'

Daisy was pushed aside as he ran for the stairs. She returned to Antonia's room at a slower pace, not wanting to hear or see what was going on inside.

'What is it? What's happening? Is it the baby coming?' Lavinia Phipps had come out of her room, looking a fright in her shabby flannel dressing gown, with her hair twisted up in rags.

'Something's wrong with the baby, I think,' Daisy whispered. 'They've sent for the doctor. The master's gone in the car to fetch him.'

The two women stared at each other and then glanced fearfully at Antonia's door. A shriek of agony came to their ears, followed by the soothing tones of the midwife.

'I don't think I can bear this,' Lavinia muttered.

'Nor me, either. The master will go out of his mind if they lose another one.'

'It's not him I'm thinking of, Daisy! At least, you know what I mean. It's that poor soul in there, and what she must be going through.'

'It's woman's lot,' Daisy countered piously. It was something she'd heard Mam say often enough but it occurred to her now that it was no comfort.

CHAPTER 26

'THERE'S TERRIBLE ABOUT poor Mrs Morgan!'

'What do you mean? Has something happened?' Ellen stared at Megan, with all sorts of thoughts going through her mind.

'You haven't heard, I suppose. She's dead, poor soul.'

'And the baby?'

'They managed to save her, but they say she's a poor, puny little mite. I doubt if they'll manage to raise her.'

Ellen sat down suddenly, feeling sick. Poor, poor Harry! How could he bear it?

'How do you know all this?'

'My Mam told me. She had it from her friend, Mrs Powell, whose daughter was lady's maid to Mrs Morgan. Out of a job now, she is, and had to go back home. Nowhere else to go. And her brother, who works down the pit with my Merfin, said they're all wondering what's to happen next. Quite worried they are.'

Ellen frowned. 'What do you mean?'

'Will Mr Morgan stay around here after the funeral, with all the sad memories? If the house is closed up, what's to become of the staff? And what if he decides to sell up and go abroad? There's a lot more jobs to be considered besides what's up at the house. All the men down the pit, and the people on the estate.'

'He'll have to live somewhere,' Ellen said doubtfully. 'He'll need staff to look after the baby, won't he?' Wealthy folk needed several people to care for their offspring. A nanny and a nursery maid at the very least, and a housemaid to see to their needs!

'They do say there won't even be a funeral here,' Megan went on. 'She's being taken back to her own people, in Gloucestershire. So nobody here can even go to pay their respects. Of course, there'll be lots coming to the funeral from London and places like that, so there wouldn't be room for any of us even if it was held in Cwmbran. Still, I'd have liked to stand outside and see the comings and goings at the church.'

Ellen wished that her friend would stop talking and go away. Fortunately Mariah started to cry just then, a loud wail which intensified when she wasn't picked up at once.

'I'll have to go, Megan. She wants feeding, I expect.'

'So I hear. See you later, then.'

Ellen wondered how Harry was coping now. Whatever love he had once had for his wife had died, or so he had indicated in their walks around Barry Island, but surely you couldn't live with someone for ten years without feeling something for them? He must be feeling bereft, just as she had done when the news of Bertie's death had come in that awful telegram. At least he would have a grave to visit afterwards. Nobody knew exactly where Bertie was buried, or indeed if he had a proper burial place at all.

She wanted Harry to come to her. She would hold him close to her while he poured out his feelings, and she would comfort him. But the days passed, and there was no word from Harry, and soon Ellen began to despair. Perhaps it was as the others feared and he had gone abroad, and she might never see him again. And if he did sell up, what would become of her? Would a new owner let her stay on here, or would she be sent packing? It was all very worrying.

At the house, Harry had summoned both the indoor and outdoor staff. They stood in front of him, wearing black arm bands, all looking very serious.

'I expect you are wondering what is to happen here,' he began. 'There will have to be changes, of course, but for the moment your jobs are safe. I shall be away for a few days staying with my wife's parents, but in the meantime, I expect you to carry on as usual.' There was a murmured response as they all visibly relaxed.

Lavinia Phipps was in her room, wringing her hands. Where was an elderly spinster to go? Mr Morgan had kindly suggested that she might stay on as nanny to his daughter, but it had been only right to refuse. She didn't really like babies and a motherless infant needed some kindly body who knew what she was doing.

'Then I'm afraid you'll have to go, Miss Phipps,' he'd said. 'I'll make sure that my newspapers are passed on to you so you can look at the situations vacant columns, and you may certainly remain here until you find a new post, but that's all I can do.'

She could hardly expect to receive anything under the terms of Antonia's will because her late mistress had owned nothing of her own. Everything belonged to her husband. Thus Lavinia was extremely thankful when Mr Morgan mentioned that she would receive a small honorarium from him, a token of appreciation for her devoted service to his wife. Some old retainers were fortunate enough to be pensioned off with an annuity, but in her case she hadn't been with the family for long enough. She counted herself fortunate to be given anything at all; many in her position were not.

Harry considered that he had treated his wife's servants more than adequately. Daisy had been sent off with a month's wages in her pocket; she would be all right. At her age she'd soon find another job, and if that didn't happen, she had family in the district. He had a vague idea there was a brother working in the pit.

It didn't occur to him to wonder if anyone would take Lavinia Phipps on, at her age. He knew she was the daughter of a clergyman, long since dead, but he had no idea if she had any living relations. Perhaps if she wasn't fit to work she could go into one of those homes for distressed gentlewomen? In any event, she was not his problem.

The few days he spent with his in-laws were a great trial to him. Antonia's mother kept saying she hoped he would be able to manage without the wife he adored, although his little girl would surely be a comfort to him. He nodded and made all the right noises, while thinking how meaningless the words were. How could a young baby be a comfort to him? She didn't know he existed!

As for Antonia, he supposed he had felt something for her in the early days of their marriage, but it certainly hadn't been a grand passion. He regretted the fact that she was dead, and he felt some passing guilt that he had been the instrument of her demise since she had died in childbirth, but that was what any right-thinking man would feel.

Where did he go from here? He was a middle-aged widower with two infant daughters. Some day he might consider marrying again; in fact he had to if he meant to produce a son, but where was a suitable bride to be found?

Unlike the working classes, who could fall in love and marry anyone they chose, people like Harry Morgan had to follow prescribed rules. What was known as 'the season', with its balls and parties and race meetings, was little more than a marriage mart, where young girls were paraded before eligible men in the hope of making an advantageous marriage. Having a pretty face was not enough. Social connections, a good dowry, a spotless reputation; all these played a part in the marriage game.

Antonia had been presented at Court, making her curtsey in front of King Eddie and Queen Alexandra. She had attended all the best balls where her chaperone had made sure that her dance card was always filled, although she must never get talked about by partnering the same man too often.

Harry had carefully played the field. He wanted a wife who would play the lady of the manor to perfection, be a gracious hostess to his friends, and provide him with children, preferably boys. He approved of Antonia's modesty and sweet nature, and approached her father in the approved manner.

At first her mother refused to let her husband make a commitment. As she never tired of reminding him, Antonia was third cousin to an earl. Harry 'wasn't quite one of us'. He was wealthy, he had a beautiful old house, and he owned large estates in Wales, but he also owned a colliery, and that smacked of trade!

It was only when the season neared its end that she relented. No other man had offered for Antonia. She didn't sparkle as other girls did. To be passed over was considered a disgrace, and Antonia had no intention of spending the rest of her life as the unmarried daughter who stayed at home, waiting on elderly parents hand and foot. She pleaded with her father to let her accept Harry Morgan's proposal, and at last he agreed that it was for the best.

'We should like your baby to be christened here, in our church,' Antonia's mother told him, when the funeral was over. 'When would you like it to be done?'

'I don't know. I hadn't thought.'

'We think it should be soon, Harry, and with dear Antonia's grave being nearby, it would be as if she were present, don't you agree?'

This maudlin thought almost made him choke, but he reminded himself that the woman was grief-stricken over the loss of her daughter. He glanced at Antonia's father, who looked away.

'Have you thought of a name for the child?' his mother-in-law continued.

That had been the last thing on his mind, and he had to come up with one quickly. 'Oh, Meredith, I think, since that was her mother's maiden name, and Anne, after my own mother.'

She brightened at once. 'How very nice! Meredith Morgan. It has a certain ring to it, don't you agree, Paul?' Her husband grunted. His wife ignored him. 'And what about a nanny, dear? Have you engaged one yet? The Osbornes have a very good nanny who has to look for a new post now that the boys have gone off to their public school. Shall I have a word with her for you?'

CHAPTER 27

Harry had no sooner arrived home when the butler appeared, with a message.

'The nurse asks if you'll go up and see her as soon as you can, sir. I told her that it is certainly not for her to summon you, but the other way about!' The man looked so affronted that Harry had to hide a smile.

'All right, Perkins, no harm done. I expect she didn't want to leave Miss Meredith.'

'Then she should have rung for one of the maids to stay with the child. Still, the woman will be gone in three weeks, so we'll hardly have time to train her in our ways.'

'Thank you, Perkins.' Harry bounded up the stairs, two at a time, and entered the nursery without knocking. He found the monthly nurse sitting down with the baby on her lap. She had apparently been trying to feed the infant but the bottle was full and the child set up a faint wail. Harry had never heard such a sad sound.

'Oh, sir, I don't know what to do! She won't take any nourishment. We've tried her on goat's milk and even given her a sugar bag to suck, but all she does is turn her head away. She wants her Mam, of course; that's what it is.'

Harry winced. 'Well, there's nothing we can do about that, Nurse! Perhaps she'll eat when she's hungry.'

'She must be hungry by now, but she's just not interested in the bottle. Look at her. She's fading away.'

Harry knew little about babies, but even he could see that this was a pale specimen compared with rosy-cheeked little Mariah. A wave of compassion washed over him.

'So what's to be done, Nurse?'

'In my opinion, if she's to have any chance to thrive, the only thing is to get a wet nurse in. There must be a suitable woman somewhere in the district.'

'I'll have to think about that,' he said. It was still the practice for women of their class to employ wet nurses, but he had no idea what Antonia might have done. She certainly would not have discussed such delicate matters with him.

'We cannot leave it for long,' the nurse cautioned. If any other servant had spoken to him in such a manner she would have felt the rough side of his tongue, but he decided to excuse her because she had the baby's best interests at heart.

'I fully understand that, Nurse! It's a question of finding the right person. She would have to live in, and most married women have enough responsibilities at home, with husbands and other children to care for.'

'Perhaps a young mother with her first child,' she ventured. 'Her husband might be glad of the extra income this would bring in.'

An idea struck him. They would have to be very careful indeed, if nobody was to suspect anything, but it could work, indeed it could.

'I do know of one young woman,' he said slowly, 'who has a baby just three weeks older than Miss Meredith. Her husband was killed at Ypres, so she has no ties.'

'Shall I write to her, then, or go to see her?'

'No, no. You leave that to me, Nurse.'

Ellen stared at Harry in disbelief. 'You mean you want me to come to look after your daughter?'

'Not to look after her, exactly. The nanny will come soon. They'll do the everyday care. Meredith needs feeding, if you think you can manage it.'

'But I'd have to bring Mariah, too.'

'Of course you would, Ellen. What did you think I was suggesting?' He tried to keep the impatience out of his voice. Obviously she was overwhelmed by the idea. He also had to make it plain that she wasn't coming into the house as his mistress.

'People hereabouts already believe that you're a war widow, Ellen. We'll use the same story when you come to the house.'

'And what about Mariah, Harry? Whose daughter will they think she is?'

'Why, your husband's, of course.'

'There's no question of you acknowledging her as yours, then?'

'Come on, Ellen. You know I can't do that.'

'Oh, no, of course you mustn't.'

'Don't be like that, Ellen. I've done my best by you, where many a man would not. I've provided you both with a roof over your heads, and the means of making a living. What more do you want?'

A great deal more, she thought, staring down at her carpet slippers so he couldn't see the expression on her face. After a long while she looked up at him. 'And after? If I do come, what happens to us when your child doesn't need me any more?'

'You move back here, I suppose.'

'I need time to think this over, Harry. Can you come back tomorrow?'

'She needs you,' he pleaded. 'I don't want her to die, Ellen.'

'Come back tomorrow,' she repeated. 'I'll let you know then.'

'Wasn't that Mr Morgan I just saw?' Megan had come into the shop carrying two Welsh cakes wrapped in greaseproof paper. 'I've been baking, see. Thought you'd like something with your cup of tea.'

'*Diolch yn fawr*, Megan. Yes, that was him.'

'So what did he want? Not collecting his own rents these days, is he?'

'His baby isn't thriving and she needs a wet nurse. He wants me to move into the house and see to it. I can't make up my mind. I said I'd let him know tomorrow.'

'Why not do it, *bach*? There'd be a bit of money in it for you, and you wouldn't say no to a little nest egg for your Mariah, would you?'

'I'm not used to living in a place like that.'

'You'd get used to it in a hurry, I know I would! Think of it, waited on hand and foot, and eating off the fat of the land.'

'Just a bird in a gilded cage, Megan. What would I do up there all day long, with nobody to talk to?'

'Oh, I'll come calling, *bach*, never fear. Give me a chance to see how the other half lives, it will. You do it, Ellen. What do you have to lose?'

Little do you know how much I have to lose, Ellen thought. She already knew what her answer would be when Harry came back in the morning, but was it wise? She risked getting even more deeply involved if she was living under his roof and seeing him on a daily basis. She was dimly aware that she had reached a turning point in her life, but not being endowed with psychic abilities she had no way of knowing where her decision would lead her.

'Have you made up your mind, then?' Harry was on the doorstep before Ellen was dressed and she hastily pulled on her dressing gown before coming downstairs.

'Yes, I'll come.'

'Good, good! Then hurry up and get dressed and you can come with me now.'

'But all my things! I'm not leaving my rocking chair behind.'

'Never mind that. I'll send a man to collect it later.'

'But I can't leave yet. What about this place? Megan's been attending to the customers but she has a family to look after. She can't be in here all day.'

'I've made arrangements for that. Someone is moving in here this after-noon.'

'What!' Ellen was annoyed at being taken for granted like that.

'It's my wife's former maid. I had to dismiss her when Antonia died and she hasn't been able to find another post. You're coming to the house and Miss Powell will be coming here. Exchange is no robbery, as they say.'

On hearing that Harry had returned to Cwmbran, Daisy had trudged up to the house, asking to see him. Her mother had been very difficult, saying that no daughter of hers was going to lounge around the house all day like lady muck. This was unfair because Daisy had more than pulled her weight since moving back home, washing her brother's filthy pit clothes, for a start.

'I'm sorry to bother you, sir,' Daisy began, although why she should have to apologize was beyond her. She was as good as the next person. 'I haven't been able to find another job, sir. There's nothing in Cwmbran for a woman, see?'

'It's unfortunate that we aren't allowed to send women down the pit these days,' Harry joked, but Daisy took this at face value and glared at him.

'I have a suggestion to make,' he told her, thinking quickly. 'Do you know the little sweet shop on Jubilee Street?'

'Oh, yes, sir. I used to go there for Mrs Morgan's sweets.'

'How would you feel about serving there?'

Daisy brightened. 'I'd like that, but what about the woman who's there now?'

'Mrs Richards? She's moving, Miss Powell. As a matter of fact she's coming here, as wet nurse to my daughter. I need somebody to take over the shop for a few months.'

'Would I have to live in, sir?'

'You can please yourself, as long as you're there in time to open in the morning.'

'I'll live in, sir. *Diolch yn fawr!*'

This would be one in the eye for Mam, she thought, and the bargain was struck.

CHAPTER 28

SETTLING INTO THE house was easier than Ellen had feared. The other servants were curious but she answered their questions without hesitation. She didn't want to appear standoffish; the time might come when she would need their friendship.

'Adhere to the truth as much as possible,' Harry had advised, and this she did. When did your husband join the Army? What regiment was he in? Where was he killed? All these things were easy to respond to. She had Bertie's photo on display beside her bed and the others accepted the fact that this was her late husband.

'Quite a nice-looking young chap,' Ruth reported to the cook, who was all agog to know more about Ellen. 'No oil painting, mind, but pleasant, if you know what I mean. That baby has a look of him, no doubt about that.' And so she should, Ellen reminded herself, when this was repeated to her, Bertie being Mariah's uncle.

Ellen had been given two rooms, a bedroom and a small sitting room. Mariah remained with her all the time but Meredith stayed in the nursery except when she was brought to Ellen to be fed. Peering anxiously at her small foster child, Ellen hoped that the two little half-sisters did not resemble each other too much.

'She looks just like any other baby to me,' Harry told her, 'but if anything she takes after Antonia. See, she has a few wisps of brown hair, whereas Mariah is definitely going to be a redhead. Actually, neither one looks like me at all!'

By the time Ellen had been in residence for a month, baby Meredith had filled out a great deal and when the monthly nurse was leaving, she stated that she was well satisfied with the condition of her charge. 'I would never have said so to Mr Morgan,' she announced, 'but I had my doubts as to whether we'd manage to raise that one, she was that puny. It was a good thing you came along when you did, Mrs Richards.'

Sometimes Ellen put the babies down on the carpet, side by side, and she was charmed by the way they took notice of each other. They were too young to smile but they waved their arms about and gurgled in the most amusing manner.

'Do you know you're sisters?' she whispered. 'Daddy's girls, that's what you are, you pretty dears. Little loves!'

Harry was delighted with them, too, and he took to visiting them in the afternoons. The only person who wasn't pleased with this arrangement was Nanny Burton, a stuffy creature cast in the same mould as that midwife who had been foisted on them.

'Remember her, old Starchy Drawers?' Ruth fussed, when Nanny sent a curt message downstairs about the quality of her food.

'How could I forget?' Cook grumbled. 'Always sending down for trays of tea, she was, and this one's no better. She don't like semolina pudding, indeed, and that's the master's favourite. If it's good enough for him, it's certainly good enough for her, I said, but who listens to me? I'm only the cook here.'

Bossy as the nanny was, she soon learned she couldn't argue with her employer. Her first complaint was that her charge was allowed to play with the wet nurse's child, although lying beside another infant on a rug could hardly be termed playing.

'It's not seemly, sir, and I won't have it. Miss Meredith has to go in there to be fed, but she should be brought back to the nursery immediately afterwards.'

'I don't see what the problem is, Nanny.' Harry frowned. 'Are you afraid of germs? Mariah is a perfectly healthy child. Meredith isn't likely to catch any infection.'

'It's the principle of the thing, sir. In my last place, Mrs Osborne would never have permitted her boys to mingle with the servants' children! It is a very high-class establishment, as Mrs Meredith must have told you when she recommended me.'

Harry's eyes were cold as he waited for her to finish. 'Are you suggesting that my household is a less superior establishment than the Osbornes' home?'

'Not less superior, of course, I did not mean to imply that, but shall we say that order has yet to be established in the nurseries? I intend to establish a proper routine, Mr Morgan, and I'm sure you'll agree that this is absolutely necessary if Miss Meredith is to grow up into a proper young lady, as befits her background.'

Harry was glaring now. 'Of course you must have complete control in your nurseries, Nanny ...'

'Thank you, sir. I knew you'd see this my way.'

'Please allow me to finish. Miss Meredith will spend time with Mariah. I intend for the two of them to be brought up together. That is my final decision.'

But Nanny was determined to have the last word. 'You surely do not mean to place Mariah Richards in my nursery, Mr Morgan? I must protest ...'

Harry held up a hand for silence. 'That will do, Nanny. I will brook no argument. For the moment Mariah will stay with her mother, but I shall reassess the situation when she is a little older. Have I made myself clear?'

'Yes, Mr Morgan.' Nanny flounced off, to bully the little nursery maid, Polly.

'She's got it in for you, Miss, good and proper!' Polly muttered, the next time she brought Meredith in to be fed.

'It's true she doesn't seem to like me very much,' Ellen answered, as she smiled down at the baby. 'Still, we shan't let that bother us, shall we, Merry, love?'

'Oh, you mustn't call her that, Miss! Nanny don't allow it.'

'It's just a sign of affection, Polly, and while we're speaking of names, you must remember to call me Mrs Richards, all right?'

'Yes, Miss. Sorry, Miss. But Nanny wants Miss Meredith given her proper name, you see? Slapped my face she did, yesterday, cos I didn't give the baby her proper title.'

'I expect you'll get used to it soon, Polly. And as for me, I'm not answerable to Nanny Barton, so she can fuss all she likes and I shan't take a blind bit of notice.'

'Ooh, Miss, you are bold!' Polly beamed her admiration. 'There's that bell again. I s'pose Nanny wants something as usual.'

'You'd best be off, then, before you earn another slap!'

Ellen frowned. It was all very well for her to make a show of bravery in front of Polly, but talk was cheap. She was increasingly worried about the older woman's attitude, and she didn't know what to do about it. She hardly liked to carry tales to Harry, yet it was unpleasant living in such an atmosphere and she was afraid that the stress might cause her milk to dry up.

Eventually the situation boiled over, as Ellen had feared it would, and over such a silly little thing. Polly had just returned Meredith to the nursery after her morning visit to Mariah, when Nanny came bustling in without bothering to knock.

'I don't know what you think you're playing at, Mrs Richards, but I'll have you know that I'm in charge of Miss Meredith!'

'Of course, Nanny. Have I ever suggested otherwise?'

'Oh no, not in so many words, my fine lady, but you take good care to undermine my authority every chance you get. If I were Mr Morgan I'd send you packing at once, and so I shall suggest to him.'

'I hardly think he will agree to that. The child is thriving on my milk. She may not take kindly to another wet nurse.'

'Nor does she need one. I shall put her on the bottle until she's weaned.'

'She didn't get on with a bottle before, and that's why I was brought in.'

'Stuff and nonsense, Richards! She'll take it and like it in my nursery. That fool of a monthly nurse didn't know what she was doing, that's all I have to say.'

'What is it I'm supposed to have done, Nanny?'

'You sent that poor child back to the nursery with bare feet! Don't you know that draughts can kill a child? It's for me to decide how that child should be dressed, and if I say she should be kept bundled up, so be it!'

When the babies had lain on the rug, exercising their little legs, Meredith's bootees had come off. She'd forgotten to put them back on before handing the child to Polly.

'If that's all that's worrying you, here they are!' She reached down and retrieved the offending articles. If Vesuvius had erupted it could hardly have made more commotion than Nanny Barton made then. Spluttering with rage, she spat out a tirade which had Ellen taking a few steps back.

'What in the name of all that's holy is going on here? I could hear shouting all the way down in my study!' Harry had come up behind them, unheard. The two women spoke at the same time, causing him to blink.

'Richards is undermining my authority with Miss Meredith, sir!'

'Nanny is upset because the baby kicked her bootees off, Mr Morgan!'

'There's much more to it than that, and well you know it, Richards!'

'Yes, there is. You're a tyrant and a bully. I've seen Polly's poor face where you slapped her, and all for calling that baby by a pet name.'

'That will do!' Harry roared. 'I will not have this kind of dissension in my house! You can go to the nursery where you belong, Nanny, and as for you, Mrs Richards, I'll speak to you later!' He strode away, fuming.

Casting a triumphant look at her adversary, Nanny bustled away, leaving Ellen to comfort Mariah, who was shrieking with fright. Ellen found that she, too, was beginning to shake. It just wasn't fair! None of this was her fault and she wished that the awful woman would leave her alone.

CHAPTER 29

ELLEN HAD BEEN waiting in trepidation for Harry to speak to her. She was surprised when he came into her sitting room, carefully closing the door behind him.

'I've come to a decision,' he announced.

'Oh, yes?'

'I want my daughters to be brought up together, under my roof.' He held his head on one side, with a grin of pleasure on his face. Ellen was puzzled.

'But they are together, aren't they?'

'For the moment, yes, but that's not what I mean. I want Mariah to live in the nursery with Meredith. They'll be company for each other. Later on they'll share a governess. Eventually I may send them to finishing school, but all that is in the future. In the meantime I want to know what you think.'

'Did you not think of consulting me? I am Mariah's mother, you know!'

'But I'm consulting you now. You seem displeased. I thought you'd be delighted.'

'Then you thought wrong! I will not allow my child to go anywhere near that Nanny Barton! She's a tyrant.'

'With her nursery maid, perhaps; young servants must be trained up. But she wouldn't harm a baby!'

'Not physically, perhaps, but emotionally, yes, I'm sure she'd treat her like a poor relation, because I know what she thinks of me. And while Mariah is too young to know the difference now, she'd certainly be hurt as time goes by.'

'I think you're making too much of this, Ellen. Don't you see, this would be a wonderful opportunity for Mariah. What does she have to look forward to otherwise, as a fatherless child?'

'I'd manage somehow.'

'I'm sure you'd do your best, but look at it this way. You can make a new life for yourself, secure in the knowledge that your daughter will be well provided for.'

Ellen was horrified. She was to be sent away, and she would be separated from her beloved child. She certainly hadn't expected anything like this! She fought down the urge to scream and shout, but something told her to take a more cunning approach.

'And just how are you going to explain this to the rest of the staff? And what on earth will they think of me if I go away and abandon my child?'

It seemed that Harry had already considered that. 'Unless I remarry, Meredith will grow up as an only child. I don't approve of that. Many such youngsters are either selfish or timid. I shall tell people that I'm bringing another child into the nursery to be a companion to her, not that it's anyone's business to question my motives.'

Ellen's eyes flashed. 'Then you'll have to adopt a child from an orphanage, because I am certainly not going to leave Mariah here without me!' (And you can put that in your pipe and smoke it, Mr Harry Morgan!)

'I expect you'll feel differently when you've had time to think it over, Ellen. Take a few days to dwell on my proposition, and then we'll discuss this again.'

Ellen kicked the table leg as a way of relieving her frustration, and immediately wished she hadn't, for the pain in her foot was excruciating. Was she being selfish in denying Mariah her true heritage? And what if Harry, thwarted of his plan, refused to let them return to the sweet shop? She would be able to find other work, but there was the problem of finding someone to care for the baby. She had heard of the terrible baby farmers, women who took in children for a price, neglecting them while drugging them to keep them quiet. Children died mysteriously in such circumstances.

That evening she went down to the servants' hall, carrying Mariah, who lay babbling happily in her basket. She often went downstairs to join the others when they gathered to enjoy the hour or two between work and bed. On this occasion she was glad to find that the butler and footmen were not present, having gone out to some meeting at the chapel.

'Just a lot of men gossiping, I expect,' the cook muttered.

'It's their temperance meeting, Cook,' Ruth told her.

'Huh! Why do they need to get together on their own, then, no women allowed?'

'There's lots of women in the temperance movement, Cook.'

'I know that, girl, but what I'm saying is, why separate meetings? I'll tell you why,' she went on, 'it's because men are useless. Women gets things done while men sit around cackling like a bunch of old hens.'

'Geese cackle, Cook; hens cluck.'

'When I want your opinion, my girl, I'll ask for it! Now then, Baby

Mariah, how are you getting along? Let's take a look at you, then!' She lifted the infant up to her lap, clicking her tongue to make her smile.

'Growing like a bad weed, isn't she, Mrs Richards? But what's the matter with you? By the look on your face something's happened to set you off. That Nanny Barton been up to her tricks again, has she? We won't let that woman come near you, my little love, will we?' she told Mariah, who gurgled happily in response.

'Mr Morgan has offered to have Mariah brought up with Miss Meredith, but how can I leave her here, especially when it means leaving her in Nanny Barton's hands!'

'Oh, I say,' Ruth gushed. 'That's ever so kind of him! Them two little girls will have everything, dolls and pretty dresses, and ponies, even. You must say yes, Mrs Richards.'

'You don't know what you're talking about!' Cook snapped. 'How can you possibly know what's in a mother's heart? Of course Mrs Richards don't want to go off and leave her baby behind!' She turned to Ellen. 'Mind you, you'd better not make any quick decisions. It would be a marvellous opportunity for the child.'

'Unless it don't work out and the master sends her away,' Ruth sniffed.

'Oh, don't talk such rubbish! He wouldn't do that, would he? Of course, with a man, one never knows, Mrs Richards. You'd best make sure he adopts her, all legal and proper, like, and then she'll be safe.'

'It's not just that, Cook. Suppose she grows up, thinking herself a lady. What happens next? What will she do for the rest of her life?'

'I see what you mean. What's the point of giving her ideas above her station? She won't marry into the gentry and she won't suit an ordinary working chap. No man wants a wife who's better educated than himself. No, you'd better take her with you when you go, and send her to the board school like everybody else.'

Ellen put forth this view the next morning. 'It's true I haven't thought that far ahead,' Harry mused, 'but surely there's a happy medium? She might marry a clergyman, or a teacher, say, someone who'd be glad to have a well-educated wife. And if she doesn't marry, she'd be well fitted to become a companion or governess somewhere.'

'And a thankless task that would be!' she moaned.

'Now it's you who are not thinking clearly, Ellen. Thousands of young men are being killed every week. In the years to come there will be many women left single, and those people won't have families, so there will be fewer prospective mates for girls like Mariah and Meredith. It may be vital for them to be qualified to earn a living.'

Ellen thought resentfully that Miss Meredith Morgan would have to do no such thing. Married or not, she would be well provided for by Papa, and if she didn't marry, she'd have a home for life.

'Don't think I'm not grateful, but can't you see I don't want to give up my child? What will you say when she wants to know where her mother is?'

'I daresay Meredith will ask the same question.'

'And she'll get a good answer. Her mother is dead. I'm very much alive, Harry, and I don't want her thinking I just walked away and abandoned her!'

It was now that he played his trump card. 'Very well, Ellen! How would you feel about staying on here, as nanny to the two girls?'

'What? But you've got Nanny Barton!'

'I really think that Nanny Barton would be happier somewhere else. As she never ceases to inform me, she's been used to better things. I shall give her a month's notice, and after that you can take over the job. Well, what do you have to say?'

'I don't know – um – yes, I'll do it!'

'Good! Then we'll proceed on that assumption.'

Everyone was pleased with the arrangement with the exception of Nanny Barton.

'I hope that man knows what he's doing, letting a chit like you into my nursery,' she grumbled. 'Not that I mind going. This is not a well-regulated household at all!'

'I'm used to better things!' Polly mouthed, behind Nanny's back. The other female servants were just as pleased.

'I'm glad he's come to his senses,' Cook said, smiling. 'Imagine him wanting to keep your child and send you packing. I never heard of such a thing! Now you can look after Miss Meredith as well. I never did like the thought of that poor motherless mite being in that woman's power. No wonder the child is so pale and quiet!'

So Ellen was left feeling happier. Their immediate future was assured, and she could sleep at night without worrying what the next day might bring forth.

CHAPTER 30

ELLEN SOON SETTLED down into a routine with the children, assisted by young Polly. Their little kingdom was a suite of rooms, comprising a day and night nursery as well as bedrooms for the two women.

'I'm not very happy with this arrangement while the babies are so young,' Ellen told Harry. 'I'd like to move their cots into our bedrooms so we can hear them if they wake in the night. Mariah will come with me and Meredith can share with Polly.'

'That's entirely up to you, Ellen. You are in charge now; do as you think best.'

Ellen had been quite contented while she had only Mariah to think of, but with her new responsibilities came certain fears. Cook was one of those people who relished hearing about disasters which had happened to other people, and she took delight in retelling the stories to anyone who would listen.

'My cousin's daughter lost her baby when she was only three months old,' she told Ellen. 'She went to pick him up in the morning and there he was, lying stone cold dead in his little bed. She sent for the doctor, even though there was nothing could be done, and he asked her a lot of nasty questions, such as had she given the tot laudanum to make him sleep.' Laudanum was a tincture of opium, and some unscrupulous child minders dosed fractious children with the stuff.

'She's never forgiven herself for little Dewi dying, but it wasn't her fault,' Cook went on. 'Things like that just happen sometimes. The good Lord wants to call them to Himself, I suppose,' she finished piously.

Personally, Ellen couldn't see why God would allow a woman to go through nine months of discomfort and the agony of childbirth, only to snatch away the infant not long afterwards. She meant to do everything she could to ensure the survival of the little ones in her charge. She said as much to Cook.

'Oh, well, they should be healthy enough, living up there at the top of the house, Nanny Richards. It's different when children live all crowded together in the towns where they can catch scarlet fever or diphtheria and that! It's when they go to school that the trouble starts! One gets measles and they all catches it. Goes round like wildfire, then, it does. Them two upstairs won't be exposed to that.'

'No, they won't. Mr Morgan means to engage a governess in a few years' time.'

'Your Mariah's fallen on her feet, then. Along of Miss Meredith she'll be learning languages, I shouldn't wonder! Of course, the board school's not that bad. I went to one, so I should know. They taught us girls good plain sewing, for one thing. The pity of it was, my parents couldn't afford the penny a week to send me, so I only stayed there long enough to read, write and cipher. Still, I ended up here, didn't I, so I've nothing much to complain about.'

'It was the same at my school in Cardiff,' Ellen agreed. 'Learning to sew, I mean. Knitting, as well. My Nan taught me that when I was four years old, so when I went to school and they started us off on making dishcloths I got on well.'

Cook laughed. 'I don't suppose that governess will have them two upstairs making dishcloths! More like tackling fancy embroidery, I expect!'

The day nursery reminded Ellen of those she'd seen pictured in story books. There was the brass-topped fire guard in front of the fireplace, and, tucked away in a corner, the folding clothes horse used for airing the baby garments. Her own rocking chair took pride of place by the fire. There were two tables, one for meals and the other for changing the babies and giving them their daily baths. Ellen had to speak crossly to Polly for changing a dirty nappy on the wrong one.

'But what's the difference, Nanny? They're both tables, aren't they?'

Ellen pointed out just what the difference was, but the stupid girl couldn't take it in. For once Ellen felt a sneaking sympathy with the dear departed Nanny Barton.

There were toys galore. Ellen especially liked the big dapple-grey rocking horse, and the fine doll's house. How she would have loved those when she was young! The house even had miniature bathroom fittings, made of real porcelain, and there were little jugs and a teapot made of pewter. Those would have to be kept on a high shelf for now in case one of the babies put them in her mouth and choked.

It was a quiet house during the year Harry spent in mourning. He paid regular visits to the nursery and these precious minutes were the highlights of Ellen's day. She knew that her face lit up with joy when he came through the door, but if he noticed this he said nothing, confining his remarks to comments or questions about his daughters. Of course he couldn't say anything more personal with Polly standing nearby with her hands behind her back, like a good child facing a vicar during a scripture examination.

Harry had insisted on putting their relationship on a proper footing so Ellen received a regular wage. There being little to spend it on, she saved her money against the day when she might have to provide for herself again.

After the accepted mourning period was over, Harry began to entertain, giving dinner parties which delighted Cook.

'There's wonderful to be preparing company meals again, even if we do have this old rationing!' Cook said. 'And the master seems so much happier these days. He was that upset when the poor mistress died. Time heals, of course. How about you, Mrs Richards? Getting over your poor hubby, are you?'

'I don't think I'll ever get over Bertie's death,' Ellen said truthfully.

'Ah, but it's different for a woman, isn't it? Our poor hearts are easily broken and not so easily repaired.'

The war came to an end at last in November. Sometimes Ellen thought of her friend Mari, wondering if she was still back in Glamorganshire now there was no longer any need for making munitions. She might even be married by now. Occasionally she felt the impulse to write to her, but sadly decided it was best not to give in to her feelings.

She had kept her pregnancy a secret from Mari and now that she actually had Mariah with her it was even more important to avoid contact. If Mari knew where she was, what was to stop her coming here to seek her out?

She was known here as Mrs Richards, the widow of Bertie Richards from Cardiff, but Mari knew better and if she chose to, she could spill the beans! It wasn't just that Ellen's own reputation was at stake, she reminded herself. There was Mariah to consider as well. Ellen wanted the child to grow up believing she was the daughter of a fallen war hero, not as Harry Morgan's bastard child.

Ellen's delight knew no bounds when Mariah took her first steps. After moving around the nursery, clinging to the furniture, she managed to stagger a few paces before sitting down suddenly. The heavy towelling napkin prevented her from suffering any hurt, but the shock made her roar her displeasure, which in turn caused Ellen and Polly to chuckle.

Meredith crawled rapidly towards her sister, but she made no effort to copy her performance. In fact, she hadn't yet mastered the knack of pulling herself to her feet and moving from one chair to the other. This worried

Ellen a little, although she knew that all children developed differently. It was just that she tended to think of the girls as twins; they were half-sisters and had been born within three weeks of each other. Of course, they had different mothers, which might account for their different behaviour.

'Look at her, Nanny! She's doing it!' Ellen had gone down to Cwmbran on a rare day off, wanting to change her library books. Polly had been left to look after the babies in her absence and Meredith had found her feet and was staggering about like a drunken sailor.

'Wouldn't you know it!' Ellen mourned. 'I turn my back for a minute and just see! I did want to be here to see it when it finally happened.'

There were many such pleasant incidents in the Morgan nursery, and as the months went by Ellen became complacent, feeling that she had her feet firmly under the table, as Nan would have said. She felt an occasional pang when Harry had friends in, however, in case he was entertaining some lady who might aspire to becoming the second Mrs Morgan.

One summer day she and Polly were walking through the grounds with the babies in their wicker perambulators, when they saw Harry and just such a lady walking towards them.

'And are these your little girls? The pretty dears!' the visitor asked, bending over to coo at each baby in turn, and Ellen felt relieved to know that whoever she was, the lady was not yet in Harry's complete confidence. Nor did he trouble to explain that only one of the infants was his daughter.

Polly stared after them as they walked away. 'She looks nice, don't she? I wonder if they'll be getting wed? The master could do with a wife, in my opinion.'

'Who asked you?' Ellen snapped, so that Polly lapsed into a sullen silence for the rest of the outing. Ellen marched on, all pleasure in the lovely day wiped out. 'I'm just like that Jane Eyre in the book,' she told herself. 'She had to act like a mousy little governess when that snooty woman came to stay and treated her like an underling.'

Not that this visitor had behaved unkindly; indeed, she'd been perfectly nice. Nevertheless, she could be a threat, Ellen decided.

Part Two

CHAPTER 31

1938

ELLEN LOOKED APPROVINGLY at her two girls, who were twirling around to display their new frocks. Meredith and Mariah were almost twenty now, young women, but she still thought of them as girls. After all, she felt like a youngster herself, although she could hardly believe she was past forty!

They were out of the school room now, and the governess had long since left. Harry had wanted to send his daughter to Switzerland to be 'finished' but she had steadfastly refused to go, even when he offered to pay for Mariah to accompany her. Of the two, Meredith was the shy one; Mariah had far more self-confidence.

They were different in appearance as well. Meredith's complexion was pale and her mousy hair was straight. Mariah had glorious auburn curls and when she talked her green eyes twinkled and her expression was animated, causing those around her to smile in appreciation. She was a kind girl, her mother thought, and she didn't mean to upstage her half-sister, but it just happened.

Ellen had done everything she could to bring Meredith out of her shell. A qualified instructor had been brought in once a week to teach the girls to dance. Birthday parties and tennis parties had been given when suitable young people had been imported and in turn she had been asked out to their events, although as often as not Mariah was left out. This grieved Ellen but Mariah took these snubs in her stride.

'It's all right, Mam, I don't mind. They ask Meredith because she's Mr Morgan's daughter. I don't belong to their world, not really.'

This saddened Ellen but there was nothing she could say to this.

'Anyway,' Mariah went on cheerfully, 'I won't be staying here for ever. I want to go and train as a children's nurse. Not one like Polly; a real hospital nurse. I should have gone sooner, but Meredith begged me to stay.'

'I doubt very much if Meredith will stay at home for ever, either. I know that Mr Morgan hopes she'll make a good marriage before she's very much older. Then she'll go to live wherever her husband chooses to make a home for her.'

'Yes, Mam, but she says that if she marries a wealthy man she wants me to live with them too, as her companion, you see.'

Ellen was taken aback. A paid companion, at the beck and call of her half-sister for the rest of her days? Once upon a time it had been the custom for young married women to take a sister to live with them, but surely not nowadays!

'Oh, no, Mariah, I don't think you want to do that, dear! Newly-weds need time alone to get to know each other. Going in for nursing sounds like a wonderful idea.'

'I'm glad you think so. I mean to write to some hospitals in Cardiff and see what they have to say. I'd love to live in that area, where you and Dad came from.'

Ellen fought down the panic which threatened to overwhelm her. 'Oh, I think you should go to London to do your training, don't you? You'll see a bit of life there, and I'm not so sure that Cardiff has a hospital just for children.'

She caught herself just in time. She had been about to say that her brother had gone into hospital when he was small, and he'd been placed on a men's ward because there wasn't one especially for children.

'I might fancy London,' Mariah mused, 'but how do I find out about hospitals there? I shan't know where to start.'

'I should make enquiries at the library. Perhaps they have directories or something. Or Mr Morgan may know. He has contacts in London. In fact, he may be able to give you a recommendation. I'm sure that hospitals want references, just like any other job.'

But before anything could be done about this, Harry Morgan made a decision which was to alter all their lives. He had grown used to having Ellen as his confidante, and so she was the first person to whom he voiced his plan.

'I don't know if you've ever considered what will become of this place when I'm gone?' he began.

'No, not really.'

'I'm getting on a bit, *cariad*, and I have to think ahead.'

Ellen demurred politely but he only shook his head.

'I'm well past sixty, and I can't live for ever. I shan't have a son now. This property is entailed, which means it will go to Chad Fletcher after my death.'

Ellen frowned. 'Do I know him?'

'No. He's a distant cousin of mine. I've invited him to pay us a visit. I want him to get a feel for this place, find out what he'll be responsible for when he inherits.'

'I see.'

'I don't think you do. Chad is much younger than I am; just twelve years older than Meredith, in fact. What I'm really hoping is that they'll take a liking to each other and decide to marry.'

'An arranged marriage! That's a bit Victorian, isn't it?'

Harry reacted with annoyance. 'I'm not going to arrange anything, as you put it. But if nature happens to take its course and they fall in love, it will be all to the good. Have you thought what will happen to Meredith otherwise? This is her home. Let's say that Chad brings a wife here and she and Meredith don't see eye to eye. Then what?'

'I assume you've left her well provided for, Harry. She's not a child any more. If she doesn't marry, she can take a house somewhere and live quite contentedly with a cook and a maid or two. Meanwhile, she may be quite upset when this Chad arrives. Nobody likes to think of a parent dying, and that's what this is all about, isn't it?'

'I'm only being prepared,' he said testily. 'I may live to be ninety, and I hope I do! By that time the girl could be married and a grandmother! Meanwhile, I've written to Chad, and I expect to hear from him any day now. I want you to break the news to her, Ellen. Soften the blow, if you like.'

'All right, Harry,' she sighed, 'but I don't see why you can't do it yourself. You don't need to mention all the ins and outs as you've explained them to me. Just say that you're expecting a visit from a cousin, and you want her to help entertain him. What could be simpler than that?'

'I'd still like you to do this for me, Ellen,' he insisted, and she was forced to agree.

'Why haven't we heard of this Chad person before?' Meredith asked, when Ellen broached the subject.

'Because he lives miles away in England, I suppose. On top of that, he's hardly your father's generation so I don't suppose they have a great deal in common.'

'How old is he, then?'

'In his middle thirties, I believe.'

'A doddering old man, then,' Mariah laughed. 'Is he bringing his wife with him?'

'I understand that he's a bachelor.'

'But how can we entertain him?' Meredith worried. 'I mean, what do men like to talk about? I don't know anything about business, or motor cars, and I don't suppose he reads the sort of books that we do.'

'You can show him the estate. I expect he rides, or there are many pleasant walks in the neighbourhood, as of course you know.'

'He won't care about that when he sees us!' Mariah giggled. 'He'll be so overcome by our beauty that he'll be struck dumb and we won't have to say anything!'

'You'll mind your manners, miss!' Ellen could see exactly which way the wind was blowing. Mariah wasn't a flirt but she did have a bubbly personality, whereas Meredith tended to become withdrawn when faced with a difficult situation. Ellen resolved to have a quiet word with her daughter when they were alone together.

'I shouldn't really be telling you this, Mariah, so this is in absolute confidence. Do you understand me?'

'Of course, Mam. What is it?'

'Very well, then. Mr Morgan is bringing his cousin here to view the property because when he dies – Mr Morgan, I mean – this Mr Fletcher will inherit everything.'

Mariah opened her eyes wide. 'But surely this place comes to Meredith?'

'No, it doesn't. It has to go to a male member of the family.'

'Good grief! Does she know about this?'

'I'm not sure. The thing is, Mr Morgan has the idea that his cousin may decide to marry Meredith and the pair of them can stay on here after her father dies.'

'What rubbish! Meredith may be a bit shy, but she's not stupid. She won't let herself be pushed into marriage and if her father believes that, he's in for a disappointment!'

'I know, love, but all I'm asking is that you give this a chance. Try to stay in the background as much as possible, and don't always be butting in on their conversation.'

'In other words, remember that I'm the daughter of the old nanny, not the daughter of the house!'

'Mariah!'

'Oh, don't worry, Mam; I know my place. I can't deny that sometimes I've envied her for being born with a silver spoon in her mouth, but I know I'm lucky to have been brought up with all the same advantages. But it's time for me to make my own way in the world now, and that's why I want to go in for nursing. I won't spoil things for her.'

CHAPTER 32

'I WANT TO KEEP Meredith here with us for a few weeks, Harry.' Henrietta Meredith was arranging flowers in a crystal vase as she spoke.

'Perhaps later in the year, Mother-in-law. It isn't convenient just at present.'

'Then you must make it convenient, Harry! Paul and I have discussed the matter and we are agreed that the girl needs to spend time away from Mariah.'

'What on earth for?'

'You can't tell me you haven't noticed how much she's in that young woman's shadow! Mariah may be a perfectly nice girl, but she's not our class. Where you made your mistake was in allowing her mother to remain as housekeeper after Meredith had outgrown the need for a nanny. If you wanted a chaperone it would have been better to retain the governess. She, at least, was an educated person.'

'My domestic arrangements are my own business.' Harry spoke stiffly.

'Naturally, but if Mrs Richards had left, her daughter would have gone with her, and Meredith would have come into her own. And she should have been sent to the continent, where she could have acquired a little polish. Of course, it's too late for that now, but we may be able to do something here. I propose to introduce her to our friends so she can meet some suitable young men. You mustn't leave it too long if she's to find a suitable husband. You may depend on me to steer her in the right direction.'

'That won't be necessary, Mother-in-law. I have plans for Meredith myself.'

'Oh? And what might those be?'

Harry cleared his throat. He had always been slightly nervous when having to deal with Antonia's mother.

'As you know, I have no sons, nor will I have now.'

'I'm sorry about that, but Antonia's father and I have always been grateful that you've remained faithful to her memory.'

Harry closed his eyes. Such sentimental twaddle! 'Yes, well, the estate is entailed. In due course it will go to a distant cousin of mine, Chad Fletcher.'

'You may have mentioned that in the past,' Henrietta murmured.

'I feel it's important that Chad should become familiar with the estate and my various businesses while I'm still here to explain how things are done. Therefore I've invited him to visit us, starting next week. He's not married, and it would please me greatly if he and Meredith were to make a match of it.'

'Surely you're not serious, Harry? This is positively feudal! You can't force the child into marriage with a man she's never met!'

He gritted his teeth. What was the matter with these women? First Ellen and now Henrietta. What was wrong with wanting to see his daughter happily settled in life?

'Nobody is forcing the girl to do anything, but if they do take a liking to each other I shall be very pleased.'

Henrietta backtracked slightly. 'All the more reason for her to meet some other young men first. This Chad may be quite suitable but she really must get to know others to give her a standard to compare him against. She hasn't had the chance to mingle with many people of her own age. Young women these days go out to business, or train for the professions, but you've kept her cooped up in your house like a princess in an ivory tower!'

Harry Morgan knew quite well why he had sheltered his daughter from the world. Every time he looked at Ellen and Mariah he was reminded of what can happen to an innocent young girl if she gets swept away on a tide of passion. Or even if she meets some unscrupulous man. That was not about to happen to his motherless daughter. It was up to him to shield her, to save her from shame and disgrace. She would get to know Chad under his careful supervision, and she would be safe, which was more than he could count on if she stayed with her ageing grandparents.

'It's good of you to offer,' he said now, 'but my mind is made up. I was pleased to bring Meredith here to attend your niece's wedding, but we leave the day after tomorrow, as planned.'

Henrietta knew she was beaten, and in some ways she was glad. She was no longer young, and somehow her energy had seeped away during recent years. The offer had been made in all sincerity, and she would gladly have carried out the tasks required, for dear Antonia's sake, yet it was a relief to have been turned down. A tear came to her eye as she thought of her poor daughter, who had not lived to see her child grow into a beautiful young woman. 'I expect you know best, Harry,' she murmured.

Mariah had been out riding. She had been all over the estate and now was more than ready for her lunch. As she neared the house she slowed her mare to a trot, heading for the stable yard. She was puzzled to see a smart roadster parked outside the front steps. Surely the Morgans hadn't returned early? That wasn't Harry's car, unless he had exchanged the Lanchester for this red vehicle.

She brought Black Bess to a halt beside the car, looking at it for some clue as to who the owner was. She hoped it wasn't some ancient business partner of Harry's, whom she would have to entertain in his absence.

Before she could move on again, the front door opened and a young man bounded down the steps. Youngish, she decided, as he came closer. In his thirties, at least. He was dressed in country clothes; awful, tweedy plus fours and a silk cravat. He was quite tall – lanky, almost – and he had sandy hair, a trifle too long.

'Hello, I'm Chad Fletcher,' he announced, holding up his hand. 'How do you do?'

'How do you do. I'm sorry, we weren't expecting you until next week.' Mariah realized that sounded ungracious, so she smiled warmly. 'Of course, you're most welcome now.'

'Thank you. Margaret, is it?'

'Mariah.'

'Ah, yes. Perhaps I should not have turned up unannounced but I happened to be in Llanelly, visiting an old college chum, so it seemed silly to go all the way back to Wiltshire only to turn around and come back next week.'

'Yes, I see. It's unfortunate that Mr Morgan is away from home, but it can't be helped. Well, Mr Fletcher, please excuse me while I take Bess to the stable. She'll get chilled if she's kept standing about.'

'Chad, please.'

'Chad, then. I'll see you at the house in a little while. Where have they put you, by the way?'

'The morning room. I'll look forward to it.'

Having seen her horse taken away by the groom, Mariah slipped into the house through the kitchen and raced up the back stairs. She found Ellen in the linen room, getting out clean sheets for the guest room and looking annoyed.

'Why on earth did the wretched man have to come now, without letting anybody know? His room isn't ready. I was going to get Sally to give it a good turn-out later but we'll have to drop everything and see to it now.'

'I suppose we'll have to put up with him now he's here.'

'We certainly will, and you mind your manners, my girl!' She turned back to the shelf, hesitating over the choice of sheets. Plain linen or the monogrammed ones?

Mariah changed out of her habit, selecting a pretty cotton frock in eau de nil green which went well with her copper-coloured hair. While she had no particular interest in Chad Fletcher, she did intend to look her best, and she took the time to brush her hair until it shone. If he had to cool his heels waiting for her, serve him right for having turned up without warning.

His face, when she finally drifted into the morning room, told her that he found her appearance worth the wait. 'What a lovely house. I suppose you're quite fond of it?'

'Yes, I am, rather. I shall miss it when I go.'

'Go? Go where?'

'Oh, I'm thinking of applying to train as a children's nurse.'

'Surely not. A lovely girl like you? You'll get married, of course. In fact, I'm surprised that hasn't happened already!'

Mariah smiled, accepting the compliment as her due.

'Are you married, Chad?'

'Heavens, no! Didn't cousin Harry say? Seriously, though,' he went on, 'do you really think there's any point in this nursing thing? You'll get married and have to give it all up. All that training wasted. Married women aren't allowed to nurse.'

'Do you ride?' she asked, casting about for a safe topic of conversation. 'If you'd like to, we can go out this afternoon and I'll show you some of the estate.'

'I do ride, of course, but why don't we take my car? I haven't had her long and I'm rather taken with her.'

Mariah was relieved when the gong sounded. She hadn't had much practice at light-hearted conversations with the opposite sex, and she was afraid of appearing gauche.

'Shall we go in? I'm so hungry after my ride I could eat my hat!'

'Allow me,' he said, taking her by the elbow, steering her towards the dining room as if he was the host and she the guest. Keeping her face impassive, Mariah tried to hide the discomfort she felt at his touch.

CHAPTER 33

Ellen wondered how Mariah was coping downstairs. She herself had never eaten a meal in the dining room. When she had been a nanny she had eaten in the nursery, and when she had taken on the role of housekeeper, her meals had been served in her own suite of rooms, brought up on the dumb waiter. Once Meredith was out of the schoolroom she'd graduated to eating downstairs with her father, and Mariah had been allowed to accompany her. Often, though, when Harry was away on business, the two girls had joined Ellen upstairs for a relaxed meal.

She sighed. Once Meredith had been weaned she should have found the strength to go back to her former life, taking Mariah with her, but she had lacked confidence and had been only too glad to lean on Harry. She asked herself now if she had made a terrible mistake. Her daughter was well educated, but what was the use of being brought up like a lady? How would a knowledge of French and music help her in the life she would have as a nursery nurse? It could only lead to the girl feeling dissatisfied.

Just think of Mariah having to entertain the gentleman who would inherit the hall in due course! At least she knew which fork to use, and didn't eat peas with her knife. Ellen smiled, imagining what Nan would have said about that! 'If there's one thing I did for you and Bertie it was teach you proper table manners. There were no bad habits in my house and don't you forget it!'

Downstairs, Mariah was holding her own very well. When asked if she had seen any of the latest London shows she simply smiled and remarked that she wasn't keen on that sort of thing. She much preferred the country, where she could ride to her heart's content. Had he been to the theatre lately?

The plot of the latest play took them safely through the soup course, and then Mariah asked if he'd travelled much. Again, he went into a long account of his experiences. He was easy enough to entertain as long as he could talk about himself, so she nodded and smiled and murmured inconsequential things in all the right places. By the time they rose from the table, Chad had decided that she was a delightful young lady, and the young lady herself had him pegged as a stuffed shirt.

That afternoon they flew round the countryside in his car, and if Chad paid more attention to Mariah than he did to the farms he was supposed to be looking at, he felt he was none the worse for that. Cousin Harry would no doubt explain everything about his estates in boring detail when he returned from wherever it was he had gone.

'He's been attending a family wedding, and staying with the Merediths in Gloucestershire,' Mariah informed him.

Chad frowned. 'And you didn't want to accompany him?'

'No, why should I? I'm much happier here.'

'Ah, riding your horse, of course,' he responded, feeling that he must have missed something. Perhaps she didn't get on with her grandparents. He vaguely recalled his mother mentioning something about Mrs Meredith being a managing sort of woman. Verona Fletcher had been present at cousin Harry's wedding, and had met the bride's mother then.

His mind flew ahead to the day when he would introduce Mariah to his mother. It was early days yet, of course, but when that day came his mother would approve.

'These old estates take a lot of keeping up,' she'd told him before he left Wiltshire. 'There'll be death duties when Harry goes, and I can only hope that doesn't wipe out everything. Of course, he has the colliery, and all those railway shares, or whatever they call them, so he's far from being a pauper.'

'What are you saying, Mother?'

'I'm saying that he's sure to leave that girl of his well fixed. Whoever marries her will be well off financially, that's all.'

He didn't need his mother to spell it out to him. He'd have to get a look at the girl first, of course, but unless she turned out to be positively ugly he'd throw his hat in the ring. He'd had numerous affairs but he'd never been in love and never expected to be. The French had the right idea, viewing marriage as a business arrangement. Living on a shoestring wasn't his idea of happiness.

'What the devil is the boy doing, turning up here before he's expected?' Harry grumbled. 'Couldn't you have got rid of him, Ellen, told him to come back later?'

'I could hardly do that, Harry! I'm just the housekeeper here, remember? You'd have been livid.'

'I suppose so. Where is the chap now?'

'Gone riding with Mariah, I believe. She's done her best to keep him entertained.'

He grunted. 'I'll be in my study for the next hour or so. I'll leave orders for Fletcher to see me if they return before I go out again.'

Meredith was left with Ellen in the meantime. 'What's he like, Nanny, this Chad?'

'Quite good-looking, I believe, and fairly personable.' Ellen didn't want to get into this; it was better for Meredith to form her own impressions. 'How was the wedding? Did you meet any nice young gentlemen?'

'I suppose so. Grandmama wanted me to stay on and get to know them all, but Father put his foot down as usual. Not that I cared, really.'

The clatter of hooves in the drive made her run to the window. 'There they are now. I can't tell what he looks like from here. I think I'll run down and greet them.'

'Yes, dear, you do that, only don't run outside; it's not ladylike. As I've always told you, it doesn't do to throw yourself at a man. Go and knock on the study door instead. Your father will want to introduce you to Mr Fletcher, I know.'

Harry was standing in the open door of his study when Chad and Mariah came in. At the same time, Meredith was halfway down the stairs.

'Good to see you, Chad.' Harry held out his hand as Meredith hurried to join them. 'This is my daughter, Meredith.'

Puzzled, Chad glanced at her, and then back at Mariah, who was standing awkwardly in the background. 'But Mariah – I thought ...' His voice trailed off.

'You thought Mariah was me!' Meredith laughed unpleasantly. 'Oh, no, she's only the housekeeper's daughter!'

'Meredith!'

'What's the matter, Father? I'm only speaking the truth, aren't I?'

'I must apologize, Miss Morgan,' Chad said crossly. 'I was led to believe ...'

'You were led to believe what, Mr Fletcher?' Mariah's tone was cool as she stared him down. Not for a million pounds would she let him see how humiliated she was. 'I most certainly said nothing that was calculated to give you the wrong impression about my place in this house! Now, if you'll excuse me, I have things to do upstairs.'

She managed to hold back the tears until she reached her mother's domain, where she broke down into wrenching sobs.

'What on earth is the matter with you, Mariah? Did Bess throw you?'

'Chad Fletcher thought I was the daughter of the house,' she gulped.

'How did he get that impression, I wonder?'

'By jumping to a conclusion, Mam! I didn't say anything to give him that idea.'

'I'm sure you didn't, love. Never mind; it's nothing to get all worked up about.'

'It's not that, Mam. It was Meredith. She was so condescending! "Oh, she's only the housekeeper's daughter, how could you possibly mistake her for me?"'

'Surely she didn't put it quite like that?'

'She wasn't far off it.'

'But she didn't say anything that isn't true,' Ellen said sadly. 'You are the housekeeper's daughter, aren't you, love?'

Chad had gone up to his room to fetch a notebook, having been told by Harry that they might as well start at once to discuss the things he had to learn about the business. Harry turned to his daughter, fury written all over his handsome face.

'That was a very ill-bred remark, my girl. What on earth were you thinking of, to speak about Mariah in such a way? Can't you see how upset she was? And Chad was taken aback as well. I doubt you made a very good first impression.'

Meredith pouted prettily. She'd always been able to wrap her father round her little finger, and she had no doubt that she could wriggle out of this little difficulty now.

'But Father! I didn't say anything untrue, did I? She is the housekeeper's daughter!'

He had never longed to acknowledge Mariah as his daughter more than at this moment, but he knew he could not. He and Ellen hadn't kept their secret for all these years to have it spilled out now, in a moment of irritation. Meredith had led a sheltered life. She would never understand why her father had betrayed her mother in such a way. The knowledge would cause so wide a rift between them that their relationship could never be the same again.

Unnerved by the long silence, Meredith tossed her pretty head. 'She should have made it plain to him who she is.'

'It was merely a misunderstanding. I suppose he jumped to a conclusion. I don't think for a moment that Mariah meant to mislead him.'

'She should have known. I think she did this on purpose, but it won't do her any good. You've brought Chad here for me, haven't you, Father?'

'Meredith!' Harry was completely taken aback by this assumption. 'He has been invited here as my heir, to learn something about the estate while I'm still here to explain everything. I thought you'd understood that.'

They were so deep in discussion that they failed to notice Chad hovering outside the door. A small, satisfied smile crossed his face as he summed up the situation.

CHAPTER 34

THERE WAS NO avoiding the fact that Mariah had to face Chad, sooner rather than later.

'I know it's awkward,' Ellen told her, 'but what else can you do? You can't hide up here for ever. And you haven't done anything wrong, despite what Meredith says. It's hardly your fault if Chad jumped to conclusions.'

'It just didn't occur to me to explain who I was,' Mariah moaned. 'I did introduce myself but should I have said "I'm the housekeeper's daughter, only here on sufferance"?'

'Don't be silly, dear.'

'Somebody had to entertain the man. I couldn't just let him cool his heels for two days until Mr Morgan came back.'

'Now you listen to me, my girl! If you never meet anything worse in life, you'll do well! If anyone should apologize it's Meredith. She had no call to be unkind, as I'm sure her father will have told her. I can't imagine what came over her, unless she was disappointed at not being allowed to stay on in Gloucestershire. Even so, that's no excuse for unladylike behaviour. Now you go down and behave as if nothing has happened.' She patted her daughter on the shoulder, and Mariah took the hint.

She went out to saddle up Black Bess, thinking that a gallop in the fresh air would blow away the cobwebs. She was just tightening the girth when Chad appeared in the entrance to the loose box, blocking Mariah's retreat.

'I say, Mariah, I'm sorry if I landed you in trouble with cousin Harry. Friends?'

'It doesn't matter.' Mariah buried her face in the horse's mane, pretending not to notice his outstretched hand. 'Will you stand aside, please? When she's tacked up and knows she's going out Bess doesn't like to be kept standing.'

'Don't be like that, Mariah. We can still see each other, can't we? Look, just hang on a minute and I'll come with you.'

'I don't feel like company, thank you!'

'What's the matter? Queen Victoria's dead, you know.'

'What do you mean?'

'Well, I'm my own man. Cousin Harry can't very well tell me I can't go out with one of the servants. All that sort of thing went by the board after the war.'

Mariah gasped. 'Are you telling me I'm one of the servants, then?'

Chad had the grace to look uncomfortable. 'Well, you are a sort of companion to Meredith, aren't you?'

Without bothering to answer, Mariah turned the horse's head and the animal lunged forward. Chad was forced to move aside to avoid being stepped on. Once in the yard, Mariah put her foot in the stirrup and swung into the saddle, urging Bess forward. Open mouthed, Chad watched her go.

Mariah was absolutely furious. A servant, indeed! As for being a companion to Meredith, she hadn't seen it in that light before. That was a paid employee, someone who fetched and carried and took orders! It was true she'd been given her place in this house, and the education and other advantages that went with it, to be company for Meredith, but that wasn't the same thing, was it? She felt belittled somehow.

She patted Black Bess, who responded with a whinny. The mare had been bought for her, or so she'd thought, but was it possible that she didn't own the animal at all? Perhaps it was just one of the perks of the job, like having food and a roof over your head when you were in service!

She made up her mind to begin her hospital training as soon as possible. She would send off her applications that very day. She'd always known that she'd have to leave home sometime. Home! The word didn't seem to have the same meaning as before.

When she eventually went back, she found the place in a turmoil.

'It's your poor Mam,' Polly gasped, her eyes bright with the excitement of passing on bad news. 'Fallen on the wet floor she has, and done something to her ankle. Cook put a wet cloth on it but it's swollen up so bad she can't get her shoe back on. She must have broken it, see?'

'Has the doctor been sent for?'

'Mr Morgan has gone in the car,' the little maid said proudly. 'There's good he is, to do that for one of the servants.'

There was that word again! Mariah gritted her teeth and ran upstairs to Ellen. She found her mother sitting with the injured limb up on a footstool.

'Just see what I've done!' Ellen groaned. 'Oh, I do hope I haven't broken it!'

But when Dr Lawson arrived, he grunted, and confirmed that she had indeed fractured the injured part, and would have to go to hospital to have it put in plaster.

'This job will take several weeks, I'm afraid.'

'I can't go!' Ellen whispered. 'There's so much to do here, I can't be spared!'

'Nonsense!' Harry told her. 'It's a poor lookout if we can't manage with a houseful of servants. Now you swallow that tablet James has just handed you, and don't worry about a thing. I'll telephone for an ambulance, and Mariah shall go with you.'

'I can't go into hospital!' Ellen hissed, when she was left alone with her daughter. 'Once I'm out of the house and they find they can manage without me, that'll be the end. I'll be dismissed, you mark my words!'

'Oh, Mam! There's silly you are! Mr Morgan would never send you away, not after all these years!'

'Don't you be too sure, my girl. Now listen. Once they've got me in that hospital I'll be done for. I know I'll have to go there now, to get the cast on, but after that I'm coming straight back here and there's nobody going to talk me out of it!'

'But Mr Morgan ...'

'I shall tell him I don't want to go to the expense of a long hospital stay, nor do I want to be beholden if he offers to pay. I don't want charity.'

'I don't know about that, Mam. How will you manage?'

'You can look after me, girl. I'm not ill. I just won't be able to get about very much. I can do my job just as well from this chair, if you'll do some of the leg work.'

It wasn't a request; it was an order. Mentally shrugging her shoulders, Mariah decided to put her plans on hold. It wasn't much for a mother to ask of her daughter, was it? In any case, she wouldn't have to sit facing Chad and Meredith in the dining room; she'd have her meals up here with Mam. Meredith would be delighted to have Chad all to herself, no doubt.

'Of course I'll help,' she murmured. 'How will you get yourself downstairs?'

'They could always send me down in the dumb waiter,' Ellen said bravely, trying to make light of the situation.

'There'll be no need for that!' Harry, coming back into the room, had heard this. 'The footmen will carry you downstairs.'

'I couldn't let them do that! They'll rupture themselves!'

'Nonsense! Two strapping young men like that, and you as light as a feather? You'll do as you're told, and we'll soon have you tucked up in hospital, snug as you please.'

'I'm not staying there. I'm coming straight back here as soon as they've put the cast on. I shan't sleep unless I'm in my own bed.'

'It'll be all right,' Mariah hastened to add, seeing that Harry was about to argue the toss. 'Mam's not ill. I can look after her, and run errands about the house.'

'Well, if you're sure …'

'This would happen now, just when there's company in the house,' Ellen moaned, wincing as the ambulance negotiated a pothole in the road. 'What Chad Fletcher will think of us I don't know.'

'Don't worry about him!' Mariah sniffed. 'He'll never know the difference as long as his bed is made and his food is on the table. He's so condescending, Mam. He treated me like a human being as long as he thought I was the daughter of the house but now he sees me as a sort of servant.'

'You're not, of course, love, but what if you were? There's no disgrace in being in service. It's a job like any other.'

'But I'm the same person now as I was when he met me. Why can't he see that?'

'Perhaps he does, Mariah, or perhaps he doesn't. The plain fact is that we do have class distinctions in this country, and ignoring that can only lead to trouble. Things have changed to some extent since my young day, when people thought of the gentry as our betters, but there's still a big gulf between the classes and it's wise to remember that.'

'Our betters! There's an expression! How are people with land and money better than those who have to work for a living, Mam? Is Mr Morgan any better than his miners, or the people who rent the farms on the estate?'

'Don't you go getting all Bolshie, my girl. As for being better, quite often young gentlemen, so-called, think they can take advantage of girls of a different class. It's quite wrong, but it happens all the time, and society always blames the victims. Young men are just sowing their wild oats; girls are no better than they should be. That's what you have to remember, Mariah.'

Mariah failed to see the point of this little homily. If Chad Fletcher had any ideas concerning her, she'd soon send him off with a flea in his ear. She wouldn't touch him with a ten-foot pole!

CHAPTER 35

'YOU'LL REGRET THIS, Mariah!' Chad Fletcher scowled, holding a hand to his smarting face, where she had delivered a resounding slap.

'You're the one who'll regret it if I tell Meredith about this!' she retorted, holding her foot poised in case he tried to handle her again. Black Bess was not the only one who could deliver a painful kick when she was annoyed.

'As if she'll believe you!' he sneered. 'She'll think you're making up a tale out of jealousy, especially when I tell her what really happened here. You made a pass at me, which of course I turned down, being committed to Meredith. That's when you hit me.'

'Of all the rotten lies! You gave me the shock of my life when you jumped out at me like that, and as for what you did, no gentleman grabs at a lady in that way, never mind forcing his tongue down her throat! I've a good mind to go straight to Mr Morgan and let him know what you're really like!' She pushed him away from her and hurried down the stairs, fuming.

Chad had been away in Wiltshire, putting his affairs in order, as he put it. Harry had suggested that he move into the hall permanently, in training, as it were, to take over the estate. Chad had been quick to agree. It was certainly in his best interest to make Meredith fall in love with him when she was an heiress in her own right. Meanwhile, a little dalliance with the delectable Mariah would not go amiss.

Ellen's ankle healed well, and by the time Christmas arrived she was able to be up and about, supervising the decoration of the house and encouraging Cook to get on with the Christmas baking. Mariah was happy to hear that Chad would not be returning for the festival. Meredith had had a letter, explaining this.

'He says he wants to spend Christmas with his mother,' she pouted. 'It may be the last one they have together.'

'Why, is she unwell?'

'No, Nanny, but once he's living here he won't see so much of her. At least, that's what he says.'

'That's a bit silly, isn't it? The woman could always come here, and of course he could return to Wiltshire for a visit. He's not chained to this place, after all.'

Meredith simpered. 'I have a feeling that he may propose when he comes back.' She turned to Mariah with a warning look in her eyes. 'You won't mind, will you?'

'Of course not,' Mariah murmured, resisting the impulse to say that Meredith was welcome to him. 'I hope you'll be very happy.'

'He was dropping all sorts of hints before he left, saying that it was time he got married and settled down.'

An imp of mischief took possession of Mariah. 'He's been in Wiltshire a long time, hasn't he? What if he brings a bride back with him?'

'Oh, what a beastly thing to say!' Pressing a handkerchief to her mouth, Meredith darted from the room.

'Was that really necessary, Mariah?'

'It was just a joke, Mam. Still, wouldn't it be funny if he did bring a wife with him?'

'Never. He knows which side his bread is buttered, does that young man.'

Not enough to keep him from trying to seduce me, Mariah thought grimly. And he'd better not try anything again, or this time I really will go to Mr Morgan. She wouldn't like to see Meredith tied to a bounder, to use her mother's expression.

She was very wary of Chad when he did return, and was careful not to be left alone with him. Sometimes, when they happened to meet in one of the passages in the house he deliberately brushed up against her although there was nothing which would have actually justified a complaint to Harry.

She was delighted when Meredith burst into the housekeeper's room, holding out her left hand on which reposed a large diamond solitaire.

'Look, Nanny, I'm engaged! Chad spoke to Father last night, and he agreed we can be married in June!'

'I'm pleased for you, dear, if that's what you want,' Ellen murmured, leaning forward to admire the ring. It was too ostentatious for her taste, but then she wasn't the one who had to wear it!

'Of course it's what I want! I fell in love with Chad the moment I saw him and he says he felt the same about me. Isn't it wonderful?'

What romantic bilge! Mariah thought. Still, Chad would behave himself now, so she herself could stop looking over her shoulder all the time.

Meredith noticed her sour expression. 'You don't approve, do you, 'Riah?

I suppose you wanted him for yourself, but it's me he's chosen, and don't you forget it!'

There was no acceptable answer to this, so Mariah excused herself and left the room.

'Poor Mariah,' Meredith said, gazing smugly at her ring. 'Never mind, Mariah is sure to find someone when she goes to London, don't you think?'

'I expect she will,' Ellen sighed. Mariah had told her about Chad's little games and she hoped and prayed he wasn't thinking of having his cake and eating it too. Surely he wouldn't do anything silly once he was married to Meredith, though?

The wedding was planned for June of 1939. There was a great deal to do because the reception was to be at the house. This meant refurbishing the place from top to bottom, opening up seldom-used bedrooms to accommodate guests coming from a distance, and ordering new linens. The grounds would be groomed meticulously in order for them to look their best on the big day.

The menus were drawn up and discarded a dozen times. Endless lists appeared as she and the girls discussed the floral arrangements, the dresses, the guests. Harry had to smooth down his mother-in-law's ruffled feathers when she learned that she would not be taking charge of the arrangements. As Meredith's grandmother, she wanted to know that everything would be done properly, and she had volunteered to move into the house for a few months. Harry quailed at the thought.

'Everything is under control, Mother-in-law,' he told her. There is absolutely no need for you to come to Wales before June. Mrs Richards is well able to organize matters here.' He held the earpiece of the phone away from his head to avoid the agonized squawking coming from the other end of the line. In the end he agreed that she should help Meredith with the selection of her wedding gown. 'But as I said, there is no need for you to come here. The girl can come to you.'

'Well, of course. We'll have to go to London for that. If you think I'm going to allow my granddaughter to go to the altar wearing a frock run up by some little dressmaker, you're sadly mistaken. I wish Meredith to have the best, and I expect you do, also.'

Meredith was thrilled when she heard the news. 'And you must come too, 'Riah!'

'I don't think that would be appropriate,' Ellen said firmly. She had only met the grandmother on one occasion, and she was quite sure that the dreadful woman would have something to say about 'the housekeeper's daughter' being included in the expedition. Unless, of course, she chose to rope Mariah in as a lady's maid!

'But I want 'Riah to be my bridesmaid, Nanny. I have to have someone grown up and sensible. The others are much too young to be reliable.'

These were two small cousins on Harry's side, little girls who Meredith had never met. There was also some talk of a distantly related toddler boy being brought from Gloucestershire to act as ring bearer. Ellen was sure that would lead to trouble.

'I need Mariah here,' Ellen said. 'I'll make a note of her measurements for you to take with you to London. Just make sure they understand that the dress must be delivered here in plenty of time, in case it needs to be altered.'

'What colour were you thinking of for the bridesmaids' frocks?' Mariah wondered.

'Oh, a lovely rose pink, I think, with chaplets of tiny rosebuds on their heads.'

Mariah's face fell. With her hair, that would be absolutely ghastly. Normally her glossy tresses could be described as copper, or auburn, but they mysteriously faded to a sandy shade when she put on anything pink, and Meredith knew that, blast her!

'That would be lovely for the two little girls,' Ellen said diplomatically, 'but I think the maid of honour should be dressed differently. What would look sweet on someone small would look odd on an adult. How about blue, say a lovely shade of delphinium?' She had a pretty shrewd idea what Meredith was up to, but if Mariah looked less than her best, it was only for one day, after all. The expensive dress could be dyed another colour, or consigned to the rag bag if need be.

Harry was to drive Meredith to Gloucestershire, and she and her grandmother would travel on together from there. He had offered to take them all the way to London but Henrietta had refused with a little shriek of horror, preferring to go in state by train, short though the journey was.

'Because you can arrange for us to use your private coach, I'm sure!'

It was easier to give in to her whim than to argue, so Harry complied.

'Oh, well, it won't be long now, Mam,' Mariah said when they had gone. With Chad and Meredith living in the house when they returned from their European honeymoon, there was no way she'd stay under the same roof. As it was, she meant to steer clear of him while his bride-to-be was away from the house. She had seen the glint in his eye when Meredith had left and shivered at the thought of what he might do.

CHAPTER 36

'I HOPE THAT'S GOOD news,' Ellen said. 'I could tell by the crest on the envelope that you've heard from the hospital.'

'Well, it is in a way, Mam. They've accepted me into the training course.'

'But that's wonderful! When do they want you to report there?'

Mariah bit her lip. 'That's the problem. I'm to be part of the October intake.'

'So? The autumn will soon come around, and meanwhile we have this wedding to pull off. It's just as well, really; if they'd taken you right away you might not have been given time off to act as maid of honour.'

'I'll stay until after the wedding, Mam, and then I'm off.'

'Off? Where will you go? If you leave you'll have to pay for board and lodging.'

Mariah rolled her eyes. 'If you think I'm staying within a mile of Chad Fletcher you've got another think coming. He's a creep, Mam, a slimy, oily creep!'

'That's a bit extreme, dear. In any case, they'll be leaving for their honeymoon as soon as the wedding is over, and the house will settle down again.'

Mam doesn't know the half of it, Mariah thought. Chad had returned to the house while Meredith was in London and he'd renewed his attack.

'Can't we start again?' he'd suggested. 'We got off on the wrong foot in the beginning, I know, but for Meredith's sake we can at least be civil to each other.'

'Yes, we can certainly try to do that,' she responded.

'Then how about a drive into the country? We can stop for a meal somewhere.'

'You shouldn't be taking another girl out while your fiancée's back is turned!'

'Don't look at me like that, Mariah! And you're hardly just another girl, are you?'

'One of the servants, you mean?'

'That wasn't what I meant at all. I'm not married yet. I don't have a ring through my nose, Mariah.'

'The answer is still no, Chad.'

'Oh, suit yourself!' he said crossly. 'Eligible men are not exactly lining up to ask you out, are they?'

He strode away, leaving her fuming. Did he believe she was that stupid? She'd read enough romance novels to know what would happen next. His car would mysteriously break down in the middle of nowhere and she'd be at his mercy. She could do without the melodrama. Mam didn't know what he was like. Chad behaved like a perfect gentleman when he was in her company.

Mariah took a deep breath and broached a subject which had been on her mind. 'I feel that the time has come for you to be moving on, Mam. We'll look around for a little place and I'll help you to move in. I'll keep you company until I start at the hospital.'

'Moving on! What on earth has put that idea into your head?' Ellen looked extremely puzzled. 'I'm quite settled here. The hall has been my home ever since you were born; since I was a girl myself, as a matter of fact. Has Meredith said anything to you? Nothing has been said about my having to leave!'

Ellen looked so worried that Mariah almost wished she hadn't said anything, but she had started now, so she soldiered on.

'Steady on, Mam! Nothing's been said, only can't you see things are going to be different now? Meredith will be mistress here. She'll want things done her way.'

'If she does, she'll give me orders. She'll still need a housekeeper. I can't see her dealing with the linen and chivvying the maids about. In any case, Harry Morgan is still in charge. Do you think he'd give me my marching orders after all these years?'

Ellen glanced around the housekeeper's room, which had been home to her for so long. She loved the chintz fabrics, the polished furniture, the clock with its Whittington chimes, the fresh flowers which were cut daily by the gardener. The thought of exchanging all this for some drab little terraced house was painful.

Watching her mother's set face, Mariah knew she had failed. All she could do now was stand by, ready to pick up the pieces if necessary. Her real fear was that Chad, infuriated by having been met by a cold refusal, would somehow take out his anger on Ellen, forcing her out of the house. He might bring his mother to live here, on the pretext that she could help his new wife to run the house as it should be run. Or he might do something worse, such as accusing Ellen of theft. The possibilities were endless, and Mariah's worries ran riot in her head.

Meredith returned from London, full of excitement over the things she had seen and done. Her wedding gown, made from ivory satin, was being prepared by a well-known couturier. The garments for the small attendants were also in the process of being made; rose-pink dresses for the little girls, who were to be attired like Watteau shepherdesses, and blue satin for the ring bearer, who was to look like a tiny cavalier.

'Blue for a boy, of course, and he'll carry the ring on a matching pillow.'

'Not a satin pillow, surely!' Ellen cried. 'The ring might slip off and roll away!'

'And what about my dress?' Mariah asked. Meredith clasped her hands together.

'Oh, they had the loveliest chiffon, in a sort of deep coral. I simply couldn't resist it.'

Mariah groaned. 'Not with my hair, Meredith! I'll look a fright! Have they started on the dress yet? Is it too late to change?'

'I'm sorry you don't care for my taste, Mariah!' Meredith's tone was cold. 'As it happens, Grandmama thought the colour wouldn't look well with the rose pink the children are wearing. She said it would balance the picture better if you wore blue, like the ring bearer only in a deeper shade. Hyacinth, I think the vendeuse called it. I'm having the coral made up as an evening gown, for myself. Part of my trousseau.'

Mariah hadn't realized she'd been holding her breath. 'I'm sure it will suit you very well, with your hair, Meredith.'

Meredith's attention was taken by the tall vases of flowers which stood around the room. She gave a small shriek. 'Should you be bringing all these flowers indoors now? Don't forget we'll need hundreds of them for the wedding!'

'Don't be an idiot!' Mariah exclaimed. 'The wedding is weeks away. All these will be dead long before that time. There'll be plenty more to come, won't there, Mam?'

'Yes, indeed,' Ellen agreed. 'There's absolutely no need to worry, Meredith. Watts knows what he's doing.'

'I know, I know. Don't listen to me. I'm just getting jumpy. This will be the best day of my life and I want everything to be just perfect.'

'Wedding jitters, dear. Every bride has them.'

'I suppose so. Were you nervous on your wedding day, Nanny?'

For a few minutes Ellen couldn't decide what to say. 'I suppose I was, dear, but it was so long ago, I can hardly remember.'

'Did your husband wear his uniform when you were married?' Meredith had picked up the framed photograph of Bertie which stood on the mantelpiece.

'Yes. The war was on, you see. Most men were married in uniform in those days. They were proud to be seen wearing them.'

Fortunately Meredith lost interest in this line of conversation and returned to the subject of London. Ellen let the words flow over her head as the girl babbled on about having seen Buckingham Palace, Covent Garden and Madame Tussaud's. Mariah was interested because once she started her training she'd be able to see these places on her days off. Not that she'd be going to the opera, as Meredith had done. She'd be lucky if she could afford to go to a Lyons Corner House for beans on toast.

'What will you be wearing to my wedding, Nanny?' Meredith asked suddenly.

'Oh, will I be there?'

'Of course you will. All the servants will be coming, except for Cook and the kitchen maids, of course; they'll have to keep an eye on the food. They can see me in my glad rags when we come back from the church. Father is arranging for a car to take the rest of you to the church.'

Ellen's face fell. You rotten beast! Mariah raged silently. How could you talk to Mam like that, after all she's done for you? Who saved your worthless life when nobody thought you'd survive your first week of life? Who sat up with you in the long nights when you had measles and chickenpox?

Meredith was supremely unaware that she'd said anything wrong, and if she'd been challenged she would have raised her eyebrows in non-comprehension. Her father was one of the wealthiest men in South Wales and she had been born into luxury. Ellen had a regular wage, and was provided with a good home; what more should she require?

Mariah vowed to herself that some day she would take Ellen away from all this. She wasn't in a position to do much about it now, not when her mother refused to see the writing on the wall, but they wouldn't be penniless for ever. When Mariah was finished with her training she'd start to make money and then she'd get a little flat somewhere, which they could share.

Mariah was unaware that storm clouds were gathering in that spring of 1939. She didn't trouble to listen to the wireless. She had only a vague idea that, over in Germany, the Nazi movement, led by an evil man named Adolf Hitler, was gathering strength. What people did over there was of little concern to her. Their political goings-on would soon fizzle out and they certainly wouldn't affect life in Britain.

CHAPTER 37

'I WANT A SERIOUS talk with you two,' Harry announced, coming upon Chad and Meredith as they sat in the library, poring over an illustrated travel book.

'Oh, not now, Daddy!' Meredith protested. 'We're planning where to go on our honeymoon. I want to go to Paris and Venice, but Chad thinks we should take in as many countries as possible.'

'Like the Grand Tour the Victorians sent wealthy young men on,' Chad said, smiling.

'That's what I wish to discuss. In view of the current political situation I don't think you should go to Europe at all. As far as I can make out, Hitler has some very nasty plans up his sleeve and I would not want the pair of you getting into difficulties.'

'Oh, Daddy, that's silly. We don't want to go to Germany anyway, do we, Chad?'

'No, but I would have liked to see the Tyrol. However, since Austria was annexed to Germany last year, perhaps it might be best if we stayed away.'

'The writing is on the wall,' Harry said, his face sober. Meredith noticed with a pang that her father was getting old. His hair, which had been steel-grey for so long, was beginning to turn white. New lines had recently appeared on his handsome face, and his waistline had begin to thicken. It was a shame that these worries – unfounded as she believed them to be – should seem to hasten the ageing process.

'Chad, you read the newspapers. You must have realized what is going on. The Nazis took over Czechoslovakia two months ago, and they've signed a pact with Italy. I can't imagine they'll stop at that. If this doesn't come to war, I'll eat my hat!'

'I don't doubt there will be trouble over there, sir, but it won't affect Britain, thanks to Mr Chamberlain. "Peace in our time," he said, after meeting Hitler at Munich.'

'That's right, Daddy,' Meredith chimed in, determined not to miss her lovely honeymoon. 'We can still go to France; nothing is happening there. And I know you wanted to see the Tyrol, Chad, but we can always go to Switzerland instead if you want to see that sort of country.'

Harry could have wept for his daughter's innocence. Hitler, that spawn of Satan, was not to be trusted. Anybody who could treat fellow human beings as he was treating the Jews – ordinary, good-living people – would stop at nothing. Men, women and children were being torn from their homes and sent to concentration camps. Who knew what was happening to them there?

'I still think you should avoid Europe,' he said, his face set in stubborn lines. 'How about the Highlands of Scotland? They were good enough for Queen Victoria so they should be good enough for you!'

'Is that where she went on her honeymoon?' Meredith was momentarily diverted.

'How should I know, *cariad*? She spent a great deal of time up there, though.'

'There can't be a war, Daddy. Our governess told us all about the Great War, and how it was the war to end all wars.'

'Obviously that was a mistake. What about the Spanish Civil War, then? That ended just a few years ago.'

'I suppose people meant a world war.' Meredith frowned, out of her depth now. 'I mean, it was only a civil war they had in Spain, wasn't it?'

'I don't have a crystal ball,' her father snapped. 'All I'm saying is, the outlook is grim, and I'd prefer you to stay here.'

'I suppose we could compromise,' Chad suggested. 'We'll go to Paris and have our honeymoon there. If anything happens we can nip back over the Channel in no time. We can still have a tour of Europe at a later date, once things settle down with this Hitler chap. What do you think, Meredith?'

'I suppose so. You're unkind, Daddy, trying to spoil things for me like this.'

Sensing at least a partial victory, Harry patted her on the hand, smiling now. 'At least you have your lovely wedding to look forward to, child. Take it from me, it will be the most lavish affair our guests have ever seen.'

'Look, here's a picture of Versailles.' Meredith had been turning the pages of her book while they talked. 'We must go there, Chad. I wonder if it's open to the public?'

Harry slipped away, unnoticed. He had done what he could to steer his wayward daughter in the right direction, and the rest was up to Chad.

'We can't have the honeymoon we wanted,' Meredith complained to Ellen and Mariah when she went upstairs later. 'Father says we mustn't go.'

'What! No honeymoon at all?'

'Oh, we can have a holiday of sorts, but we can only go to Paris.'

'Only go to Paris!' Mariah mocked. 'What wouldn't I give to go there?'

'I expect he's a bit worried about the situation in Europe,' Ellen murmured. Harry had already shared his fears with her and she had to agree that things didn't look promising. The British government already had complicated plans to evacuate children from the cities in case war broke out and there was large-scale bombing.

'Surely it will never come to that,' she'd told him, horrified at the thought of bombs raining down on defenceless civilians, perhaps on a much larger scale than had occurred during what they thought of as 'their' war. 'Parents will never permit their children to be taken away to live among strangers.'

'They may not have much choice, *cariad*. And you'd better brace yourself, because if it comes to that we'll probably have a dozen children billeted on us, in a house this size. You'll be pressed into service as a nanny again!'

'I was expecting that in any case,' she countered. 'By this time next year Meredith might be a mother, and that will make you a grandfather!'

'I don't think I'm ready for that,' he groaned, but he smiled as he said it.

'No more gloomy thoughts!' she counselled. 'This is a happy house now, with the wedding so close. Let's keep it that way, shall we?'

A member of the fashion house travelled up from London in a hired car, carrying the partially finished wedding garments for a fitting. Harry had arranged this so the girls did not have to return to London.

There was great excitement as the grey-and-burgundy-striped boxes were unpacked, revealing the dresses swathed in yards of tissue paper. 'Just make sure that Chad doesn't come up here,' Meredith ordered. 'It's bad luck to see me in my gown before the wedding day!'

'It would be bad luck for him if he burst in here to find us all half dressed!' Ellen threatened. Her outfit was being made by a local dressmaker, who had a good reputation for producing excellent work.

'Although she isn't a patch on Madame Blanche,' Meredith had scoffed. 'It's all in the cut, you see.'

Even in its half-finished state, the bridal gown looked wonderful on Meredith, setting off her slim figure to perfection. The seamstress clasped her hands in admiration. 'You'll look wonderful on the day,' she gushed.

A discontented look marred Meredith's pretty face. 'I don't know at all. I wish now I'd requested a train. What do you think, Nanny?'

'It's not too late,' the seamstress murmured. 'I'm sure it could be done in time,' but Ellen spoke up firmly.

'This is Cwmbran, Meredith. You're getting married in All Saints church, not Westminster Abbey. And what happens if it rains? They don't call this Wet Wales for nothing. Do you want to drift down the aisle dragging a soaking wet train?'

'Don't be silly. The car will stop right outside the church door and the train wouldn't drag on the wet ground. The bridesmaids will hold it up, of course.'

'Oh, really! The little girls are much too small, and Mariah won't be able to manage by herself. It takes two, one on each side. Where are we going to find another grown-up girl at short notice, and how would we get her dress made in time?'

'I hadn't thought of that.' Meredith twirled around once more, gazing at herself in the long mirror. 'I suppose this will have to do. You haven't tried your dress on yet, Mariah. Go and do it now, will you? I want to see how we look together.'

Mariah had to admit that she liked her dress. It was a lovely shade of deep blue which didn't clash too badly with her hair. She would have preferred pale green, but that was said to be unlucky for weddings, or did that only apply to the bride? She tried to remember the old rhyme about the colour of wedding dresses.

'Married in blue, something, something. Married in green, not fit to be seen.' She removed her old gingham house dress and slipped the pretty frock carefully over her head, patting her curls back into place.

'What will you be wearing on your head?' Ellen wondered, when Mariah had displayed her dress, to the accompaniment of murmurs of approval. Mariah looked at Meredith, with her head on one side.

'Oh, a chaplet of little roses, to match what the little ones are wearing. Pale pink rosebuds will go quite well with that blue.'

Fortunately the seamstress spoke up before Mariah could explode.

'I would suggest white rosebuds, miss. You want to think of the effect coming down the aisle, like. The maid of honour should look completely different from the little girls, you see?' Ellen breathed a sigh of relief, and peace reigned.

CHAPTER 38

THE DAY OF the wedding arrived on a gust of wind. It had rained during the night and now small clouds were scudding across the sky.

'What's it doing out there?' Meredith inquired anxiously, when Ellen roused her with a cup of tea. 'I couldn't bear it if it rained on my wedding day! Happy the bride the sun shines on!'

'Rain before seven, dry before eleven,' Ellen chanted. 'I've run your bath for you, so you'll have to get up in a minute. The hairdresser will be here at nine.'

'I wish I wasn't getting married, Nanny. Everything's going to change, and I don't want that to happen.'

'Nonsense! You love Chad, don't you?'

'I suppose so. No, I'm not sure.'

'It's not too late to change your mind, you know.' Many a bride had last-minute doubts but there was always the possibility that a mistake had been made. Better to back out while there was still time, rather than endure a lifetime of regrets.

'I can't do that. What am I going to tell people? A lot of the guests have already turned up. The bedrooms are full, in case you've forgotten!'

Ellen muttered something about not being likely to forget, since she was the one who had had the work of getting them all settled.

'Are you getting up, or not, Meredith? If you don't get a move on soon your grandmother will be in here fussing about, and we don't want that.'

'But what am I going to do about Chad, Nanny? I can't decide about that.'

Ellen decided that great cunning was called for. 'Call off the wedding if you like, my girl, but just you remember that all those wedding presents will have to go back. You won't catch me packing them up for the post! *And* you'll have to write a letter to go with each one!' Writing letters had never been Meredith's strong point.

'Can't we just put one of those notices in *The Times*, then? You know,

"The wedding which was arranged will not now take place?" They did that when Charlotte Frobisher broke off her engagement and went to India.'

'Yes, I expect we shall, but those notes will still have to be written, thanking people for sending gifts in the first place.'

Meredith swung her legs out of the bed. 'Will you go and tell my father, Nanny?'

'I'll do no such thing! You can tell him yourself. But there's something else you have to remember. Married or not, Mr Fletcher isn't going to go away. He's come to live here for a purpose. How do you fancy facing him over the breakfast table after this, knowing you've shamed him in front of all his friends and relations?'

'I hadn't thought of that.'

'No, I don't suppose you had. Now then, into that bath you go, before the water gets cold. Some of us have a wedding to go to!'

Grumbling, Meredith did as she was told, leaving Ellen standing in the middle of the floor, biting her lip. Was it only wedding nerves? Had she done the right thing in steering the girl towards her marriage, or should she find Harry and let him deal with it? Finally she made up her mind to say nothing. Meredith was a grown woman and must make her own decisions.

Ellen rode to the church in a hired car, accompanied by several chattering maids. They were greeted by a little crowd of miners' wives, who had gathered there to see the bride. Several of them had babies in their arms, carried in the traditional way under huge shawls which enveloped both child and mother.

The staff were seated at the back of the church, which pleased them because they could watch the other guests coming in, and marvel at the fashionable garments and lovely hats worn by the ladies.

'Look at that one!' Ruth giggled, pointing out one particularly striking headpiece. 'It looks like a flower pot upside-down, with all them roses coming down the side.'

'Ssh! She'll hear you!'

The bridegroom and his friend were now arriving, ready to take up their places at the altar steps. They looked very grand in their morning suits, carrying top hats which they had removed at the door. No doubt about it, Chad and Meredith would make a handsome couple.

A distant cheer was heard, followed by the strains of 'Here Comes The Bride' from the organ. Meredith came down the aisle on her father's arm, then came the two little bridesmaids, followed by Mariah, resplendent in blue. She seemed to be having trouble keeping the little ring bearer in order. Instead of keeping to his assigned place, he was trotting down the aisle, grinning, occasionally stopping to stare up into the face of a guest. Ellen longed to take him by the arm and put him back where he belonged. She could hear murmurs of 'how sweet' and 'dear little chap' but they'd soon change their tune if he started to roar, and then she'd be to blame for causing a commotion.

In another moment, what she had feared all along came to pass. Not looking where he was going, the child tripped over his own feet and the ring fell off the satin pillow and hit the floor with a tinkle. It rolled merrily towards a grating and disappeared from view. There was a concerted gasp from the assembled guests as a church warden peered into the depths and then, straightening up, shook his head. Totally unperturbed, the little boy lowered the pillow to the floor and sat on it, sucking his thumb.

Ellen couldn't understand how the ceremony proceeded from that point without further ado. She would not have been surprised if Meredith had rushed from the church in floods of tears. It wasn't until the Fletchers were safely married, and everyone was back at the house, enjoying the reception, that she knew the full story.

'I could see that coming a mile off,' the best man was proclaiming. 'Letting a toddler carry a ring on a pillow was asking for trouble! So I kept the ring safely in my pocket, and no harm done.'

'But what about the ring that got away?' someone asked.

'A curtain ring from Woolworth's. Nobody could tell the difference!'

Ellen smiled. What a lovely young man he seemed to be. Just the sort of husband she'd choose for Mariah. And it was traditional that the maid of honour and the best man should pair off later, when there was dancing....

She could sit back now and enjoy the reception. Harry had decreed this. 'After all, you've been a second mother to the bride,' he told her, bringing happy tears to her eyes. 'Let somebody else do the work for once. With all the extra help we've hired you won't be needed to fetch and carry.'

She noticed with amusement that Chad's mother and Meredith's grandmother were practising a form of one-upmanship. Both dressed to the nines, they wore fixed smiles on their faces as each strove to do the other down.

'Of course, this will all belong to my son one day,' Verona Fletcher remarked, when someone had praised the house, saying how lovely the bride's home was. 'He is Harry Morgan's heir, you know.'

'Naturally, I'm aware of that,' Henrietta said stiffly. 'My poor daughter was married to the man, after all. It was a great tragedy that she died so young, giving birth to Meredith. Had she not done so, there would have been a son to inherit, I'm sure, and poor Harry would not have had to pass on his wealth to a distant branch of the family.'

She managed to imply, by tone of voice, that the branch was far removed from the Cwmbran Morgans in more ways than one, Ellen noted, amused. She watched Chad's mother struggling to come up with a suitable rejoinder, and failing. Round one to Mrs Meredith! They reminded Ellen of two dogs competing for territory, circling each other as they tried to make up their minds whether to go for the jugular.

'I fancy that shrubbery needs to be cut back,' Verona announced, to nobody in particular, as she gazed out of the window. 'It should be seen to at once. It's far too overgrown for my taste. I must tell Chad to see to it.'

'As far as I know, my son-in-law is still master here,' Henrietta sniffed.

Fortunately it was at that moment that Meredith came downstairs, having been to powder her nose. Mariah followed, looking lovely and unruffled. The two tiny bridesmaids had been chasing each other in and out of the drawing room and were now in a state of disrepair. One of them had spilled orange squash all down her front, and the other had her chaplet of rosebuds hanging over one ear.

'Do look at those two!' Meredith grumbled. 'They're turning the place into a circus and I won't have it. Go and sort them out, Mariah!'

Mariah only smiled. 'I'll do nothing of the sort! They must have nannies or mothers somewhere. Let them take charge. I'm going for a glass of champagne. I'm so thirsty my tongue is sticking to the roof of my mouth.'

At last it was all over. The speeches were made, the cake was cut and Meredith went to her room to change into her going-away outfit. This was a very smart costume in royal blue, with a tiny feathered hat to match. She and Chad were being driven to the station, where Harry's private coach awaited.

'This time tomorrow we'll be in France!' Meredith exulted, as she kissed Ellen goodbye. 'I can't believe it's really happening!'

'Goodbye, dear, good luck! Goodbye! Goodbye!'

CHAPTER 39

ALL OF BRITAIN was shocked by the announcement which was made on 3 September. Britain, as well as France, Australia and New Zealand, had declared war on Germany, and Canada followed suit a week later. Hitler's forces had invaded Poland on 1 September, and they had already overrun Austria and Czechoslovakia several months before.

'And of course they won't stop at that!' Harry declared, when they had switched off the wireless and were sitting about, looking grim.

'But I don't see why we have to go to war, Daddy.' Meredith frowned. 'Or France, either.' She had fallen in love with France during her brief honeymoon and could not believe that something as dreadful as war could happen there.

'These people have to be stopped, *cariad*. The rest of the civilized world cannot stand by and watch them take over. Somebody has to go to the rescue.'

'But Mr Chamberlain said peace in our time, Daddy!'

'Chamberlain was wrong. Oh, I don't suppose it was his fault. Herr Hitler deliberately pulled the wool over his eyes, I don't doubt. Well, we'll soon be in the thick of it now. We'll see some changes as the men get called up into the services, and women too, this time around. They won't have me, of course, I'm too old, but Cwmbran will be affected. Fortunately the miners won't have to go but those in other jobs will soon find themselves in uniform.'

Meredith turned to her husband, her eyes wide. 'They won't make you go, will they, Chad?'

He shrugged. 'Not if I can help it, dear.'

Harry lowered his head so Chad couldn't see his look of disgust. He had always suspected that his son-in-law was a selfish individual, but this was too much. Words such as shirker and slacker came to mind.

'Don't tell me you're a conscientious objector,' he said coldly.

Chad opened his eyes wide. 'Don't tell me you're one of those people who'd like to imprison anyone who can't see things your way, cousin Harry! As it happens, I don't see why a man should have to go and get himself shot at if he doesn't choose to.'

'That's not the same thing as refusing to fight because of one's religious beliefs or moral principles, Chad! Would you sit here at home, safe and sound, while others go off to fight for you?'

'They wouldn't be fighting on my behalf, because I don't believe in this stupid war to start with!' Chad snapped, going red around the ears.

'So you'd sit tight until the Germans come marching into Cwmbran and take over this place, pillaging and raping, would you?'

'Don't be a fool. That won't happen!'

'Stop it! Stop it, both of you! I can't bear it!' Meredith had leapt to her feet with her hands clenched. 'Isn't it bad enough there's a war on, without you two going at it?' She ran to her husband and buried her face in his cashmere pullover.

Exasperated, Harry strode out of the room. His mind went back to that unfortunate man who had deserted from the army in the last war. What was his name? Parry? He'd been a footman at the hotel at Barry, and had become involved with Antonia's maid. The fellow had come to Cwmbran and actually got himself taken on in the colliery office. The chap had gone to gaol, and was extremely lucky not to have been executed.

Harry wondered where he was now. The man had married a local girl, to give their expected child a name, and she was most likely still living in Cwmbran. He really didn't care much one way or the other. The man had behaved badly and been punished for it. What was distressing was the thought of the shame Chad Fletcher could bring on the Morgan name.

Meredith would probably expect her father to pull strings so that Chad could be kept safe at home, perhaps stating that his presence was vital to the running of the mine, which in turn was a vital part of the war effort. But how would Harry appear to his employees then, a man who had dealt harshly with some poor wounded soldier, yet helped his own son-in-law to avoid doing his duty? He could hear the complaints now, that such treachery was only to be expected of 'them' up at the hall.

Mariah was filled with patriotic fervour. 'I'm going to join up,' she told her mother. 'It's a good thing I hadn't started on my training yet, or I might not be free to go.'

'You could sign on as a probationer nurse instead,' Ellen suggested. 'There will be plenty of useful work looking after the men who've been wounded in action.'

'What, and spend the war scrubbing bedpans and dealing with dirty laundry? I'd never get near a wounded man, Mam, that'll be left to those already trained. No, I'll be better off joining one of the women's services, perhaps the Air Force.' She went to a recruiting office, but soon returned, chagrined.

'What happened?' Ellen wanted to know. 'I should have thought you'd be snapped up at once!'

'Oh, they'd have taken me, all right, but only as a glorified skivvy, Mam. Apparently I don't have any skills or qualifications. The officer didn't have much time for a girl who'd been educated by a governess and hadn't even sat any exams. I can't type or do shorthand, I can't drive a car, and I haven't even held down a job! It seems all I'm fit for is to peel potatoes and do the washing up in some canteen. If I wanted to do that I'd take a job as a scullery maid!'

'What are you going to do, then? If you wait until you're called up you'll have to go where you're sent.'

'I suppose I could learn to drive, perhaps, or go and learn to type. It's too bad the cavalry will be mechanized in this war, or I might be able to look after their horses. At least that's something I would be good at.'

'You don't have to go into the services,' Ellen said. 'I'm sure there'll be a great demand for people to do factory work. I did that for a while in the last war.'

'I know, you've told me, Mam. I'll bear that in mind.'

Predictably, Meredith was less sympathetic. 'It's so ridiculous, expecting women to taken part in the war.'

'No, it's not!' Mariah told her. 'We'll be freeing men to go and fight. And you'll have to do your bit as well, Merry. As Mam says, if we wait until our call-up papers come, we may not have much choice in what we do for the next few years.'

'Oh, I shan't have to do that,' Meredith replied, trying to hide a smile but not succeeding. 'I'm expecting a baby, you see.'

'How wonderful! What fantastic news!' Ellen flung her arms around Meredith, delight written all over her face. 'When is it due?'

'Early April, I think.'

'I must get out the knitting needles at once! Is Chad pleased?'

'I suppose so. You can't tell with men, can you? They never let you know what they're thinking.'

Harry would be a grandfather. Probably he and Chad would be hoping for a boy, to inherit the estate in due course. That's if there was a due course! She knew it was wrong to have defeatist thoughts – and of course the Allies would win – but what if some day everything that Harry now owned was to fall into enemy hands?

'I suppose you think I'm foolish to have a baby when there's a war on.' Meredith had somehow divined what was on Ellen's mind.

'No, no, of course not. It's lovely to have something to look forward to instead of listening to all this talk of rationing and hardship.'

'And wherever I am when it's born, I'll come back home for the christening,' Mariah remarked. 'I hope you'll ask me to be one of the godmothers.'

'Oh, you can't leave me, Mariah!' She sounded so alarmed that Ellen and Mariah exchanged puzzled glances. 'Promise me you'll stay until after the baby's born.'

'But you'll have your husband, and your father, and Mam as well, not to mention a house full of servants. I'll be coming back on leave from wherever I happen to be, and I'll write nice long letters to tell you what's going on in my life.'

'Everything is changing, and I can't bear it! I want everything to stay the same.'

Meredith looked as if she was about to burst into tears, and Mariah hastened to reassure her. 'I won't be going anywhere for a while, Merry. Of course I've had to register, the same as everyone else, but I don't suppose I'll be called up yet. I'm going to take driving lessons in the meantime.'

'And how is that supposed to stop Hitler?' Meredith scoffed. 'And what good will it do? Women don't make good drivers, Chad says, so they'll hardly let you drive a tank or something, will they?'

'Chad!' Mariah was furious. 'I don't see him rushing off to drive a tank! Ideally I'd like to drive an ambulance, but even if I'm only detailed to drive some general around, at least I'll be doing something for the war effort.'

'Better to stay home and grow potatoes,' Meredith remarked. 'Apparently we have to dig up the west lawn and turn it into a gigantic vegetable garden. Daddy says that food is going to be rationed and we'll have to produce all we can.'

'We?' Mariah raised her eyebrows. 'Do you plan to get busy with a hoe?'

'Hardly!' Meredith patted her stomach. 'But your mother will help, won't you, Nanny? It can be your war work.'

'I suppose so,' Ellen replied, startled. She'd never had anything to do with gardening, but she could learn. Before this war was over, everyone would have learned to cope with things they'd never have thought possible in the old days.

CHAPTER 40

A T FIRST THE war moved slowly, and people were lulled into a false sense of complacency. Many parents who had allowed their children to be evacuated to the country brought them home again, and life went on much as usual. When rationing was imposed early in 1940, the effects were not felt too badly at first.

Some people were building air-raid shelters in their back gardens, but Harry Morgan decided it wasn't necessary at the hall, which had deep cellars. The servants made these comfortable, and air-raid drills were held under his leadership.

'Is this really necessary?' Cook grumbled. 'Surely to goodness they won't bomb us here. There's not enough of us to make it worthwhile. They'll go for the cities, I expect. Swansea, and Cardiff, perhaps, where the docks are.'

'You may be right, Cook, but who knows what Hitler has up his sleeve? We do have the colliery nearby, remember.'

'How are they going to find it, then?'

'Spies!' the footman told her.

'Don't be stupid, boy! Any spy who came to Cwmbran would soon find himself in the lock-up. A stranger would stick out like a sore thumb.'

'Don't underestimate the Nazis,' Harry told them. 'It's my belief they've been planning this war ever since they lost the last one. They'll have sent their spies over here in peacetime. They could have poked their noses in anywhere, and certainly they'd have been able to buy maps and charts.'

'Cheek!'

'Yes, well, all I'm saying is, we must be prepared for anything.'

'If them Nasties come here I'll give them what for with my rolling pin!' Cook announced, causing the smallest housemaid to break into a fit of giggles.

'That's the spirit!' Harry grinned, but inwardly he felt heartsick at the thought of lorries filled with enemy soldiers rolling up the long driveway to his home. It would take more than a rolling pin to stop their advance.

When spring came, it brought both joy and horror with it. On 9 April, Harry and Chad sat glued to the wireless while upstairs Meredith laboured to give birth to her child. Germany had invaded Denmark and Norway; what would come next?

'I can't stand much more of this!' Meredith gasped, in a lull between her pains.

'Everything is going quite normally, Mrs Fletcher,' the midwife soothed.

'How much longer, then?'

'It will be a little while yet, Mrs Fletcher. As I said, you're doing very well.'

'Oh, here comes another one!' Meredith's words were cut off as another contraction came. Ellen knew that the girl would soon be entering the second and most painful stage of labour.

'I'm going to die, aren't I?' Meredith panted.

'Nonsense! Of course you're not going to die!'

'My mother did. She died giving birth to me.'

'I know. You've told me,' the midwife replied. 'But you've no need to worry. These things don't run in families.'

The midwife sounded quite cheerful, so Ellen supposed that everything was all right.

At three o'clock in the morning, Meredith was delivered of a little boy, to be known as Henry Morgan Fletcher. Having satisfied herself that the baby had the requisite number of fingers and toes, she fell into an exhausted sleep. Ellen went downstairs to share the glad news. Harry was pacing the floor, a glass of whisky in his hand, and Chad was slumped in an armchair, sound asleep.

'It's a boy! Both well!' She smiled.

'Thank the Lord for that!' Harry shook his son-in-law awake. 'You've got a son, my boy! And Meredith has come through it safely!' The fact that his little girl had survived her ordeal was such cause for celebration that the fact of his becoming a grandfather had yet to sink in properly.

'Is it all right?' Chad asked doubtfully, staring at the crushed red face of his son. 'Its head is a bit of a funny shape, isn't it?'

'Your head would be a funny shape if you'd just travelled through a confined space!' the midwife said, with indignation written all over her homely face. 'And your son is not an it, Mr Fletcher! He's a lovely little boy.'

'But what about his head?' Chad persisted. 'It seems to be squashed. He will be all right, won't he?'

'He'll be as right as ninepence after a day or two,' she said, smiling. 'Just you wait and see. Wouldn't you like to hold him for a moment? Then you can pop in and see your wife, but don't stay long. She'll be needing her rest.'

Ellen tried to hide a smile. He really did look a bit green. If looking at a newborn baby made him feel so squeamish, how on earth would the man cope on the battlefield, if he eventually ended up there? And they called men the stronger sex!

Little Henry was a month old when the German army invaded France, Belgium, Luxembourg and the Netherlands. Winston Churchill took over as prime minister of Britain, vowing to lead the people to victory. Petty irritations beset them on the home front. 'You'd better brace yourself!' Harry growled, when Ellen entered his study with some newly washed ash trays.

'Why, what's the matter now?'

'There's a man coming down from the ministry, to inspect the place.'

'Whatever for?'

'To see if they want to take this place over, I imagine.'

'What ministry is that, then?' Ellen frowned.

'How the hell should I know? I was so angry when I read the letter I just crumpled it up and threw it on the fire.'

'Just as well it's a cold day, then, or you wouldn't have had a fire to throw it on.'

But Harry was in no mood for jokes. 'Where do you suppose we'll all go if they turn us out of here, Ellen? The family, and the servants, not to mention Meredith and the baby!'

'Turn us out! They couldn't do that, could they?'

'Don't ask me! It depends what they want the place for; if it's some secret government department they won't want civilians wandering about.'

'I heard they're taking valuables from museums and art galleries and storing them in disused mines,' Ellen said hopefully. 'Perhaps that's why this chap is coming, to ask if you've any disused mine shafts about.'

The man from the ministry, when he came, was an officious fellow in a shiny suit, wearing small, round, wire-rimmed glasses. He trotted about from room to room, looking as though there was a bad smell under his nose.

'Honestly, if he'd put on white gloves and tested for dust on the furniture it wouldn't have surprised me at all,' Ellen grumbled later.

'That's the war for you,' Harry sniffed. 'Give some minor civil servant a clipboard and a bundle of forms, and they turn into little tin gods.'

'But are they going to put us out, or what?'

'We'll be hearing in due course, that's what he said. Now we have to wait for some pundit in Whitehall to decide our fate. That's all I can tell you, Ellen.'

At that moment the door opened, and the aged butler stood there, puffing from the effort of having clambered up from below stairs.

'Excuse me, sir. There's someone to see you. It's a woman. I've put her in the morning room, sir.'

'Thank you, Perkins. I'll be down in a minute.'

Harry didn't recognize the woman who scrambled to her feet when he entered the morning room. She was one of the miners' wives, he supposed. She wore a shabby beige coat and her feet were painfully crammed into peep-toed shoes which looked too small for her. A big toe, adorned with chipped nail varnish, protruded from each shoe. Blonde hair escaped in wisps from the brightly patterned headscarf on her head. A bottle blonde, Harry decided.

'Yes, can I help you?'

'It's my son, Trevor.'

'Yes?' He didn't know where this was leading.

'Trevor Parry?'

'I don't think I er ...'

'You don't remember me, do you?'

'I'm sorry, I can't place you. Mrs Parry, is it?'

'Then perhaps you remember my husband, the one you helped put away, Mr Magistrate Morgan!'

Harry could understand why the woman felt bitter, but it was hardly his fault that the man had deserted from the army in the first place.

'I want you to see to it that my son doesn't have to join up, Mr Morgan. I won't have him being killed, or shellshocked like his poor father was. You've got influence in high places; I'm sure you can pull strings. Please, you owe us that much, Mr Morgan!'

CHAPTER 41

HARRY BLINKED ONCE or twice before answering. Then he chose his words with care.

'I'm sorry, Mrs Parry. I do not have any such influence, and even if I had, I should not use it in such a way. Surely you realize that every mother in Cwmbran would want to keep her son safe at home? If I helped your son – and again, I must stress that there is nothing I can do – everyone would want the same treatment.'

He was aware that he sounded pompous, but the woman should have known better than to come with such a ridiculous request. Bronwen Parry narrowed her eyes.

'So that's the way the wind blows, is it? Let everyone else die on the battlefield so long as you can stay at home, safe and sound!'

'That's a bit thick, Mrs Parry! I'd be only too glad to do my bit, but they're not likely to have me, at my age.'

'I didn't mean you, Mr Morgan. It's that son-in-law of yours, isn't it? Talking about him in the village, they are, see? Nothing wrong with him, fit as a fiddle, but will he go? Well, my Trevor has plenty of reasons for not joining up, Mr Morgan. He's grown up with no father on the scene, and me having to explain how poor Tom was called a rotten coward, and punished because he couldn't take no more after what he'd seen and done in the war. Now the boy is supposed to go through the same thing! You've got to help us, Mr Morgan. You must!'

Harry rang the bell. 'Mrs Parry is leaving, Perkins. Kindly show her to the door.'

'You haven't heard the last of this, Mr Morgan!' she bawled, looking back at him over her shoulder. 'And that Fletcher better watch out, or they'll get him some dark night when he's least expecting it!'

It was an empty threat, of course, but all the same, having Chad here when others were in uniform was an embarrassment.

'It might be best if you went away somewhere for a bit,' he told Chad later.

'What on earth for? I've plenty to do here, and my wife has just had a baby. She won't want me going off on holiday without her.'

'She'll be back on her feet soon. Why not take her and little Henry to Wiltshire, to visit your mother? I'm sure she's longing to see her grandchild.'

'I might do that later, although Mother has mentioned coming here. That would be less of an upheaval than taking Meredith and the nurse all the way to Wiltshire, not to mention all the equipment Henry seems to need.'

'I don't think you quite understand, my boy. According to the Parry woman, feelings are running high in the village. Why, in the last war, someone would have presented you with a white feather by now!'

'They can't make me go,' Chad said sullenly. 'Aren't I doing war work here? Mining and farming are reserved occupations, and I am helping to see that it all runs smoothly. If I'm actually called up, that will be a different matter. I suppose I'll have to explain it to a tribunal and see what they have to say.'

'Nevertheless, I believe it would be best if you leave for a while. The talk might die down if people believe you've gone to join up. It's not just you I'm worried about, Chad. If there really is unrest in Cwmbran, it could lead to a strike in the pit.'

'Highly unlikely!' Chad scoffed. 'They know which side their bread is buttered, cousin Harry! And they may not like what I do, but I'm management. The way I live my life is none of their business, and they'd better not forget it!'

'Perhaps it is a bit far-fetched,' Harry admitted, 'but there could be sabotage, nothing to do with the colliery. Hay ricks on the farms, mysteriously set on fire, that sort of thing. I really do think it best if you leave the district for a while, my boy.'

'Oh, very well, then! I suppose I could go to Kent and spend a few days with Aubrey Mortimer but Meredith won't care for it!'

As it happened, his wife listened to the plan with a most unflattering display of disinterest. 'How long will you be away, Chad?'

'A couple of weeks, perhaps.'

'Oh. Have you been to say hello to Henry today? I could have sworn he smiled at me this morning, even though Nurse says it's only wind. I can't wait until he's sitting up and taking notice!'

Harry had warned Chad to say nothing to Meredith about the real reason he was leaving. Since the birth of the baby she was inclined to be a bit weepy at times, and if she had any idea of trouble brewing she could become hysterical.

'We're not really in any danger, are we?' Ellen demanded, when she was put in the picture by Harry.

'No, no. It's just a question of justice being seen to be done, that's all.'

'Honestly, that's a bit much! That business with the Parry chap happened a lifetime ago, and you only did what you had to do at the time.'

'I know that, but the point that's being made now is that there's one law for the working man and another for the moneyed classes. It's bound to cause resentment.'

Ellen could not agree. 'If Chad were to go into the army and deserted, it wouldn't make a jot of difference that he'd been to Eton instead of the local council school. He'd still have to face the music. Not that they shoot deserters these days, do they?'

'Not as far as I know. The truth is, I'm embarrassed by the fact that my son-in-law doesn't want to go and do his bit.'

'Then what do you mean to do about it?'

He sighed. 'Nothing, I suppose. In any case I don't know why I'm so anxious about some minor uprising which may or may not take place in Cwmbran! We've more to worry about with the threat of invasion hanging over our heads.'

'Do you think that will happen, then?' Ellen's face turned pale.

'The government believes that Hitler's been thinking about it for years. Our only hope is that Winston Churchill can lick us all into shape now they've made him prime minister. He's been the voice of doom long enough, and they've called him a war monger, but now he's been proved right, hasn't he?'

Ellen wondered what they would do if the invasion did happen. Would they all go up into the Black Mountains and hide, just as people had done when the Romans came, or the Normans? It didn't bear thinking about.

Chad left for Kent, and the house seemed quiet without him. A letter came from the ministry to say that after due consideration, 'they' had decided that the house wouldn't do, being too small for their plans.

'I'd like to have known what those plans were,' Harry said.

'I wouldn't!' Meredith shuddered. 'I was so afraid they were going to turn us all out, just when Baby and Nurse are getting nicely settled.'

It was decided that some of the rooms would be closed up for the duration. Several of the servants had been called up, and there were too few left to do all the work.

'Although we may have to open them up again if they send us any evacuees,' Ellen realized.

'I don't know how you'll manage if they do!' Mariah pointed out. 'What if you have half a dozen little Cockney boys billeted on you?'

'That's why you're needed here, my girl! Between that and keeping up the new vegetable gardens you'll be worth your weight in gold. If the powers-that-be try to take you away, I shall have something to say to them!'

Then, towards the end of the month, something momentous happened. Allied troops were sent to land at a place called Dunkirk, but something went terribly wrong. They were driven back to the sea by the Germans, and thousands upon thousands of them were left stranded on the beaches, where they were at the mercy of enemy guns on the ground, and the Luftwaffe from the skies. British ships waited nearby, but they were unable to get close enough to pick up the survivors. The soldiers were sitting ducks, waiting to be massacred.

The whole dreadful episode was a resounding defeat for the Allies and yet, forever afterwards, what happened next would be referred to as the miracle of Dunkirk, and remembered as a triumph, and a tribute to the endurance of the human spirit. Drake's victory over the Spanish Armada paled by comparison.

In addition to the sterling work performed by the British navy, hundreds of small boats set out from England, manned by civilians of all ages. Fishing boats, pleasure craft, even a boat belonging to a group of Sea Scouts. Working gallantly under fire, these men and boys spent the next few days ferrying soldiers from the beaches to the waiting ships. Some were them-selves wounded. Others would never see home again.

By 3 June it was all over. More than 338,000 men had been taken off the beaches of Dunkirk and brought to safety. How, people asked each other, could that be regarded as anything but a victory for Britain?

Meanwhile, the Luftwaffe conducted a Blitzkrieg on Paris, in preparation for Hitler's triumphant entry into that beautiful city. Before a week had passed, Norway was forced to surrender to the Nazis, and soon afterwards Italy declared war on Britain.

'We're in the thick of it now,' Harry Morgan declared, but even he had no way of knowing that the war was about to come much nearer to Cwmbran. It was to hit home in a way that none of them could have fore-told.

CHAPTER 42

'THERE'S SOMEONE TO see you, sir!'

'Oh, not Mrs Parry again!' Harry groaned.

'No, sir, it's young Mr Mortimer, him that was Mr Fletcher's best man last year.'

'Well, what are you waiting for, man? Show him in!' Harry was not prepared for the serious expression on the younger man's face but it slowly dawned on him that Chad was supposed to have been in Kent with this man, so why was he here alone?

'I'm so sorry to be the bearer of bad news, Mr Morgan, but I thought it best to come and let you know in person. I'm afraid that Chad is dead.'

'Dead!' It was a moment before Harry found his voice. 'A car accident, was it? He always did drive too fast. My daughter was always complaining about it.'

'Nothing like that, sir. The fact is, he was killed on his way back from Dunkirk. I've only recently got back myself, or I'd have let you know earlier.'

'Dunkirk!' Harry was aware that he was repeating Aubrey's words like an echo, but this was so unexpected. 'You say he went to Dunkirk! I had no idea.'

'Yes, well, I have a boat, you see, so when the call came for volunteers to go over and bring those chaps off the beaches, naturally I had to fall in! Chad said he might as well go along too. He said it would be a bit of a lark. I'm sorry, that's not the right thing to say in view of the circumstances, but I'm only quoting him, you know.

'Well, we made a few sorties and took a few of them back to the ships, and right glad they were to see us, I can tell you. The problem was, we were being strafed from above and that's when poor old Chad bought it.'

'What – er – happened to him? To the body?'

'Oh, he wasn't buried at sea, if that's what you're thinking, sir. He was brought back to England. We just need to know where he's to be sent. I mean, will he be buried here, or in Wiltshire?'

'That's something I'll have to discuss with my daughter. I don't know if you're aware that Meredith gave birth to a baby quite recently. In fact, that's why she stayed at home instead of accompanying Chad on his holiday.'

'Oh, yes, he told me about his boy! Delighted to be a father, of course.'

Harry pulled himself together with an effort. 'I haven't asked you to sit down, Aubrey. You must excuse me; this has come as a dreadful shock, as you can imagine, and how I'm going to break the news to Meredith I just don't know. Look, you'll need a stiff drink after this, I'm sure. Just sit back and I'll ring for Perkins.'

'That's very kind, but I should be on my way. I have a train to catch, if someone will be kind enough to drive me to the station, and I ought to get started.'

'I won't hear of such a thing, my boy! You must have been on the road for hours and you'll be ready to collapse. You'll stay the night, of course, and perhaps for a day or two after that. Meredith will be bound to have questions, once the first shock is over.'

Leaving Aubrey dozing in his chair, Harry went to find Ellen. 'Is there a bed made up somewhere? We have an unexpected guest.'

'Of course. Who is it?'

'Aubrey Mortimer.'

'Chad's best man? That's odd. Wasn't Chad going to stay with him?'

Mariah came bursting in on them. 'Is Chad back? I've just seen his car in the forecourt. Shall I let Meredith know? She was asleep the last time I peeped in, but she'll want to be awake to welcome him home.'

'Sit down, Mariah. You as well, Ellen.'

Mystified, the pair did as they were told. 'Is it the invasion?' Ellen quavered.

Harry patted her shoulder. 'It is bad news, but it's not what you were thinking. You've heard about Dunkirk on the wireless, and seen what the newspapers have to say about it. Well, Chad was there, helping to rescue our gallant men, and I'm afraid he didn't make it back.'

'You mean, he's still in Dunkirk, Harry? Has he been captured?'

'Worse than that, *cariad*. He's been killed.'

Ellen swayed. Just before she lost consciousness she was aware of Harry snapping at Mariah as he ordered her to fetch the smelling salts.

'I'm all right! Take that horrid thing away!'

'Are you sure, Mam? Just take another little sniff, to make sure.'

'I've said I'm all right, haven't I?' Now it was Ellen who was snappy. Mariah sank down on the pouffe, as she tried to digest the awful news. Poor

Meredith, how was she going to take it? Chad was her husband, the father of her child.

'How did Chad's car get home, Mr Morgan?'

'Aubrey Mortimer drove it up from Kent. It was he who brought the news to me. In fact, he was with Chad when he died. At least Meredith can take comfort from that.'

'Where is Aubrey now, then?'

'I left him in my study when I came up here.'

'I'd better go and ask him if he'd like something to eat, then. He may be hungry if he's been on the road all day.'

'That's right, dear, you go and see to things. We'll look after Meredith.'

Aubrey Mortimer jumped to his feet, looking dazed, when Mariah entered the study.

'Oh, Mariah, hello! Did you just come in? I must have dropped off.'

Mariah smiled down at him. She had met him at Meredith's wedding, of course, and had taken an instant liking to him then. 'Are you hungry? I happen to know there's some cold ham in the larder and I could fry some up with an egg or two.'

'What it is to live in the country! Don't you have rationing here? A ham sandwich would do me fine. I could kill for a nice hot cup of tea to go with it!'

'Coming right up!' She smiled. She was soon back with a plate piled high with delicious-looking sandwiches and a pot of tea.

'Good grief! Do you expect me to eat all that?' He could feel his mouth watering.

'You'd better not!' she said, grinning. 'One round of those is meant for me. I could eat a horse!' Sensing that he might not want to talk about the Dunkirk expedition, she cast around for something else to say, and asked him if he was serving in the navy now.

'Good Lord, why on earth would you think that? Oh, I suppose because I can handle a boat. No, I'm in the RAF, actually, training to be a pilot.'

'How thrilling! What sort of aircraft?'

'Hurricanes. I learned to fly them at St Athan's.'

Mariah was impressed. She knew that this was extremely dangerous work.

'How about you?' Aubrey mumbled, through a mouthful of home-baked bread. 'Been called up yet, have you?'

'I've just passed my driving test, so it'll probably be a toss-up between the Women's Land Army and the ATS. Mam would like me to stay here, to grow potatoes. Most of the gardeners have already gone, you see.'

'That would make more sense than carting you off to work on someone else's farm, certainly, but ours is not to reason why, and all that.'

'Do you like it in the Air Force, Aubrey?'

He shrugged. 'It's a bit like being back at school, really. A lot of spit and polish and physical jerks. I'm up in the air most of the time, of course, so it's not too bad.'

A thought struck Mariah then. 'But we thought that Chad was staying with you, and that was why he – um …'

'Why he got roped into the Dunkirk business, you mean? As it happens he just turned up on the off-chance and luckily for him I was at home on sick leave at the time. Busted ribs, after I pranged, you know. It didn't turn out to be so lucky in the end, of course,' he muttered, his voice trailing off suddenly.

Feeling awkward, Mariah got to her feet. 'I'm sure you're tired and longing for your bed, and here am I keeping you talking. We've put you in the blue room, where you stayed the night before the wedding. Can you find your way up?'

He assured her that he could. 'I wonder if they've told Meredith yet?' he asked.

'I'm not sure. They may have decided to let her sleep until morning.'

'I suppose so. Well, good night, Mariah, and thanks for everything.'

'Good night, Aubrey,' she responded, as she watched him climbing the stairs. Every movement he made spoke of weariness and resignation.

Far away at the top of the house there was the thin wail of a baby. Henry had apparently woken up and was demanding to be fed. Poor little chap, she thought. It's a good job he's too young to know what's happened to him.

Would he miss growing up without a father, or would Harry live long enough to be a father figure to him? Of course, in time, Meredith might marry again.

Mariah was beginning to realize just what war meant to families such as theirs. Before it was all over, a great many children would be left fatherless, perhaps orphaned altogether. As it was, families were being torn apart because so many city children were being sent away to live with strangers, for fear of bombs. And what if their mothers, left behind, were killed? What would become of the children then?

She herself was a war baby, and she was a posthumous child, her father having been killed at Ypres. She was lucky to have grown up in this house, with Harry Morgan as a role model. She shuddered to think of what her life might otherwise have been.

CHAPTER 43

THEY HAD EXPECTED Meredith to sob and wail when the news was broken to her, but instead she became unnaturally quiet, hardly speaking for days. It was almost as if she had expected something to happen, and now that she had been proved right she needed time to take it in. When she did speak it was to ask the same questions over and over again. 'Like a stuck record,' Ellen commented.

Aubrey was very patient with her, explaining that death had been instantaneous, and that Chad did not suffer. 'I don't think he even knew what hit him,' he said firmly, staring back at Harry, whose eyes showed disbelief.

'That's good,' Meredith murmured, before lapsing into silence again.

Aubrey had agreed to spend what remained of his leave in Cwmbran, to see them through this difficult time.

'Mother won't mind,' he assured them. 'All in a good cause, what?'

Ellen suspected that the unknown Mrs Mortimer would mind very much, as her son's days might well be numbered, but she held her tongue.

'Is there anything I can do to help?' Aubrey asked, when Meredith had gone back to sleep, curled up in a ball as if she could crawl back into the womb.

'You can come and help me dig for victory,' Mariah told him, quoting the slogan from the posters which were plastered all over the country, along with such admonitions as 'Be like Dad, keep Mum' and 'Careless Talk Costs Lives'.

'Do you enjoy gardening?' Aubrey wanted to know, as they worked side by side in the unending battle against weeds.

'I suppose I do, if you don't count my aching back and blistered hands!' Mariah laughed. 'When we were little – Meredith and me – we were allowed to have a little patch where we grew radishes and nasturtiums. I managed to grow one or two plants but Meredith was too impatient and kept digging things up to see what was happening. Then she got upset because my little plot was successful while hers failed.'

'Oh, dear! So what happened next?'

Mariah laughed again. 'Oh, Mam let her grow mustard and cress on a bit of old flannel and that worked because she saw instant results, but when I had all of six radishes to show, she was quite put out!'

'You two truly are like sisters, Mariah,' Aubrey observed. 'All that sibling rivalry on the outside, when underneath you're as close as two peas in a pod. I'm sure Meredith will be glad of your support now.'

'I expect she will,' Mariah agreed, but she knew they weren't as close to each other as Aubrey believed. They had been born only days apart, and Mam had fostered Meredith almost from birth, yet they'd grown up knowing there was a gulf between them. Meredith was deeply conscious of being Miss Morgan, the daughter of the house and there had been times when she'd twitted Mariah about being 'only Nanny's child'.

'You've got to let me pick first because this is my house,' she'd say, or, 'You can't sit on my Daddy's lap, 'Riah, cos he's my father, not yours.'

Ellen found herself in a dilemma over this. Meredith had to learn to treat other people with respect, but what the child said was true. She could hardly be given a smack for calling Mariah a servant's child, because that was what she was. Only two people knew that the children were half-sisters, and neither wished to enlighten them.

The governess did her best, but she knew how quickly she could lose her job if she wasn't careful, so she erred on the side of favouring Meredith. Not that Mariah minded too much; she was the sort of child who went about happily ignoring anything she didn't choose to hear.

She now came to with a start, realizing that Aubrey was staring at her.

'What's the matter?' she asked, putting a hand up to her face. 'Do I have mud on my nose or something?'

'No, Mariah. You look perfectly beautiful.'

'Oh, don't be silly!' She felt the blush spreading over her face and neck.

'I'm not! You are beautiful, Mariah, whether you realize it or not. Look, I have to go away tomorrow, but I don't want to do that without saying something to you first.'

'It's all right, Aubrey; I've already promised to keep an eye on Meredith.'

'No, it's not that. Let me speak, will you? I've enjoyed these past few days we've had together, and I'd like us to keep in touch. There isn't anyone else, is there?'

'No, there's nobody else.'

'Then may I write to you, Mariah?'

She suddenly knew that if she never saw him again, the world would have lost some of its brightness. She had never been in love, yet now the feeling that burst over her was like the sun coming out after the rain, complete with a glorious rainbow.

'I've enjoyed being with you, too,' she told him, 'and if you write to me, I'll certainly answer your letters. Not that I'll have anything exciting to say. It'll just be a progress report on how well the garden is doing!'

Looking down from an upstairs window, Meredith frowned at the sight of Mariah being kissed by the handsome Aubrey Mortimer. A wave of fury swept over her as she watched them, knowing she shouldn't be spying on them but unable to turn away.

It wasn't fair! She had lost her husband before they'd even reached their first anniversary. Why should Mariah have a man dancing attendance on her now? She didn't need Aubrey, not like Meredith needed to have Chad here at her side. And Aubrey had come here to see her, not Ellen's daughter! Of course she didn't look at Aubrey in 'that way' but he was a link with Chad and she'd welcomed his sympathetic conversation and kind interest in her baby son. Why, she'd even considered inviting him to stand godfather to the child.

When Aubrey left the next day she refused to go downstairs to see him off, pleading exhaustion. It was Mariah who drove him to the railway station – in Chad's car, if you please! – and Harry, no doubt sensing which way the wind was blowing, declined to go along, leaving the pair together.

When Mariah returned, looking bleak, Meredith couldn't resist putting the knife in.

'What's the matter with you? You've got a face like a wet week!'

Mariah looked at her in surprise. How did the girl expect her to look? Biting back an indignant retort, she went in search of her mother, whom she found in her sitting room, cradling baby Henry on her lap.

'Meredith's in a foul mood,' she complained. 'She just about bit my head off just now, Mam, and I'm sure I haven't done a thing to upset her.'

'You'll have to make allowances, *cariad*. She's just had a baby and her hormones are all over the place, and on top of that she's lost her husband. It's better if she flies off the handle once in a while, rather than sinking into depression.'

'I suppose so. How long did it take you to get over Dad's death?'

'Quite a while,' Ellen muttered, her eyes going to Bertie's photograph. 'But I had you to take care of, and then Meredith as well, and that kept me busy. This little chap will be a consolation to his mother, won't you, my darling?' She bent down to kiss the baby on his fuzzy little head. 'Aubrey got off all right, did he?'

'Yes, although the train was late, and then when it did come it was packed out.'

'You really like him, don't you?'

'How can you tell?'

Ellen laughed. 'I'm your mother, aren't I?' And no more was said.

True to his word, Aubrey wrote at once, and when Perkins came into the breakfast room, carrying the post on a silver salver, Mariah got up from the table and snatched up the blue envelope before anyone else had the chance to look at it.

'Anything for me?' Meredith asked. She had just started coming downstairs after keeping to her boudoir for days, taking her meals on trays.

'Quite a few, by the look of it,' Harry said, passing a small bundle to her.

'One from Grandmother, one from Mrs Fletcher, and I suppose these are all expressions of condolence. You'll have to reply to those, Mariah, I can't face it.'

'I'll be glad to help if I can, but I'm not prepared to write to your grandmother, or to Chad's poor mother. You'll have to do that yourself.'

'Quite right, too,' Harry interjected. 'Having Mariah do it would not be the thing at all, and you know that very well, my girl.'

'To hell with etiquette!' Meredith snapped, earning a surprised look from her father. 'I've just lost my husband! Why can't you people understand that!'

'And Verona Fletcher has just lost her only son,' Harry reminded her gently. 'Try to imagine how she must be feeling. You're a mother yourself now, you know.'

Meredith said nothing, but after her father left the table she turned a sour glance on Mariah, who had remained quiet during this exchange.

'I suppose that's a letter from Aubrey you shoved in your pocket.'

'I don't know; I haven't opened it yet.'

'If you take my advice, you won't answer it.'

'Why ever not? You can write to him too, if you want to. He'll be pleased to hear from friends while he's stuck in that camp, living in a draughty Nissen hut.'

'I can't be bothered. Nor should you. He's only going to get himself killed in this rotten war and then you'll wish you'd never set eyes on him. Believe me, I know!'

'Oh, Meredith!' Mariah reached over to take her friend's hand, but the other girl rushed out of the room before another word could be spoken.

Mariah wiped away a tear. Yes, it was highly possible that something would happen to Aubrey, buzzing around in his small, vulnerable aircraft, but she couldn't let that stop her loving him.

CHAPTER 44

THE BATTLE OF BRITAIN had begun. The valiant men of the Royal Air Force began the fight in the air which would ultimately help to decide Britain's fate. Mariah shuddered to think of what Aubrey must be going through, and she refused to contemplate Meredith's horrid prophecy that he wouldn't come safely through the war.

True to his word, Aubrey wrote to Mariah on a regular basis – cheerful, funny letters which said little about the horrors he must be witnessing every day. When his crew were not in the air they were playing football, or listening to the gramophone in the hut. One of his friends had just bought a new record by Vera Lynn, the Forces' Sweetheart, but was foolish enough to leave it on a chair, where it was smashed when someone sat down on it.

He complained that the food was awful, but at least there was plenty of it, and they were always given a good feed of bacon and eggs when they returned from a mission. Mariah tried to think of amusing stories to tell him in return, but she couldn't find much to say. Rabbits had terrorized the garden and she'd had to plant the lettuce again; she was thinking of getting a guard dog to frighten them off. Hardly deathless news.

'Mr Morgan has joined the Home Guard and is in charge of a detachment. They've had to stop ringing the bells at All Saints, because they're supposed to use them to warn us when the invasion happens.' Biting her lip, she crossed out 'when', replacing it with 'if'. Harry insisted that no defeatist talk was allowed.

'My men have to go from door to door collecting any maps that people may have,' Harry announced. 'We're supposed to have a bonfire so that potential spies and fifth columnists can't get hold of them. A lot of nonsense, really. I'm quite sure that the Huns would have collected all the maps they need long ago.'

All road signs had to be removed. The sign at the railway station was blacked out. All this was meant to slow down the advance of the enemy if the invasion did in fact take place. It certainly did not affect the locals, but it did lead to one amusing incident.

A Canadian soldier on leave had borrowed a bicycle and pedalled his way to the district, hoping to look up relatives. His grandparents had emigrated to Canada but had often spoken of cousins left behind, with whom they had lost touch. Homesick, and far away from his family, this Brian Watkins had decided to try to trace his Welsh kin.

'Here! Where do you think you're off to, then?' Watkins dismounted from his machine at the sight of the burly farmer wearing an arm band which identified him as a member of the Home Guard. The man carried an ancient shotgun under his arm. It looked as if it might be a relic of the last war, but lethal enough, in its way.

'I'm looking for Pen y Bryn Farm.'

'You're going in the wrong direction, then, boyo!'

Watkins scratched his head. 'I guess I am. I must have been going round in circles, on account of you folks taking all the signs down.'

'You'll have to do better than that, man! Looking for the colliery, were you?'

'I don't know nothing about that. I'm looking for cousins of mine, name of Watkins.' The gun was moved into a more suitable position for firing.

'Here, what's the matter with you, mister? Can't you see my uniform? We're supposed to be on the same side!'

Fortunately Harry Morgan happened to be driving by at that moment, and was able to sort the matter out. 'Have a bit of sense, man!' he said brusquely. 'Save your belligerence for the Hun, if he comes.'

'Only doing my duty, sir! And it worried me, him saying he was looking for people called Watkins. That was my wife's name before she married me, see?'

'And that's my name, too!' Brian grinned. 'Your wife and me could be related!'

While small incidents such as that were cause for a toast or two in the Red Dragon that evening, other things gave untold grief. Civilians were drawn into the war as never before in history. The bombs were beginning to rain down on British cities, partly to destroy vital installations such as docks, air fields and factories, but also to break down morale among the people.

'Swansea got it again last night,' Harry remarked, looking up from his newspaper.

'So did poor old Cardiff,' Ellen said, sad to think of the city of her childhood going up in flames. 'I hope St John's church doesn't get it. It was built back in Norman times. It's wicked to think it's lasted all this time, only to be destroyed now.'

'Perhaps it won't happen, Ellen. It's the docks they'll be going for. And don't you fear, we're giving them as good as we get. If they believe we're going to let them do their worst without retaliating, they're in for a big surprise!'

The raids continued. They were particularly bad in London, where people took refuge underground every night, not knowing what they'd find when they emerged into the daylight the next morning.

'Imagine having to go down the tube every night,' Ellen muttered. 'It must be awful having to sleep on a station platform. At least we have our cellars here where we can go if the worst comes to the worst.' She was beginning to feel guilty because so far no enemy aircraft had been sighted over Cwmbran.

It was in early July that something happened to rock Ellen's world, so terrible that a bomb falling on the house would have seemed mild by comparison. And it all came about because she had shown kindness to an orphan boy in the past.

John Stephens had come to them as a trainee footman, shortly before the outbreak of war. She felt sorry for him because his father had been killed in the Great War, and in an excess of grief his mother had gone and drowned herself. Left alone in the world, young John had been taken into an orphanage, where he'd remained until he was old enough to be sent out to work. After an unhappy stint as a boot boy in a large house, he'd been recommended to Harry as a willing worker, and he'd come to Cwmbran.

She and John took to each other at once. He particularly liked to look at her photo of Bertie, stroking it gently and asking questions.

'P'raps my Dad looked a bit like this, Mrs Richards. In his uniform, I mean.'

'I expect he did, John.'

'I wish I had a picture of him. I bet my Mam had one, but I don't know what happened to her things. I was only two when I went to the orphanage, see.'

'Never mind, John. I'm sure he was a father to be proud of. I expect he fought bravely, just like my Bertie.'

Inspired by this mental image, John was determined to follow in his father's footsteps and nobody was surprised when he announced he was giving notice.

'I'm joining up, see. They say if you go now you can pick which regiment to join.'

'We'll be sorry to lose you,' Harry told him, 'but we're proud of you, Stephens. You'll come back and see us when you get some leave, won't you?'

'Of course he will!' Ellen smiled. 'This is your home now, John.'

And that casual remark, which meant so much to the lonely young man, proved to be her undoing.

'I just came in through the kitchen, Mam,' Mariah announced. 'It's so freezing cold out there I had to leave the turnips and come in for a warm. Guess who's there? John Stephens, and he's brought a friend with him.'

'On leave, are they? Go and fetch them up. I'd like to hear how he's doing.'

John bounded into the room. Reaching forward to give him a welcoming hug, Ellen looked over his shoulder at the dark-haired man standing behind him. He looked vaguely familiar, but she couldn't think where she might have seen him before.

'Mrs Richards? This is my mate, Mal Williams, from Cardiff.'

Williams? All at once the years dropped away and she thought of Mari, the friend of her youth. Maldwyn! Hadn't that been the name of the littlest brother, the baby?

'And look, this was Mrs Richards' husband.' John had crossed the room and picked up the photo before Ellen could stop him. 'He was in the army, just like my Dad.'

Mal took the photo and looked at it, and then at Ellen. He frowned. 'Bertie Richards wasn't married, I know that for a fact!' Over by the window, Mariah gasped.

'What would you know about it?' John scoffed.

'Plenty. I was just a nipper when he was killed, but he was a mate of my oldest brother. Before they left they went to a studio and had their pictures taken. Bertie gave a copy to our Mam, see, and she kept it on the mantelpiece. To remember him by, she said, cos he got himself killed, over at Wipers.'

'You've got it wrong,' John protested again. 'Of course he was married. I've told you, this is his wife, Mrs Richards. Widow, I mean. I've known her ever since I came to work here.'

Ellen gulped. The cat was out of the bag with a vengeance. Of course, Mal hadn't yet put two and two together. He'd been too young when she'd left to recognize her now but in a minute he'd be wanting to know how she'd come by the photo, and why she was pretending to be Bertie's wife. She pulled herself together with an effort.

'It's been lovely seeing you again, John, and you as well, Mal. I'm sorry we can't spend any more time together but I have a great deal to do. It's this war, you know; we're short-handed in the house and that makes more work for everyone.'

CHAPTER 45

'**M**AM! IS THIS **true**?'
Ellen swivelled round to where Mariah was standing, white with shock. She felt utter despair, but there was no avoiding the confrontation which was coming now.

'Is what true?'

'What that Mal just said, that you and Dad weren't married!' There was a long silence while Mariah went over various scenarios in her mind. A young couple, desperately in love, had given in to their passion when Bertie was about to be sent to the front. The pair would have been married sooner or later, but unfortunately he had never returned and Ellen was left alone to bear their child. It was beautiful, really; like many another poor soul, she had lost the love of her life yet she did have their baby for consolation, just as Meredith did now that Chad was gone.

'Yes, I suppose it is.' Ellen said at last. 'We were not married, I'm afraid.'

'Then why do you call yourself Richards? And why is that my name, too?'

'I've every right to that name, Mariah. Bertie was my brother, you see, so I was born a Richards. I truly didn't set out to deceive anyone. It happened by accident. Someone saw that photo and jumped to the conclusion that Bertie was my husband and myself a war widow. It seemed easier all round to let it continue. I'd left Cardiff by that time and I thought it would never come out that I'd got myself into trouble.'

'Oh, Mam!'

'I did it for you, really,' Ellen pleaded. 'People can be so cruel and I didn't want you to suffer for my mistake. Cardiff is a long way away. How was I to know that Mari's brother would turn up and blow the whole story apart?'

'How dare you!'

They shot round to see Meredith framed in the doorway, her bosom heaving. 'You're nothing but a loose woman, *Miss* Richards! How could you bring your illegitimate child into a decent household like this, pulling the wool over my father's eyes? Oh, you knew what you were doing, all right! She was brought up here in luxury, given an education and everything that money could buy! And to think my father treated her like a princess! Every time I was given a new frock, or a new toy, dear Mariah had the same! It makes me sick to think of it. Why, she's nothing but a little—'

'Meredith! That will do!' Ellen snapped, and years of obeying Nanny came into play and Meredith closed her mouth. Meredith's indignation could be smoothed over later. It was Mariah's feelings which had to be considered now.

Harry had been halfway up the stairs when the two young soldiers came rushing down, almost pushing him into the banisters.

'Here, steady on, lads! Where are you off to in such a hurry?'

'Sorry, Mr Morgan, sir! We have to get going!'

'But aren't you staying for a night or two? That's what I was given to understand.'

'Sorry, sir! Got to get back to camp!' They ran out through the front door.

Harry blinked. For one wild moment he thought that the invasion had started and that all leave was cancelled, but that was ridiculous. He'd been listening to the wireless and had heard nothing. Surely there would have been an immediate interruption to regular transmission if the German army had landed!

He reached the housekeeper's suite in time to hear his daughter's strident tones.

'I do think we're owed an explanation, Nanny! If Bertie Richards isn't Mariah's father, are you going to tell us who is?'

'That's between Mariah and me, Meredith. This is really none of your business.'

'Oh, isn't it! Then I'll make it my business, and the first person I'm going to tell is my father, and I doubt very much if he'll want either of you to stay here after this. You've lived here all this time under false pretences. You can't be trusted. For all we know you could be skimming money off the household accounts, feathering your own nest at our expense. Oh, yes, my father will hear of this, make no mistake about that!'

'Meredith.' Harry's voice was low. Ellen's hand flew to her mouth, while Mariah appeared to have been turned to stone. 'If you're so keen to know who Mariah's father is, I'll tell you.'

'Harry, no!' Ellen's voice was filled with pain, but he ignored her.

'I'm Mariah's father, Meredith. She is your sister.'

'No! I don't believe you!' Tears of fury spurted from Meredith's eyes.

'That's your privilege, but like it or not it's the truth.'

'I hate you! I never want to see you again!' She fled from the room and they heard a door slam. Mariah stood still for a few seconds and then she, too, left the room.

'Well, you've done it now, Harry! Look at me, I'm shaking like a leaf. All this has been such a shock, and those poor girls must be feeling even worse. I do wish you hadn't blurted it out like this.'

'I suppose I might have chosen my words with more care,' he admitted, 'but when I heard Meredith spitting out all that venom I was disgusted with her. Perhaps it's all for the best, though. We should have come clean years ago. Then they'd have taken it in their stride.'

'What, admit that I'd borne your child, when your mother-in-law was seldom off the doorstep? A fine scandal that would have made!'

'Water under the bridge, Ellen. How did all this get started, anyway?'

'Oh, it was that chum of young John's. It turns out he's a brother of my old friend, Mari. He recognized Bertie from his photo and let slip that Bertie had never been married. They realized he'd put his foot in it somehow and ran off, but by then the damage was done. Mariah wanted to know what it was all about, and I had to explain. What was I supposed to say? Would she have believed me if I'd denied it? We've told so many lies over the years, Harry, and it had to stop.'

'And then Meredith overheard, and put her oar in! I don't know my own daughter any more, Ellen. She's become so spiteful and bitter in the past few months.'

'She's just lost her husband, you know.'

'Yes, but that's no excuse for mouthing insults like a fishwife! And while we're about it, I have to say that I rue the day I invited Chad Fletcher here! He's turned her into a snob, and that certainly isn't how she was brought up.'

'Don't be too hard on her,' Ellen said softly. 'Try to remember she's just learned that her beloved father has done something she won't be able to forgive in a hurry.'

'Go away! I don't want to talk to you!' The words struck Harry to the heart. He opened the door and went in, to find Meredith huddled in an armchair with her knees drawn up. The look she cast at him was one of pure hatred.

'We mustn't leave it like this,' he told her. 'I'm your father.'

'Then it's a pity you didn't act like it!' she countered.

'Haven't I always been a good father to you? Many a girl would have given anything to be brought up like you, with everything your heart could desire. You've been spoiled, probably.'

'You sound just like Nanny when we were little. "Eat up your crusts. Many a starving child in China would love to have them." How could you, Daddy? Isn't it bad enough that you betrayed my mother, without bringing your mistress into the house?'

'Ellen is not my mistress, nor has she ever been. What happened between us was a mistake, although I can never regret the fact that Mariah came of that. Had your mother not died when she did, I would never have brought Ellen into the house.'

'So you say!'

'Look here, Meredith! This has been an enormous shock to you, I know, but I hope that when you've had time to reflect you'll be able to understand. Ellen and I did not set out to do harm to Antonia, and that you must believe.'

Meredith made no reply. He had the urge to shake her until her teeth rattled, so he clenched his hands inside his pockets in order to gain control of his temper. Seeing that there was nothing he could do to bring her round, he left, closing the door behind him. He remained still for a moment but then, hearing a muffled sob, he walked quickly away. Time would have to do its healing work.

Still feeling stunned, Mariah hurried out to the garden and took up a hoe, but she could not settle to the work. She went to the stable and saddled up Black Bess, and took the animal out on the road at a fast pace. It was a firm rule that one did not gallop the horses on hard ground, but Bess was willing enough to break into a canter and soon they had left the estate and were heading out into the countryside. The cold air stung Mariah's cheeks, and she wished she'd put on a headscarf, to protect her ears.

So Harry Morgan was her father! It was hard to take in. So many times during her childhood she'd wished fervently that he was her father, and then been plagued by guilt out of loyalty to poor dead Bertie Richards. And now this! Did this mean that her idol now had feet of clay? She decided it didn't. She was in love herself and had learned that life was not just black and white.

Then there was Mam. It was all very sad, really; just one mistake and Ellen must have been paying for it ever since.

What would happen now? Surely the servants had heard something of the kerfuffle upstairs and would have been asking questions. How would they behave if the tale came out? Harry wasn't likely to say anything, but Meredith might! Then what?

CHAPTER 46

'COME QUICK, MISS! There's a trunk call!'
'Thank you, Polly. I'll come at once.'

Polly's head disappeared inside the window and, hastily wiping her dirty hands on her already grimy britches, Mariah hurried towards the house, hoping it might be Aubrey at the other end.

'Can you hear me?' he bellowed. 'This line is awful. You keep fading out.'

'Yes, yes. What's up?'

'I've managed to wangle a forty-eight-hour pass this coming weekend. I'm hoping we can get together.'

Mariah's heart leapt. 'How? You couldn't get here and back in the time.'

'No, but you could come to London.'

'London!'

'Yes, I know it's short notice, but I've a mate whose mother lives there and she'll put you up. What do you say?'

'Well, um, yes, I suppose I could, if the trains are still running.'

'Terrific! Look, I'll send you a letter with the arrangements, OK?'

Mariah tried to say something but the pips went, and she was left holding a dead phone. It would be wonderful to see Aubrey again at last, but the difficulty would lie in trying to persuade her mother that it was all right to go.

As she had expected, this wasn't easy.

'Oh, no, you can't do that!' Ellen was shocked.

'It's all right, Mam! I shan't be going to a hotel. A friend of Aubrey's has a mother in London, and I'll be cuckooing with her.'

'I wasn't thinking along those lines,' Ellen replied primly. 'It's so dangerous there right now, with the blitz going on. You might be killed!'

'We can't spend our lives worrying about what might possibly happen, Mam!'

'But I do worry, and so does any mother with any sense. I'm not forbidding you to go, but I do urge you to consider it very carefully.'

'I have done, Mam!' (For all of thirty seconds, Mariah reminded herself.) 'I've told Aubrey I'll be there, and wild horses can't stop me.'

'Oh, very well then!' Ellen said crossly. 'And don't blame me if you get killed!'

'Is your journey really necessary?' a stern-faced man, shown on a poster on the station wall, demanded to know. Mariah had been prepared to cycle down to the station but Harry had insisted on driving her.

'Are you all right for money?' he asked, as he drew up outside the station.

'Yes, thank you, Mr Morgan.'

'You'd better take this, anyway,' he told her, as he passed her some folded bank notes. 'And isn't it time you called me Daddy, or Father, or something?'

She smiled, but said nothing. She was beginning to come to terms with the changed view of her parentage, but the idea of calling him Dad to his face was something else. A distant plume of smoke told her that the train was on its way. 'Thanks for bringing me. I'd better go now. See you soon!'

London was a shock. It was one thing to read about the bombing raids in the newspapers but to see the devastation at first hand horrified her. Whole streets had been reduced to heaps of rubble, while in others parts of houses and shops were still left standing. She gazed up at one house which had lost its front wall. The furniture was still in place, including a framed picture hanging drunkenly on the back wall. It looked for all the world like a dolls' house, the kind where the whole front swung open.

The people she passed on the streets seemed cheerful enough, exchanging quips as they queued for buses which never seemed to arrive. How many of them had already lost everything, she wondered, or suffered bereavement? Yet there was a spirit of determination in the air, as if the bombing had only served to breed defiance in these Londoners. Mr Churchill's words, promising the British people blood, sweat and tears, were being put into action. Mariah squared her shoulders and hurried on.

'You got here, then,' her hostess greeted her. 'I'm Mrs Cairns, of course. Your young man is serving with my boy. Do come inside, dear. I've got the kettle on. It's never far off the boil, if the truth be known. Let's give you a hand with that case. My goodness, what you got in here, the crown jewels? Weighs a ton, it does!'

'Mam sent a few things,' Mariah explained. 'A pound of butter and part of a ham. I could have brought eggs, except I was afraid they'd get crushed on the train.'

'That'll be a treat, I'm sure. P'raps I should get myself evacuated to the country like all the kiddies from around here.'

It dawned on Mariah then that she'd seen very few children on her way here, but she'd assumed that they'd all be in school at this time of day.

'Sit down, take the weight off your feet, Miss Richards.'

'Mariah, please.'

'Pretty name, that. Always fancied that myself, but I got stuck with Ethel instead.' She pronounced it as Effoo. After the musical voices of the Cwmbran people, Mariah found the East End dialect hard to understand.

'My hubby's in the army,' Ethel announced proudly. 'Served in the last war as well, he did, so they've made him a sergeant now. What do your parents do?'

'Mam's housekeeper in a big house.' Mariah carefully omitted any mention of a father, but fortunately Ethel was chattering on and didn't notice.

'Ah! I was in service myself, before I was married. There's not many going in for that now, though. All the girls is making munitions or being Wrens and that. Things is going to be different once this war's over. Still, they said that after the last war, didn't they, and what happened when the chaps got home? Mass unemployment, with officers selling shoelaces and matches on the street. Ah, it's a funny old world!'

Thankfully sipping her tea, Mariah was taken aback when Ethel said something about her being engaged to Aubrey.

'Oh, I don't know about that,' she began.

Ethel chuckled. 'Let the cat out of the bag, have I? Why d'you suppose your young man's fetched you all the way down here from Wales? That's what my lad told me, anyway. "Can you put her up, Mum, he says, cos my mate Aubrey's going to pop the question, and he don't want her staying in no stuffy hotel what charges the earth."'

'I see,' Mariah said faintly.

'I hope I haven't spoken out of turn, Mariah, but it's just as well to be prepared, ain't it? Then you can work out what to say when the time comes. Now, you are going to say yes, ain't you? You'd never have come all this way in the middle of a war if you weren't soft on the chap!'

Mariah had read any number of magazine stories and she knew how proposals should be made, preferably by candlelight while soft music played. Nothing had prepared her for the offer of marriage which Aubrey blurted out while they were eating beans on toast in a Lyons Corner House.

'I say,' he said suddenly, putting down his knife and fork, 'I was going to wait until later, but I can't hold back any longer. I'm mad about you, Mariah. What I mean is, I love you. Let's get married!'

'What, now?' She half expected him to reach into his pocket and whip out a special licence, but he did nothing of the sort.

'No, but on my next leave. What do you say? You do love me, don't you?'

'Of course I do. With all my heart!'

He reached across the table, taking her hands in his. 'Then we'll start making plans, won't we! Gosh, this is the happiest day of my life!'

'Aubrey, there's something I have to tell you. There's something you ought to know about me.'

His face fell. 'What is it? Don't tell me you're already married!'

His expression was so comical that she had to laugh. 'No, of course not! It's nothing like that.'

'Then what?'

'I can't say anything here. Let's go for a walk and I'll explain everything.'

This wasn't going to be easy. He had to know about her parentage, but some men were funny about things like that. It was best to sort it out now. At last, when they were sitting on a park bench, under a tree dripping with moisture from a recent rain, she managed to find the words to tell him.

'It's about my father, Aubrey.'

'Yes, what about him?'

She took a deep breath. 'You've seen that photo of Mam's, haven't you?'

'Of course. Go on.'

'Well, Bertie Richards was my uncle. Mam wasn't married when she had me, and when people thought she was a war widow she went along with that, to protect me.'

Aubrey shrugged. 'It happens, Mariah. I'd never hold that against you.'

'Wait. There's more. I've recently found out who my real father is. It's Harry Morgan, Aubrey. He's the man Mam was in love with.'

CHAPTER 47

ELLEN HAD GONE to call on Megan. Her friend had recently welcomed her first grandchild, and was eager to show him off to Ellen.

'Here he is, then! This is young Dewi! Isn't he a lovely lad?'

Ellen had to agree that the child was indeed a fine specimen of babyhood. He already had a thatch of dark hair and was as chubby as could be.

'Weighed eight pounds nine ounces at birth, he did!' Megan exclaimed proudly. 'What do you make of that, then, Ellen?'

'He's lovely, Megan.'

'That's what I told old Mrs Proctor down the street. "It's not right to bring a child into the world at a time like this," the old cat said. And I came right back and said that babies bring joy with them, and we can all do with a bit of that when there's a war on.'

'Good for you! Listen, Megan, what's going on with that Mrs Parry? You know, the one who married that deserter in the last war.'

'She's still around Cwmbran, large as life. Why do you want to know?'

'Oh, she caused a bit of trouble a few months back. She came to the house, wanting Mr Morgan to do something to keep her boy out of the war. Trevor, I think his name is. Of course, Mr Morgan could do nothing of the sort.'

'Oh, that's Bron all over. Never interested in anyone else's problems, just as long as she gets her own way. Well, she didn't exactly get it this time.'

'What do you mean? Has he been called up?'

'Na, na. Gone down the pit. A reserved occupation, see. They can't make him go anywhere now.'

'Then what was all the fuss about?'

'Her father was killed down the pit, and her brother works there too. Bron swore she'd never let her boy do the same. In the end it was a case of choosing between two evils. At least she has him close to home these days.'

'Well, I'm glad it worked out for young Trevor, although I can't say the same for our poor Meredith. Her father blames himself for having advised

Chad to take himself off for a bit. If he'd kept quiet it might have ended differently.'

Little Dewi began to fuss and Megan turned him over to check his nappy. 'Nothing the matter there, young man, and you've been fed, so you can just go back to sleep!' She began to rock him in her arms.

'*Huna, blentyn, ar fy mynwes ...*' she crooned. 'There, he's off again. That was a bad do, all right, people saying how anyone with money and connections can avoid the call-up. Mind you, it never was as nasty as Bron tried to make out. A bit of mumbling and grumbling but they never would have acted on it. Too many of them want to keep their jobs, and if Mr Morgan turned nasty they'd have found themselves being shipped off to the war in no time.'

'I wonder what they're saying about Chad now?'

'Oh, he's a hero, of course! The idea of civilians going over to Dunkirk in all those little boats has captured their imagination.'

'Mariah's young man was there, too,' Ellen said proudly.

'Isn't he in the RAF?'

'Yes, but he was home on sick leave. Apparently he enjoys messing about in boats, so that was how he and Chad joined in the rescue effort.'

'How is Mariah now? Worried about him doing all that flying, I suppose.'

'Actually she's with him now. He has a forty-eight-hour pass, and she's gone to London, to meet him there. She's staying with a friend's mother,' Ellen added hastily, in case Megan should get the wrong idea.

'I suppose we'll be hearing wedding bells one of these days, then.' Megan smiled, thinking as she spoke that it was a silly expression. The chapel she attended didn't go in for bells, and All Saints, where presumably Mariah would tie the knot, was forbidden to ring them for the duration.

'I don't know if he's popped the question yet. In one way I hope he hasn't. When I see the way poor Meredith is moping about, I couldn't wish to see my girl go through the same thing.'

'But if he does get killed, she'll grieve just as much whether they've been married or not,' Megan pointed out.

'Maybe so, but at least she won't get left with a little one to bring up!'

Megan held little Dewi more closely, smiling tenderly at his sweet face. 'At least this one's dada is working down the pit, Ellen. That's something to be thankful for.'

Time to change the subject, Ellen thought. 'Whatever became of that young woman who moved in here after I left? Daisy, wasn't that her name? She was Mrs Morgan's lady's maid, as I recall. I haven't thought about her for years.'

'Oh, her! Living next door to that one was a real trial, I can tell you! Always moaning on about how Bron had stolen the love of her life, although by what I could make out that Parry chap had only been using her. She felt even more evil towards Bron, of course! She'd married him and given birth to his son, hadn't she?'

'So what about Daisy?'

'Oh, that was the funny part. She did get married in the end, and guess who the chap is? Glyn Pugh, Bron's brother.'

'Never!'

Megan nodded. 'A friend of Daisy's brother, Sid Powell. That's how they came together. And for a while, until they could afford a place of their own, the pair of them had to live with Glyn's mother. Imagine them being under the same roof as Bron and her infant! Poetic justice, I call that.'

Walking home, Ellen made up her mind to support Mariah to the full, no matter what her decision might be. So when her daughter flew into the house, her face radiant, Ellen was able to congratulate her in all sincerity.

'And when is it to be, this wedding?'

'When Aubrey's next leave comes up.'

'That won't leave us much time to prepare, will it?'

'We don't want a big do, Mam. There's a war on, after all. People aren't splashing out on marquees and orchestras as they did before the war.'

'I suppose not,' Ellen said sadly. Meredith's wedding had been a splendid affair, and Harry had promised that when the time came Mariah's should also be a day to remember. Ellen had dreamed of seeing her daughter floating down the aisle in a creation of snowy-white lace or satin, wearing a filmy veil on her curls, secured by traditional orange blossoms. Still, outward trappings were not important.

'There's only one thing, Mam.' Mariah hesitated, not sure how to phrase what she had to say without giving offence. 'I felt I had to tell Aubrey that I'm, well …'

'Illegitimate?' Ellen finished. She felt her face turn hot with shame.

'Oh, Mam! I didn't mean to hurt you. It's just I felt there shouldn't be any secrets between us. Better for him to find out now, than later.'

'Quite right.'

'And then I had to tell him who my real father is. Meredith would have said something, if nobody else did.'

'I see.'

'He said it didn't make a bit of difference to him,' Mariah went on. 'He loves me, and that's all there is to it. He went quiet for a bit, and when I wanted to know what was on his mind, he said it was a pity Mr Morgan hadn't married you years ago and recognized me publicly as his daughter. Then we'd have been known as Miss Mariah and Miss Meredith, instead of Miss Meredith and the nanny's girl.'

'Oh!' Ellen was taken aback. Did etiquette mean so much to Aubrey, then? Of course he was from a different background, and had gone to Eton. He might not care about these things now, but would they come between him and Mariah in the future?

Mariah seemed to know what was on her mother's mind. 'No worries on that score, Mam! He was only thinking of me, but it did make me wonder. Mr Morgan was free to marry again after Meredith's mother died. Did you never think of getting married then?'

Ellen thought back to the naïve young girl she'd been. How at first she'd thought the same thing, that Harry would propose to her after the mourning period was over. That hope had died a natural death when he'd made no move to approach her again, and after that she'd been only too glad to be offered a paid position in the house so she could be near him. And, if she was honest with herself, because she dreaded being sent out into the world to fend for herself.

Mariah was cut from different cloth. If ever things didn't work out for her, she'd go out into the world without a qualm, full of confidence, and would make a place for herself. Even Meredith might not be capable of that.

'I suppose it crossed my mind once or twice, but Harry never gave me any indication that it might be possible, and I said nothing because I didn't want to rock the boat, as they say. It was different in my day, Mariah. Women weren't expected to be too forward. They were supposed to let the men make all the decisions then.'

'It's about time things changed, then!' Mariah said firmly.

CHAPTER 48

THE AUTUMN BROUGHT continual bad tidings, and it became a nightly ritual for Harry and the rest of the household to gather together to listen to the nine o'clock news carried by the BBC Home Service. German U-boats were still attacking merchant ships in the Atlantic, and air raids were intensifying.

Lithuania, Latvia and Estonia had been taken by the Soviet army during the summer, and the Italians, who had already occupied British territory in East Africa, invaded Egypt in September. Neither country meant to stop at that, and when the news broke that a pact had been signed by Germany, Italy and Japan, it became obvious that the evil tentacles of war were becoming extremely widespread. Mariah thought of the enemy as a giant octopus, reaching out in an attempt to grasp them.

To everyone's surprise, the invasion did not come. What could be going on in Hitler's devious mind? Did he expect that the stress of waiting would drive everyone to the point where they would capitulate without resistance when his jack-booted men eventually marched on to British soil? If he did, then he was sadly mistaken. Everyone, from the smallest Scout to the oldest member of the Home Guard or the overalled ladies who manned the station canteens, was determined to fight to the last breath.

The year 1941 offered little hope that the war would soon be over. Swansea was so badly bombed in March that the decision was made to evacuate children to safer parts of the country.

'We can take six here,' Ellen assured the billeting officer. 'All the same sex, if possible, because of sleeping accommodation.'

'I shouldn't have thought that would matter, in a house this size, madam,' the woman remarked, looking around her in some awe.

'It's not a question of size. After what these children have already gone through, they'll be feeling frightened and alone. If they can share a room with other children they know, they may not feel so bad.'

'And they may cause an uproar every night!' the woman retorted, but she didn't have time to argue. She carefully wrote down 'six' on her clipboard and went away.

Six scruffy small boys were duly delivered to the door. 'Cor, this place is bigger than the orph'nage!' one declared.

'What orphanage?' Mariah asked.

'Our orph'nage, where we come from, of course! Matron made us pray every night that them Jerries wouldn't drop a bomb on us in the night, only we asked God to wipe out the orph'nage and the school. Not when we was in it, of course.'

'You little tinker!' Mariah laughed.

After the first shyness had worn off, the boys set off to explore, and she could see she'd better set some ground rules forthwith, before an accident happened. Two of them were already sliding down the banisters with shouts of glee, causing Harry to peer out of his study to see what was going on.

'Who are you, mister?'

'This is my house, young man, and I'm also in charge of the local division of the Home Guard, so you'd better be ready to salute when you see me coming! And if you're going to stay here you'll have to play your part in the war effort, is that clear? You'll be helping Miss Richards in the garden, and we can use some spare bodies to assist with the paper drive. Is that understood?'

'Yes, sir!' The replies were heartfelt and immediate. If there was one thing their stay in the 'orph'nage' had drilled into them, it was respect for authority and Harry had all the bearing of a military commander.

'How about lending a hand with our evacuees?' Ellen asked Meredith, but she might as well have been talking to the wall.

'I've got Henry to take care of, and I'm so tired all the time! Please don't ask me to do anything else on top of that!'

The monthly nurse had left long ago. There was a very capable little maid in the nursery, and Ellen had been doing as much as she could to relieve Meredith, but enough was enough.

'Henry's been sleeping through the night for simply ages. He's a dear little chap, not a bit of trouble. Surely you can manage to pitch in and help!' Ellen then made the mistake of pointing out that most women not only looked after their own children, but they also did all the cooking and cleaning in their homes as well.

'Some women don't have any choice. I do, Nanny. What are servants for? Daddy pays them, doesn't he?' The implication was clear. Daddy paid Ellen a wage so she had no business ordering the lady of the house about.

*

'Has Meredith agreed to darn the boys' socks?' Mariah wanted to know. 'I really have more than I can handle, and so do you, Mam. She should be able to manage that while she's sitting on her bottom like the Queen of Sheba!'

Ellen pulled a face. 'I did ask, and I delivered a bundle of newly washed socks, every one of which has a potato in it, but as far as I know she hasn't lifted a finger!'

'Right, that does it! Doesn't she know there's a war on?' Mariah marched into Meredith's sitting room, where she found her half-sister disconsolately leafing through a pile of magazines.

'These are no good at all!' she complained. 'They all seem to have got thinner since the war started. And the paper is poor quality, too!'

'Never mind magazines, Meredith Fletcher! Didn't Mam bring you a bundle of socks to darn? Have you finished them yet?'

'She did mention something, but I didn't think I needed to do them right away.'

'Tell that to those poor little boys playing outside in the bitter cold, with bare legs! If you're too much of a lady to do any menial work, you should get involved in volunteer work, the Red Cross or something.'

'I'm exhausted all the time,' Meredith whined. 'You don't give me any sympathy, Mariah! I've lost my husband and I've got a fatherless baby.' She began to weep.

'Crocodile tears!' Mariah snapped. 'I'll tell you about fatherless children! There's a little boy downstairs whose father died at sea when his ship was torpedoed. His mother put Evan in an orphanage so she could enlist in the WRNS. She told him she wanted to go and help kill a few of the blankety-blank people who'd murdered her man!'

'Could she do that?' Meredith was interested in spite of herself. 'Put him in an orphanage, I mean, when the kiddie had a parent living?'

'I don't know what the rules are in a case like that, but she did it anyway. And do you know what that brave little fellow says about it? "Our Mam's gone to help win the war, and I'm glad!"'

'Oh, Mariah!'

'Don't you "Oh Mariah" me! That little chap thinks the world of his Mam, even though she dumped him in an orphanage. Don't you want Henry to be proud of you? Oh, I know he's too young to understand what's happening now, but some day he'll ask, "What did you do in the war, Mummy?" and how are you going to answer that? "I just sat on my bottom, my darling, because I was too lazy to get on with things"?'

'You're very hard, Mariah!'

*

'I don't know what you said last night,' Ellen said the next morning, 'but take a look at this! Nine pairs of socks, all neatly darned, and she says if we can get hold of some wool she'll get started on knitting a few more pairs!'

'Good-oh!'

'And since your opinion seems to carry so much weight with that young woman, you can let her know what we think of her refusing to speak to her poor father!'

Mariah grinned wryly. 'I'll leave that one to you, Mam!'

'A fat lot of good that would do. Don't you know I'm the scarlet woman?'

'And what does that make me? The scarlet baby?' For some reason this struck them both as funny, and they giggled helplessly for a few moments.

'I mean it, though,' Ellen said, wiping her eyes. 'They have to be brought together before too long. Harry isn't as young as he used be, you know. He was past forty when you girls were born. How would Meredith feel if he died suddenly and the last time she'd spoken to him, words were said in anger? Somebody has to do something.'

So Mariah went back to Meredith, and a blazing row ensued.

'That man betrayed my mother, and somebody has to make him pay for that!'

'Nobody's perfect, Merry. He made a mistake, that's all.'

'It's a mistake that shouldn't have happened. And don't call me Merry!'

'And don't you bawl at me like that!'

'I'll bawl if I like! That man and your mother broke *my* mother's heart!'

'That's a load of codswallop! She didn't know a thing about it. Mam told me.'

'Of course, that's what she would say!'

'Girls! Girls! People can hear you all the way downstairs! What on earth is going on here?' Harry had come in, completely unheard.

'I'm telling Meredith to buck up!' Mariah said, her voice dripping with scorn.

'Daddy, are you going to let her speak to me like that?' Meredith flung herself into her father's arms and submitted to his soothing words.

Well, at least they're on speaking terms again, Mariah thought with disgust.

CHAPTER 49

MARIAH WAS FILLED with remorse for what she had done. Meredith cried for two days after their spat. In the end Harry sent for the doctor to take a look at her. 'Don't you think she needs a sedative or something?' he asked.

'Just let me speak to her alone,' Dr Lawson told him. 'I don't prescribe sedatives unless I have to. Meredith may simply be overwrought. A couple of days in bed and warm milk at bedtime to help her sleep may be all she needs.'

'That's the problem, old man. She's kept to her bed a great deal since Chad was killed. We all thought it was time she spent more time up and about, taking on light duties. Mariah meant well, even if she did go off the deep end a bit.'

After what seemed an age to those anxiously awaiting the doctor's diagnosis, he returned to the morning room, looking cheerful. 'Nothing to worry about! In fact, I'd say that her breakdown has done her the world of good. She's bottled everything up inside for too long, but she'll be on the mend now that the dam has burst.'

Mariah was relieved. 'I thought I'd sent her over the edge, Doctor.'

He laughed. 'Perhaps you did mention one home truth too many, but no lasting harm has resulted. Her hormones barely had time to settle down after giving birth before her husband was killed, and not long after that, my old friend tells me, she received some rather distressing news!'

'So did Mariah,' Harry said, putting an arm around his other daughter's shoulders.

'And perhaps that's why you flew off the handle when you did,' the doctor said, looking at Mariah with a twinkle in his eye. 'It's not every day that you lose one father and gain another! Never mind, I expect you'll all shake down together soon. It's not as if you're all strangers to each other, is it?'

Meredith was still rather cool towards Ellen, but Harry pointed out that she had much to be grateful for. 'Not only did she save your life, *cariad*, but she's been here for you all these years, bringing you up, nursing you through various illnesses and so on.'

'My real mother would have done that too, Daddy!' A vestige of animosity still remained like an ice chip in Meredith's heart.

'Of course she would have loved you dearly, *cariad*! But as for taking care of you, no, she would not have done that. There would have been a nanny; in fact, you did have one in the very beginning, until Ellen took on the job.'

Mariah kept her distance for a while, but once Meredith started speaking to her she realized that they were beginning to find their way back to their former relationship. She knew she was forgiven when Meredith offered to lend her the lovely satin gown which had been lovingly packed away between layers of tissue paper.

'How very kind.' Ellen smiled. 'It's lucky you two are the same size, Mariah.'

This was a tactful way of putting it, as Meredith had not yet lost all the weight she'd put on before Henry was born.

'Yes, it is kind, but I won't be having a white wedding. I know a lot of brides are making the best of a wartime wedding, cutting up old curtains and making veils out of butter muslin, but that's not for me. If I can scrape up enough clothing coupons I shall buy a nice little suit, something which will come in handy later. Let's face it, I'll probably have to wear that same suit for the duration of the war, but I shan't mind. Every time I put it on I'll be reminded of Aubrey.'

'But a suit!' Ellen gasped.

'It'll look quite nice, Mam, if I find a smart hat to go with it. I wonder where I'll be able to pick one up?'

The Swansea Six, as Mariah dubbed them, were shaping up quite well as gardeners. One of them had helped his grandfather on an allotment and was able to tell a weed from a carrot.

'Tadcu and Mamgu died of typhoid,' he explained matter-of-factly, and was pleased when she explained that her grandparents had also passed away from that disease.

The boys were interested to hear that she was getting married.

'You'll be leaving us then,' one said sadly. In his experience it wasn't safe to love anybody because you always ended up alone. They either died or went away.

'That's where you're wrong then, Dai Jones! I'll be going away for a few days but I'll be back before you know it.'

'Won't your husband want you with him?'

'He's too busy being a pilot in the RAF, and they don't allow wives in the camp. He said he'll be happy to think of me here in Cwmbran, waiting for him.'

Mariah was confident that she wouldn't be called up now she had six evacuees to help look after, as well as almost sole responsibility for the gardens. Nor would Meredith be made to enlist in one of the women's services, because she had a young baby. Ellen and Harry were too old to be eligible for active duty so it looked as though their little family was safe for the time being.

The only blot on the horizon came when one of the boys came down with measles, which all the rest promptly suffered from too. Ellen was in her element, reliving her nannying days. 'You'll have to keep them in a darkened room or their eyesight could be affected,' the doctor warned.

'Yes, Doctor. And what about Henry – is he in any danger?'

'At his age he should still have immunity from his mother, but you must keep him in the nursery, just in case. Meredith and that young nursemaid can look after him between them. Keep sponging the boys down, and give them plenty of fluids, and I'll look in again tomorrow.'

'Yes, Doctor.'

Mariah wished she'd gone to train as a children's nurse. It was interesting work, and she'd be more help to Ellen now if she knew what she was supposed to be doing. But then, if she had gone away to hospital she might never have met Aubrey!

It was due to Megan that the dilemma of Mariah's wedding garments was solved. She rang up one evening to speak to Mariah, shouting into the phone because she wasn't used to it.

'It's a friend of mine, Elsie Davies. You wouldn't know her. She's been a lady's maid up London, only she's coming home now because her Mam don't want her there with that old blitz going on.'

'Oh, yes?'

'Her lady gives her things, and this time she gave her a lovely costume, a nice beige. Ever so expensive, it was, Elsie says. She doesn't fancy herself in that colour, her being so pale, so she asked me did I know anybody who might make use of it. There's wicked to let such a lovely thing go to waste, I said, and I told her I'd speak to you.'

'Beige! I'm not sure, Megan. Would it fit me, do you think?'

Elsie is about your size, only shorter. Very handy with her needle, she is. She could alter the suit to fit, I'm sure.'

'I'll have a word with Mam and let you know. *Diolch yn fawr!*'

'*Da iawn!*'

'What do you think, Mam?' Mariah looked at Ellen with her head on one side. She had to come up with something soon, or she'd be getting wed in her nightgown.

'No harm having a look at it, I suppose. And if it's come from some smart London shop it's probably nicer than anything you're likely to find here in Cwmbran.'

The suit was made from lightweight gabardine, and beautifully cut. It fitted Mariah like a glove, except that the skirt was too short.

'There's a good hem here,' Megan said, turning it back in her hands. 'Elsie could soon let that down, couldn't you, Elsie?'

'No trouble at all, Miss Richards.'

'But won't it leave a mark?' Ellen worried.

'No, madam. I'll give it a good steam and you'll never know the difference.'

Mariah couldn't make up her mind. 'It's a bit plain. I'm meant to be getting married in this, you see.'

'It'll go lovely with that auburn hair of yours, Miss Richards, and easy enough to dress it up with a pretty blouse and contrasting shoes.'

'There's those bronze-coloured court shoes you've never worn,' Ellen remembered. Mariah had bought them for some special function before the war but had come down with a beastly cold the day before and had to stay at home. The shoes had been pushed to the back of the wardrobe.

'And a pretty blouse in a nice coffee shade,' Megan suggested.

'Na, na, Megan! Too dull altogether. My lady had a lovely green one to tone with this costume but unluckily she didn't want to give that away.'

'We'll pay a visit to Miss Meadowes,' Ellen decided. She was the local dressmaker, a little English spinster who had come to Cwmbran years before to visit a cousin, and never left. 'She may have some bits and pieces put by that she could whip up into a blouse.'

'I have the very thing,' the dressmaker said, beaming. 'Just let me see where I've put it.' After rummaging around, she came up with a length of some shiny material in stripes of dark green and navy. Mariah fell in love with it at once. Problem solved!

CHAPTER 50

IT WAS A PERFECT June day. It had rained a little during the night, but the sun had come out now and drops of moisture sparkled on the shrubs near the house.

Because so many of the staff had left to join up, Ellen had commandeered a couple of village women to help serve the modest repast which would be given to the guests on their return from the church.

'You should have asked me!' Megan protested. 'Been glad to do it, I would, and no need to pay me, either!'

'You'll be an honoured guest at the church!' Ellen reminded her. 'You were there when Mariah was born! You surely didn't think we'd let you hand round plates of food at her wedding reception!'

It was to be a quiet affair, not a bit like Meredith's sumptuous wedding two years before. The groom and his best man were smartly turned out in their RAF uniforms, and Meredith, who had managed to put aside her feelings of animosity and had consented to act as matron of honour, was wearing a pretty summer frock.

'I do wish you'd let me lend you my gown,' she murmured, as she helped Mariah into her jacket. 'It seems all wrong for you to be getting married in a costume, even though it is really nice.' She fingered the material, rather wishing that Mariah would pass it on to her when she was finished with it!

'To me, it seems all wrong for people to be putting on lavish weddings while there's a war on, Merry. So many people are suffering and going without.'

'I don't see how you wearing my gown would make it any worse! Still, it's your day. You know best what you want to do.'

'What I want to do is get married to Aubrey,' Mariah said softly. 'That's all that matters to me. Outward trappings don't mean a thing. And I'll tell you something else!'

'What's that?'

'I shan't have to change into a "going away" costume after the reception, because I'll be travelling in what I've got on now!'

'You'd better not spill jelly down your front, then!'

'Aren't you girls ready yet? It's time we should be leaving for the church. Ellen's already gone, Mariah!'

'Coming, Daddy!' Meredith called, giving a last-minute tweak to the tiny hat that sat on an angle on Mariah's bright curls. It had a little half-veil and was a perky bit of nonsense that added a festive touch to the bride's ensemble.

As always, there was a little crowd around the church gates as the local women congregated to catch a glimpse of the bride.

'Look, it's Mr Morgan!' The loud whisper floated on the breeze to reach Mariah's ears. 'He's giving the bride away!' Harry and Mariah exchanged small smiles. As a little girl she had dreamed of being escorted down the aisle by her father on her wedding day, knowing it could never be, for poor Bertie Richards lay buried in some foreign field. Now the day of her marriage had arrived, and here she was, clinging to her father's arm. Life was full of surprises.

They might be in the middle of a war, but to the small group of guests who were assembled in the ancient church, this wedding was as perfect as it could possibly be. Thousands of couples must have plighted their troth under this roof over the centuries, with mothers sniffing happily into their hankies, and bridegrooms beaming with pride as they watched the maiden of their choice arriving at the altar steps.

A little cheer went up when the newly fledged Mr and Mrs Mortimer emerged from the main door. A shower of confetti met them as they ran to the waiting car.

'Square confetti?' Mariah laughed, picking a few stray pieces off her shoulders. 'I've never heard of such a thing!'

'It took those boys hours to make that stuff,' her mother said. 'Sat in the kitchen all last night, they did, cutting up old magazines. You can't buy real confetti now for love nor money, and as for rice! That's on the ration now, of course, and we couldn't think of wasting good food, even if it is my only daughter getting married!'

Another surprise awaited them when they arrived at the house. Lined up with military precision at the foot of the front steps were the Swansea Six, each boy clutching a garden implement.

'It's an arch, see?' Dai shouted proudly. 'You're supposed to walk under it, for luck. We wanted to do it outside the church door, but he wouldn't let us!' He stuck out his tongue at Harry.

'I'll see you later, boy!' Harry roared, but he was smiling as he said it.

'I hope you washed the mud off this lot,' Mariah said, as hand in hand she and her husband ducked under the outstretched hoes and rakes. 'I don't want dirt on my lovely costume.'

'Course we did. Can't you see we shined them up proper?'

'Less of your cheek, young man!' Aubrey countered, getting a gap-toothed grin by way of reply.

It was the happiest of days, and when the guests were assembled in the drawing room, enjoying the meal which had been provided, Ellen was thankful that everything had gone so well. All her worries were behind her now, and there had been plenty to worry about! What if they hadn't been able to find enough food to feed everyone? What if the war had taken a turn for the worse, and Aubrey's leave had been cancelled?

'Stop it!' she told herself. 'Nothing's gone wrong, you idiot!'

She was surprised when the butler slipped into the room, approaching her, rather than Harry. 'What is it, Perkins? Has something gone wrong in the kitchen?'

'No, Mrs Richards. There's a lady asking to see you.'

'A lady?' Ellen was puzzled. Casting a quick look around the room she confirmed that all the guests were present, so who could this be?

'Show her in, then, Perkins, will you?'

'She said she didn't want to do that, Mrs Richards, so I've put her in the morning room. I've explained that we're in the middle of a wedding reception but she hadn't known that, and she doesn't want to interrupt.'

'Oh, very well; I suppose I'd better come and see what it's all about. I do hope it's nothing important. I don't want to miss the speeches.'

What could it be but bad news? All sorts of notions flew through Ellen's mind. Perhaps Meredith's grandmother had died, or Chad's mother. But then why send someone to break the news when a telegram or a phone call would have done just as well? Had Mrs Mortimer's house been bombed while she was here in Wales? But again, tragic though that would be for the poor woman, it wouldn't take a special messenger to let her know about it.

There was only one way to find out. Ellen gingerly opened the door of the morning room, just as the visitor rose to her feet. Both women spoke at the same time.

'Mari! What are you doing here?'

'Ellen! I came as soon as I heard! I'm sorry, though, I seem to have arrived at the wrong moment!'

The two old friends stood awkwardly in the middle of the room. It was

Ellen who found her voice first. 'Do sit down, Mari. We won't do any good standing here, wearing a hole in the carpet!'

'Why didn't you tell me what had happened to you?' Mari demanded. 'Did you think I wouldn't have stood by you?'

'I was too ashamed. Confused, too. You know what it was like back then. If I'd stayed in Cardiff women would have thrown mud at me in the streets!'

'Come, now, it wasn't that bad!'

'That's what I believed at the time, anyway. How did you find out about it now, then? It was your Mal, of course. He happened to come here with his army mate, who was a footman here for a time. They came up to my sitting room to say hello, and the first thing he noticed was Bertie's photo!'

'And according to him, he was so surprised that he just blurted out the wrong thing! He's not a bad chap, Nell! He wouldn't have hurt you for the world, but his tongue does tend to run away with him at times! When they got back to camp he wrote me a note, saying what had happened. I couldn't believe it at first; that it was you, I mean, living in a house like this! You're the housekeeper now, I understand.'

'That's right, except there's a bit more to it than that. Look, I must get back, but you must come and join the guests, and meet Mariah!'

'Oh, I couldn't just barge in!'

'You're not. I've invited you. Are you going to come quietly, or do I have to call Perkins back to carry you in?'

They both laughed at that. Perkins was wiry but he would never see seventy again, and Mari was, well, face it, a little on the heavy side. She'd put on weight since Ellen had seen her last.

'Oh, that's your daughter, is it, Nell? She is lovely! And what about the bridesmaid? An old school friend, is she?'

'That's Mrs Fletcher, Mr Morgan's daughter. I'll fill you in later. You'll stay the night, of course; we'll have time to ourselves after this lot have gone.'

'Who are all those little boys, then? Not Mrs Fletcher's kiddies, surely? She looks too young.'

'Our evacuees, from Swansea. Come on, I want to introduce you to my friend, Megan. She doesn't know about you-know-what, so not a word out of place, mind!'

Mari nodded, her bright eyes taking everything in. What a grand house! What she wouldn't give to live in a place like this! On second thoughts, maybe not. It must take a lot of dusting!

Later, when the Mortimers had been waved away, and the last of the guests had gone, the two old friends went upstairs together. 'Tell me everything,' Mari insisted, as she accepted the cup of tea Ellen held out to her.

'Not much to tell, really. I was grieving over poor Bertie, and this kind man came on the scene and showed me a bit of sympathy, and well, one thing led to another. It was only the once, mind, but that was enough. My Mariah is the result.'

'But who was the chap? Where is he now? Did he let you down, or what?'

'It was Mr Morgan, Mari.'

'What! The man who owns all this? My, you fell on your feet, didn't you!'

'It's not what you think, Mari. I've been in this house as an employee, ever since his wife died. There's been nothing more between us to this day.'

'But your Mariah; has he acknowledged her as his daughter?'

'Yes, although that didn't come out until recently, and nobody else knows but the four of us, and Aubrey, of course, and that's how I hope it will stay. But Harry's done right by her, had her well educated and provided for, and I'm grateful for that.'

'Well, I'll be blowed!' Mari gasped, and seemingly could find nothing more to say. The two old friends sipped their tea in companionable silence.

CHAPTER 51

'THIS IS LIKE a wonderful dream,' Mariah sighed happily. 'I still can't believe we're really married. I kept praying that nothing would go wrong.'

'Me as well. I was on tenterhooks right up to the last minute. I was so afraid that something would happen to make them cancel my leave,' Aubrey replied, taking her hand in his and bestowing a light kiss on her fingers.

Mariah looked around the room, her eyes dancing. 'It was so clever of Mr Morgan – my father – to think of this. I had no idea what you had in mind. I was afraid we were going to spend most of your leave travelling, and that our wedding night would take place in some awful boarding house! That's if we could even find a place to take us in, when half the population seems to be on the move all the time.'

Harry had already thought that one out. When Aubrey had arrived in Cwmbran the night before the wedding, he and his best man had shared a tiny room above the Red Dragon. Everyone knew it was bad luck for a bride and groom to sleep under the same roof the night before their wedding, so Ellen hadn't even considered letting the men over the doorstep, although there were several spare bedrooms.

'I hope you won't think I'm interfering,' Harry began, 'but I was wondering where you're taking Mariah on your honeymoon.'

Aubrey scratched his head. 'That's the worst of it, sir. I stopped at a couple of likely-looking hotels on the way here, but they're all booked solid. Jim here knows the landlady of a boarding house in Llanelly; I suppose we'll head there. You must think I'm an awful fool, sir, but you've no idea what it's like out there these days.'

'I told you we should have brought a tent!' Jim quipped, but Aubrey wasn't amused.

'Well, here's the thing, Mortimer. I have an empty cottage on the outskirts of Cwmbran. A cowman on one of the farms lived there until recently, but he's been called up and hasn't been replaced yet. His wife has gone to live with her mother for the duration. She gave it a good turn out before she left, and the upshot is, you can go there directly after the reception, if you like.'

'Gosh, can we really?' Aubrey was thrilled, and he knew that Mariah would be, too. Ellen was the only other person who was in on the secret; as soon as she heard what was happening she'd made Harry drive her to the cottage, where she stocked the larder with food.

The happy couple left in Harry's car, which caused some muttering in the ranks when the servants noticed this.

'Where'd they get the petrol coupons, that's what I'd like to know! Don't they know there's a war on?'

But Harry told them that all the guests had had a whip round in order to send the youngsters off in style. He winked at Ellen, who tried to hide a smile. She knew her daughter. Right about then Mariah would be begging her husband to let her in on the secret.

'Where are we off to, Aubrey? Not that I care, as long as I'm with you, but you might give me a hint!'

'We'll be there in a minute, old girl!'

'What? Where are you taking me? This isn't some kind of joke, is it? We won't be driving to the back of the house and sneaking up to my room?'

'Wait and see!' The car drew up in front of a small cottage, with honeysuckle growing round the door.

'I've always loved these farm cottages, Aubrey. I used to call them icing sugar houses when I was little, because that thick white coating on the walls reminded me of royal icing, you know, the kind they used to put on wedding cakes, before the war.'

'Aren't you going to get out?'

'What? You mean, this is it?' Mariah clasped her hands together as she looked around her. 'Oh, I do have a clever husband!' She flung her arms around his neck and kissed him hard on the mouth.

'It was Harry's idea, actually,' he said, delighted to see her pleasure. 'If it had been left up to me we'd probably have been spending the night under a hay stack!'

'Come on, *cariad*,' Mariah whispered, 'let's go inside.'

Later, they began to talk about their future. 'I'd like a cottage just like this one, Aubrey. In fact, if we could stay in Carmarthenshire to bring up our children, I'd be more than happy. I can't imagine any nicer place to live.'

'It's beautiful countryside, all right. Everything will depend on what sort of job I'll be able to get after the war. I was brought up in the country myself, so that's the sort of environment I favour. Perhaps I could find a job as a farm manager or something. You know, Mariah, we haven't really discussed money. People imagine I must be rolling in it, having gone to Eton and Cambridge, but Dad lost everything when the stock market crashed back in 1929, and when he passed away a couple of years later, poor Mother had to make do on a shoestring. Since those days I've always known that I have to make my own way in life.'

'I suppose there are people who might think I come from a wealthy background, too, living at the hall as I do. Even though I've recently learned that Harry Morgan is my father, and he's certainly been good to me over the years, I'm not the daughter of the house. Mam is the housekeeper, and I'm proud of that.'

'Don't worry, my love; I'll do my best to support you!'

'We'll support each other! In any case, we needn't bother about that now. That's for after the war. For now, you'll be going back to camp, to feast on powdered eggs and Spam, and I'll be returning home.'

'They haven't sent you your call-up papers yet, have they?' Aubrey looked rather worried at the prospect.

'No, but it probably won't be long. I'm hoping I can convince them that I've got enough to do here, what with supplying half of Cwmbran with vegetables, and helping Mam with the Swansea Six. Although if Meredith decides to take some of that on, it may make a difference. I've been wondering if it might be best if I joined the WAAFs or something. When I think of what you're doing, night and day, I feel a bit of a slacker.'

'I don't want you doing that, Mariah. Listen to me, will you? If you do that we may not see each other again until after the war. You can bet your bottom dollar, as the Yanks say, that we'd never get leave at the same time. That's the way the service works. They seem to make a point of not considering the individual.'

'Maybe you're right. Let's not talk about it any more, Aubrey. This is our time. Let's make the most of it.'

So for just a little while they lived in a world of their own, far away from the war and all its horrors. Like all lovers since Adam and Eve, they revelled in each other's company, safe in their own little paradise. In two days' time they would return to their ordinary lives, but whatever happened to them after that they would always have this time to look back on. Outside the cottage a strong breeze came up, causing the trees to sway and the window frames to rattle. Mariah didn't care. She was safe in Aubrey's arms, as they listened to the song of the wind together.